Magic by Midnight

Allison S. Bass

For my husband, who gave me the courage to start.
For my son, who gave me the courage to finish.

CHAPTER 1

O utside, the wind whispered and tree branches tapped lightly against the glass pane as if they were beckoning me to join them. If I paused long enough from my tedious task of shelving books, I could almost feel the breeze tickling my face. With a sigh, I ignored the wind and placed another book on a shelf, wondering if my adventures would only ever come in the form of books.

The sound of the library door creaking open, wailing in slow protest against its ancient hinges, caught my attention. I turned to eye the oak door. Grateful for the distraction, I abandoned my stack of books, lifted my long skirts, and dashed across a faded rug to tell the latecomer that the library was closing for the day.

My steps froze when I recognized the visitor. "Your Majesty?" I dipped into a low curtsy.

King Frederic stood before me, tall and domineering, and inclined his head slowly as if he agreed that he was, in fact, the ruler of Valencia. His hazel eyes were piercing, and I had to fight the rush of nervousness I felt at suddenly coming face-to-face with him. It didn't matter how many times I had met him over the years or the fact that he was my best friend's father, he was still a king.

"Felicity," King Frederic replied with a fraction of a smile, which seemed formed out of politeness than actual happiness. "How are you?"

"I am well, Your Majesty, but Prince Alexander is not here today."

"I'm not here for Alexander," the king said. "I'm here to see you."

"*Me?*"

This was the *Royal* Library of Valencia, housed in one of the wings of the palace. I had lived in the library for all of my seventeen years. It was a part of my heritage; every member of my family had been a librarian. But the king had never singled me out before.

I stood there staring at King Frederic for another moment until I finally remembered my manners. "I'm sorry, Your Majesty. How can I be of service to you today? Did you need help finding something?"

The king stepped out of the doorway, striding deeper into the room. The sheathed sword on his hip tapped lightly against his tall riding boots, and the library's wooden floors moaned under his weight. He turned to survey the rows and rows of bookshelves. He stood almost a foot taller than me, his dark brown hair was peppered with gray, and he exuded royalty from the top of his well-made tunic to the tips of his polished boots.

He turned back around to face me. "I'm sorry to give you no warning of my arrival."

Before I had time to consider my words, I replied, "A king does not need permission to visit his own library."

My candor took us both by surprise, and King Frederic let out a dry, clipped sigh. It was the sigh that made me pause. Something was troubling him.

"I suppose it is *my* library," he replied. "Is Maxwell here today? I'd like to speak with him, too."

"Of course." I gestured for him to follow me. "I'll take you to his study."

The room was quiet as the king followed me, save for the creaky floors. To be fair, it was always quiet. It was a library, after all. But since we were closing for the day, the sounds I usually heard in the background: chairs scraping across the floor as someone sat down to read, the crisp rustling of pages being turned, and the hushed whispers of people talking animatedly over a book were gone. There was only a peculiar calmness.

I caught the king glancing up to the domed ceiling with a slight look of reverence on his otherwise masked face. The library had that effect on people. With its towering oak beams, imposing dark bookshelves colored with the spines of numerous books, and a mural of constellations painted on the ceiling, the library was breathtaking. The hush that echoed across the room flooded every nook and cranny and made each visitor reverently silent when they first arrived, and a king was no exception to the rule.

We came to a stop in front of my uncle's study and I peeked my head inside, the familiar scent of old parchment and worn leather tickling my nose.

"Max?"

My uncle looked up at me from over the papers on his desk.

"Yes, Fliss?"

I had to force back a grin at the tuffs of chestnut hair curling over his ears and the ink smudge across his chin. His glasses sat skewed on top of his nose, giving him a scholarly look. Max, who was in his late thirties, somehow made his bookish appearance look handsome.

I pointed to the spot on his chin and said, "You've got a bit of ink right there. Also, there's someone here to see us."

Max rubbed at the spot and looked back down at his papers, ignoring me completely, which I took as a subtle dismissal. It wasn't that he didn't want me around; he just didn't want other people around when he was in the middle of working.

"This is important—"

"Can you handle it for me?" he asked. "I'm in the middle of something."

"Max," I breathed his name with more patience than I felt, "*King Frederic* would like to speak to us."

I pushed the door open a little wider, revealing the king on the other side. Max shot up out of his chair, nearly spilling a bottle of ink.

"Your Majesty." Max offered the king a bow. "What an honor to have you in the library. To what do we owe the pleasure of your visit? I don't believe Prince Alexander has stopped by the library today. I was under the impression he was still away from the palace."

A shadow crossed King Frederic's face. "As I explained to your niece, I'm not here looking for Alexander. He is *why* I'm here, though. I would like to discuss him with you and Felicity."

A flash of awareness dashed across Max's face, and he immediately sprang into action, clearing away stray pieces of parchment and books off a worn chair.

King Frederic brushed past me and walked into the study, side-stepping a pile of books I had told Max only yesterday to pick up because someone was going to trip over them. The king had to hunker over to avoid hitting the low ceiling.

Max and I waited to take our seats until the king found his own. After we all settled in, the king let out another long and weary sigh.

"Your Majesty, what can my niece and I do for you?" Max asked.

"The same thing that all the librarians in the past have done for the royal families of Valencia," King Frederic replied. "It's time for Alexander's fairy tale."

CHAPTER 2

The king's unusual statement surprised me and I leaned forward in my seat. I bit my lip nervously, wondering how Alexander would react if he knew the three of us were meeting in secret behind his back.

"You do know that once the librarian is made aware of the fairy tale, we cannot stop the unveiling of history," Max said.

"Yes," the king answered, after what seemed like years. "Alexander's eighteenth birthday is coming up soon. His fairy tale will need to be in place before that time. My wife and I hoped to be able to settle the disagreements Valencia has with the fairies before Alexander's birthday, but, alas, the fairies were not willing to hear our pleas. That is why I waited until the last possible moment to speak with you. I was hoping to undo Alexander's fate..."

My eyes swung over to Max. *Fairies? Fate?*

Max dismissed my silent questions with a small wave of his hand.

The sunlight from the window filtered in, casting a glow about the room and highlighting the dark circles under King Frederic's eyes, the worry lines on his forehead, and the sheen of gray that covered his hair. He seemed older than his years.

"Then we will proceed as soon as we can," Max replied.

Both men turned to me. I wanted to squirm in my seat and evade the king's gaze, but Alexander would have called me a coward for feeling nervous around his father. Instead, I made my best attempt at sitting up straight.

"Are you quite sure, Maxwell? Is Felicity capable of the task ahead? Is she even old enough to understand the gravity of the situation?"

"If I remember correctly, your librarian was no older than Felicity is now," Max said.

King Frederic's face drained of color. "Are you certain there is no way *you* could handle this? I would feel much more at ease about this if you were in charge."

Instead of responding immediately, Max got up, walked across the room, and pulled out a very old chest. The straps were worn and the metal lock looked thin enough to pry apart with your hands. He rummaged for a key in the pocket of his tunic. After he found it, he placed it gently within the lock, clicking it open. Max reached down into the chest, pulled out a thick white book with gold lettering, and walked back to the king and handed the book to him.

"Your Majesty, can you read the title of this book?"

The king peered at the cover, shaking his head. "I see no title on the book."

"Can you read the words inside? Can you tell me what the pages say?" Max asked the king, in a testing voice.

"You know I cannot." The king sounded frustrated, defeated almost.

"As I live and breathe, I cannot read these words either, Your Majesty," Max said gently, sounding as if he were explaining things to a small child. "I would never lie to you." He brought the book over to me, placing it on my lap. "Go on, Fliss." He gave me an encouraging nod when he saw the confusion on my face. "Tell us what the title says."

I looked down at the book. I caressed the binding and traced the gold letters on the front with my finger. It was the most elegant book I had ever seen. The ivory cover shined, and the lettering was a script that would rival even the most experienced calligrapher's handiwork.

"*Cinderella*," I murmured, looking up at the two men who observed me with interest.

"Are you sure you can see a title? Are there words on every page?" Max asked.

I opened the book and skimmed. There certainly were words, and my eyes caught glimpses of phrases here and there as I flipped through the book.

"Yes," I answered more confidently this time. "It says right here on the front cover: *Cinderella*, and I can see words on every page."

"Good. Good." Max smacked his hands together and exhaled in relief. "You see, Your Majesty," he said, after he sat down, "I cannot do this for you. Only my niece can. If it's any consolation, I wouldn't trust any other teenager with the fate of the kingdom or your son's future."

"It's not, really, Maxwell."

Max shrugged.

The king's eyes darted over to me. "The fairy tale itself should be easy enough to follow, so long as Alexander remains oblivious." He nodded sharply once. "I suppose I'll leave her to it then."

Fairy tale? What fairy tale? There was that term again. My mind raced through possible options of why they were talking about fictional stories.

The king got up and walked to the door. "Thank you," he said to Max with a wince before he left, like he was thanking someone for committing a crime.

Max's hands clasped together and formed a point with his fingers. He glanced at me purposefully, and then to the king again. "It is not I whom you should thank."

The king looked at me then. His eyes crinkled as he focused on me. I felt his uncertainty.

"Thank you, Felicity," the king spoke gently. "You have my gratitude, and someday you will have Alexander's."

He took a few steps forward and held his hand out for me to shake, in an awkward sort of offering. When he released my hand, my curiosity wasn't satisfied, merely ignited even more.

The king glanced at Max and then left the room with a rapid turn on his heel. I sat there for a few moments, taking all that had happened in, or at least I tried to take it in. I stared at the doorway King Frederic had gone through while Max stared at me.

"I suppose you have some questions to ask," Max interrupted my thoughts.

"Will you answer them?"

"If you ask the right ones."

My uncle was infamous for not answering questions he didn't think were worth asking. To the people who proclaimed there was no such thing as a foolish question, Max would respond that asking the right questions was often more satisfying than getting the right answers.

I started with the obvious question first, "What does this book mean?"

"This will sound odd, but the book holds Prince Alexander's destiny. It tells us what kind of woman he marries and what kind of king he becomes. However, only you can see what that destiny is. The book decides his fate and the fate of our kingdom."

I had to stifle a laugh. "Oh, that's all?"

"I know this seems strange."

"*Strange?* No, wearing a wool cloak in July is strange. This seems like absolute nonsense. It's a joke, right?" I stood up to leave, laughing at the absurdity of it all. "Alexander probably put you up to this."

He frowned at my laughter. "I can assure you that it is not a scheme. This is difficult to explain. Oh, dash it. Your mother was supposed to be the one to do this when the time came." He whipped his spectacles off his face and muttered a curse under his breath. "I suppose there's no other choice..."

I plopped back down in my seat, resigning to the fact that I'd at least have to pretend to hear him out, no matter how far-fetched his words were.

"These books we collect in our library, they aren't just fictional stories. Some of the books are quite real. The book in your hand is Prince Alexander's story and someone else's story. I assume by the title you'll be looking for someone named Cinderella. It's your job to take the story and help real events play out as they do in the book. Doing so will help ensure the future of Alexander. It will ensure the future of Valencia."

I stared at him for a long minute. Finally, I blinked. "Why would I believe any of this?"

"Why would you not?" he countered.

"Because it's impossible."

Max *tsked.* "If you are going to think of an excuse not to believe in this, at least don't make it a poorly crafted one."

"Well, it *is* impossible!"

He bit back another sigh. "It's your destiny to read Prince Alexander's fairy tale. Just as it was your mother's destiny to read his father's."

"My mother?" I echoed.

"It's this family's fate. The librarians are in charge of fairy tales."

Fate.

It was a heavy word, heavy enough to make me pause for a moment at least. "Forgive me if I come across as completely dense when I say this, but how does a librarian help orchestrate a fairy tale, something that was entirely *fictional* last time I checked?"

"You help match the pieces of the book together to coincide with what's happening in Alexander's life." Max stated this fact as if it was the simplest concept in the entire world.

I shook my head. "Even if this is true, which I'm not saying it is, I can't just interfere with Alexander's life, not in so drastic a way. This is his future we're talking about here. *His wife.* I can't choose that person for him."

"You aren't choosing for him. The fairy tale chooses," Max said, his tone gentler this time. Perhaps he could sense my calm beginning to unravel. "His father before him had a certain destiny, too. If your mother hadn't stepped in to help King Frederic with his fairy tale, the kingdom may not even exist anymore. It might not seem right to interfere, but it is far greater a risk to do nothing at all."

Max reached into his desk and pulled out a worn book. I had seen that book in his desk a thousand times. When I was little, my mother used to read me the story before I went to bed.

He handed me the book. "When Rosalind was a librarian for King Frederic many years ago, she led him to a young maiden locked in the tallest tower of the palace. She was a young maiden who lay in eternal sleep. This is their story. This is their destiny."

I traced the title with my fingertips. "*Sleeping Beauty?*" I asked incredulously. "*Mother* made this fairy tale come true? She never told me."

"She wasn't allowed to tell you. Once the librarian knows of the fairy tale, there's no turning back. The librarian *must* begin piecing together the fairy tale immediately. That's why we had to wait to tell you until the king and queen thought it was time, which according to fairies must be on or before the next monarch's eighteenth birthday."

"It doesn't matter." I heard my voice raise, unraveling in a shrill manner. "Do you hear what you are saying? This is all impossible."

"There's that senseless word again. Nothing is impossible when you have the right kind of magic, and the gift you have is a kind of magic." Max regarded me quietly for a moment. "Why would the king, who is not known for playing practical jokes on unsuspecting librarians, seek you out for a task that involves the future of his son, not to mention his kingdom, if the fairy tale was not true?"

My mind still reeled with uncertainty. How could my uncle, who was a scholar driven by facts and logic, even entertain the idea that fairy tales were real? He believed in things that could be found in his books, underlined twice, and proven true. Yet, I trusted Max more than I trusted anyone else in the world. Deep down, I knew he wouldn't lie to me.

I met his eyes. Something stood out, something that was stronger than facts and logic.

Truth.

The corners of his mouth eased into a small smile as he took in the shock on my face.

Awe filled my voice as I said, "You aren't lying."

"Of course not. I would never lie to you."

"So, these fairy tales are real?"

"Of course. You should be grateful, too. You always wanted a grand adventure. Well, there's nothing quite like orchestrating a fairy tale that impacts the destiny of this kingdom." Max tapped on the book in my hands. "One more thing. You can't tell Alexander about the fairy tale."

"Why not?"

"Because he could choose not to follow the fairy tale and tamper with the fate of the kingdom. Giving him the freedom to choose his destiny could throw everything into chaos."

"What would happen then?"

"The kingdom would perish, probably by the hands of something very evil if we are being honest." Max shrugged. "Such is the way with most fairy tales. There's good and there's evil."

"Why couldn't *you* choose to do this?" My hand tightened around the book. "Why me? I'm hardly old enough for this responsibility."

"I didn't get a choice. There's only one librarian chosen in each generation of our family. Your mother was King Frederic's librarian, and I've long suspected that you were Alexander's. Today confirmed my suspicion."

I flipped the book open to the last page of the fairy tale. Alexander's name and face flashed before my eyes on the spectacularly illustrated pages, and I caught glimpses of the name Cinderella and several images of an angelic-looking girl with long, flowing blond hair and radiant blue eyes.

"There's one thing I don't understand."

Max raised an eyebrow. "Only one?"

"What force is so great and so powerful that it has King Frederic seeking out the help of a seventeen-year-old girl? Why wouldn't he refuse to go along with the fairy tale?"

My inquiry made Max grin boldly. "Ah-ha! Now she's asking the right questions."

"Who writes the fairy tales? Where did you even get that book?"

"For goodness' sake, I said ask the *right* questions, not the foolish ones. Use your brain." Max leaned over the debris littered across his desk, eyeing me closely. "Who do you think writes *fairy* tales?"

When I said nothing, Max answered for me.

"Fairies, dear girl." His eyes wandered over to the door as though he expected someone else to come through it. He cleared his throat and looked back to me a moment later. "Seventeen years ago, the very night you were born, a fairy gave me this book to give to you. Fairies control the fairy tales. Thus, the fairies control this kingdom."

CHAPTER 3

The conversation I had with Max propelled me from the library and into the outdoors. I made my way to the palace garden. The sweet smells of honeysuckle and lilacs greeted me along with the coolness of early spring, and I wished I'd had the foresight to bring a shawl to wrap around my shoulders. The haze of twilight washed over the garden, casting a glow of pinks and purples and oranges across the exotic flora. There was a spot beneath a weeping willow at the far side of the garden that I always did my best thinking under. I sat down beneath its branches and pulled the fairy tale from my satchel. The nearby lilac bush, my mother's favorite scent, was in full bloom and the familiar fragrance brought a rush of memories back to me.

Before my mother died, she would bring me to this tree and read me stories of far off lands and daring adventures. The wispy leaves would hide us, tickling our arms and swiping at our faces as they danced around us. Together, with our heads stuck in a book, my mother and I traveled the world without ever leaving the comfort of our willow's embrace. My mother was capable of bringing any story to life. Her musical voice would drip over me like honey as she read, and I was powerless to do anything except listen.

These stories made me question the person I was, where I came from, and, more importantly, where I wanted to go. In all the thirteen years I had with my mother, she never spoke of my father, who he was, or where he came from. I would occasionally catch her staring out the window, sweeping her eyes across the landscape, her mind in another world. In those rare moments, I knew she was remembering him. She would stand straight and proud, while simultaneously seeming defeated and lost all at once.

Once I asked her about my father and if I would ever see him. She faintly told me he was dead and never to speak of him again. I was saddened by her answer but complacent with it for many years, but then I wondered what harm could come from talking about a dead man. What was she keeping from me? I badgered her more about my father's identity as I got older, but she never relented, not even on her deathbed.

For the most part, I had come to terms with not knowing my father's identity. Perhaps he had been a thief or traitor or murderer. I convinced myself I didn't *really* want to know who he was, especially not if he was horrible enough for my mother to keep his identity from me. Though part of me wondered if I was worse off not knowing who he was, even if he wasn't the person I wanted him to be.

"Fliss!" A flash of dark hair jumped out from behind the tree's trunk.

I jerked back in surprise, nearly hitting my head against the tree. Startled, I looked up to meet a pair of blue eyes that were so bright they reflected the vibrancy of the person they belonged to.

"Alexander!" His presence caught me off guard, and I tucked the fairy tale, *his fairy tale*, underneath my skirts as he peered down at me with a grin that crinkled his eyes. "Are you trying to scare me to death?"

"No. Merely surprise you. I'd say I was successful." He

shifted slightly as he hovered over me. "Can I join you? Or do you want to be alone with your thoughts?"

"Of course you can join me."

He sunk down next to me with tremendous ease for someone who was so tall. Our shoulders touched accidentally when he leaned against the tree. I scooted over to give him more space.

"I stopped by the library, but Max said that you'd probably be under your tree in the garden, doing what he called some *serious* thinking."

"He was right."

"He usually is."

Alexander stretched his legs. His riding boots were scuffed and dusty. His hands looked rough and dry. Dark circles underneath his eyes betrayed how tired he was.

"You look as though you haven't slept in a week."

He slumped against the tree and closed his eyes, leaning back dramatically. "Imagine, if you will, how uncomfortable it is to spend all day in a saddle and all night sleeping on the hard ground for an entire week. I dare say I've been living in the palace too long. It's turned me soft."

I almost laughed. Between the reckless smile, his calloused hands, and his strong build, there wasn't much soft about Alexander.

He popped back up a moment later, his energy returning. "But I'd rather talk to you and tell you about my trip than sleep."

He noticed the corner of the fairy tale sticking out from underneath my leg. I shoved the book farther underneath me, hoping he wouldn't ask me about it.

Alexander raised an eyebrow and tilted his head just enough to cause some of his dark brown hair to fall against his temple. "Why are you sitting on that book?"

17

"I'm not sitting on it," I replied quickly.

His eyebrow traveled even farther up his forehead.

"I'm propping up my leg on it."

"Why?"

"It's good for my circulation."

"Where'd you hear that?"

"I read it in a book."

"Which book?"

"The one I'm resting my leg on. Now tell me where you've been," I demanded. I really did want to know. "I thought perhaps you'd abandoned your kingdom."

Instead of badgering me about what was really going on, like he was usually inclined to do, Alexander shrugged away my peculiar behavior. "Father had me go out on patrol with some of the knights."

"That's twice in one month he's sent you on some mission. He sent you away the week before last to meet the ambassador in Aurum."

"It's his not-so-subtle way of thrusting me into adulthood, I suppose."

Alexander folded his arms behind his head, looking entirely too at ease with the world. It was mostly a façade, though. For all his perceived nonchalance, Alexander was never completely at ease. As future king, his thoughts were always preoccupied with the kingdom's affairs or his responsibilities, especially the older he got. I couldn't help noticing that those responsibilities were growing more and more each day. Though I doubted Alexander minded too much. There was nothing in this world that he loved more than Valencia and its people.

"Where did you go this time?" I tried to keep the excitement from my voice, but it was no good.

Alexander sensed my excitement and his eyes sparkled with enthusiasm as he regaled his tale, "We went to the border of Valencia and Brittolia. There were reports of, listen to this," he lowered his voice conspiratorially, "*bandits* in the area. There's a group of them living in the forest."

I pictured the map above Max's desk in the study. Brittolia was the kingdom directly north of Valencia. The two kingdoms weren't always on good terms with one another, but King Frederic had been actively striving for peace between them in recent years.

I leaned forward in hopes of hearing a swashbuckling tale of adventure and rescues. "Did you have to rescue a maiden who had been captured by the bandits? Save a carriage traveling across the border from being robbed? Duel with the leader of the outlaws?"

Alexander chuckled. "I'm afraid it was nothing so daring or romantic. When we gave chase, they narrowly escaped us. However, I managed not to make myself look like an inexperienced fool in front of the knights this time, if that's what you really want to know."

On a previous patrol, Alexander's horse had been spooked by a snake and threw him, breaking not only his wrist but also a good portion of his pride. He was sent back to the palace a week earlier than planned, giving several young ladies at court who had hopes of marrying a prince the chance to play nursemaid while he recovered in the palace infirmary. Alexander later confided in me that he had led the knights in the wrong direction, and if he'd consulted his map better, he might never have gotten the group lost and been thrown from his horse.

I fell back against the tree and sighed. "You don't realize how lucky you are. Someday I'm going—"

"You are going off to see the world and have grand adventures while the rest of us poor creatures live ordinary, complacent lives," Alexander said, waving away my words. There was a playful dryness to his voice. "I know. I know. You've told me all this before. *Felicity*, if you wanted adventures so badly, you should come see the world with me. You needn't traipse all over the kingdom by yourself."

"Who says my adventures would confine me only to this kingdom?" I asked with a smile.

"I'd rather you didn't travel alone, in this kingdom or any other."

My smile faded. "Because you think I can't take care of myself?"

Alexander lifted himself off the tree's trunk to get a better look at me. "It's because you are my friend and I don't want you to get hurt."

"I can take care of myself. You told me once that I could handle a sword better than most of your knights."

"I see that particular compliment went straight to your head."

I prodded him with my elbow. "But it's true, right?"

"*Yes*," he relented. "Of course, it's true. After all, *I* was the one who taught you how to use a sword. It doesn't mean I like the idea of you diving head first into a dangerous world all by yourself. Have you already forgotten about the bandits I mentioned earlier? It's not safe for anyone to travel alone these days."

"I *have* to go." His eyes widened at the passion in my statement. "I love the library, but I'm only a librarian because it's what's expected of me. It's Max's calling. I'm not sure it's mine, though."

"What exactly is it you are hoping to find on these adventures?"

I said nothing. I couldn't tell Alexander the truth, because I wasn't entirely sure what the truth was myself. Over the years the library, with its mountains of breathtaking stories and daring tales, had given me a sense of adventure that couldn't be satisfied by daydreams under a willow tree any longer. There had to be more to this world. There had to be more to me.

I felt the sharp point of the fairy tale's corner dig into my calf. Maybe there was already more to me. Max was right; the greatest adventure I might ever have could be literally right beneath me. I wouldn't even have to leave Valencia to seek it out.

"Felicity?" Alexander broke into my thoughts. "What exactly are you hoping to find?"

"I'll let you know when I find it."

"You aren't even eighteen yet. How can you possibly know what—"

I interrupted him before our conversation turned into a one-sided lecture. "Speaking of eighteenth birthdays, you have one coming up next month."

"Stop changing the subject."

"Stop avoiding a new one."

"You know how I feel about my birthday. The court will want to make some big celebration out of it. I'd like to enjoy my birthday without the pomp and pageantry."

"You are a prince," I reminded him. "Pomp and pageantry come with the title."

He brushed a blade of grass off his boot. "What are you going to get me? For my birthday, I mean."

I was once again acutely aware of the fairy tale lying beneath my skirts. *Well, if the things Max and your father say are true, I'll be getting you a wife.*

"What does one get a prince, who already has every material possession he could want, for his birthday?" I asked him.

Alexander looked thoughtful for a moment, scratching his chin and making a dramatic *hmm* under his breath.

Finally, he leaned in closer, near enough for me to count the few freckles that brushed across his nose.

"Can I get back to you on that, Fliss?"

"Don't wait too long."

"What I want will be worth the wait."

I started to ask him more about the patrol when an abrupt *cough* interrupted me. Alexander and I pulled away from one another.

"Your Highness!" a trill female voice called out.

Our heads swiveled around, and I had to stifle a groan as Lady Cressida, who was simultaneously the most beautiful and most conceited young woman in court, ducked her head under the leaves of my weeping willow.

"Prince Alexander," Lady Cressida said. "I thought I saw you enter the garden. I've been waiting to see you since you got back. There's something I've been *dying* to ask you." She paused when she saw me sitting on the other side of Alexander. Her smile faltered. "Oh, your librarian friend is with you. I hope I'm not interrupting something."

In fact, you are.

"Of course you're not," Alexander replied cordially without an ounce of the irritation I felt. "I was just catching up with Felicity. What can I help you with, Lady Cressida?"

I glanced through the willow's leaves at the gaggle of ladies waiting at the garden entrance. Lady Cressida's ever-present posse had followed her with their heads pressed together, whispering and giggling as they pointed to Alexander.

"Several ladies were wondering if you'd join us in the ballroom. Lady Alana was going to teach us the steps of the new dance the Avondale court is doing." Lady Cressida gestured animatedly to one of the other girls, indicating for her to come forward. "We are in *desperate* need of more men to join our little gathering, though. Will you help us out?"

Lady Alana, who had arrived as a visitor from the Avondale court earlier this year, was the vibrant young woman everyone was talking about. Her glossy auburn hair, bold gray eyes, and alabaster skin made her irresistible, but it was her soft voice and easy charm that completely won over Valencia's courtiers, making her the darling of the court from the moment she arrived. Initially, I was surprised Lady Cressida had let her into her circle of friends, seeing as how someone as beautiful as Alana would be competition for Alexander's affections. I assumed Cressida had some reason for keeping her rival close, for she was nothing if not intentional in her strategy to lure Alexander into a marriage proposal.

Alexander jumped to his feet when Alana appeared next to Cressida. "My Lady," he said politely, kissing her proffered hand while she curtsied.

Alana smiled prettily. "Your Highness."

Cressida smiled, too. More so to give the appearance that Alana and Alexander's interaction didn't bother her than actual happiness, but she did it with so much force, I was sure her cheeks were going to split apart.

Alexander probably wanted nothing more than to have a decent meal and go to bed. The court had certain expectations of their crown prince though. Even if he had just returned from a long journey, those expectations outweighed basic needs like food and sleep. It was no surprise when he said, "A dancing lesson sounds grand, especially one taught by our guest from Avondale. I'll go change into some proper clothes and meet you all there."

"Excellent!" Cressida clapped her hands together. "We'll see you up there in, shall we say, half an hour?"

"Felicity is invited, too," Alana said. All three sets of eyes turned down to me.

"Yes, of course she is," Cressida said. "We wouldn't dream of leaving the librarian out."

I liked Alana, really, I did. She visited the library on occasion and always made polite conversation about the weather or the palace or whatever book she was reading. Cressida, however, made my blood boil. I doubted I could spend the evening watching her fawn all over Alexander without gagging.

"It's fine," I said, rising to my feet. "I'm not much of a dancer."

"Which is why this would be good practice," Alexander said.

"Well, we won't force you!" Cressida trilled. She clasped Alana by the wrist, urging her along. "I'm sure you'd rather read your book anyway." She glanced down at the fairy tale with a smirk. "See you in the ballroom, Your Highness."

Alana cast me a pitying look before they took off.

"He's coming, ladies!" Cressida shouted to her friends. The girls broke out into shrill chatter and bursts of giggles.

After watching the girls flounce away, Alexander turned to me and offered his arm.

"Come on, Fliss. You are welcome to come join us, if you want to learn the new dance from Avondale."

I could feel something inside me begin to deflate and it sucked away the easy atmosphere I had been enjoying with him. I hadn't seen him in days and our time together was already over. "I'll pass. Maybe next time."

His arm slowly fell to his side. "All right then. I'll see you in the library tomorrow for our lessons with Max. I still have to finish that chapter in our astronomy book that he told us to read."

"You are a prince. Max can't tell you to do anything. Just skip the reading for tonight."

"You'd love that, wouldn't you? Then you could score higher than me on the exam he's likely to give us tomorrow."

"I'll beat you anyway."

He held a hand over his mouth and stifled a yawn. "We'll see about that." He eyed the setting sun and his gaze traveled over to me once more before he turned to leave. "Don't stay out here too late. It'll be dark soon."

"Is that an order from a prince?"

"It's a request from a friend," he said with a smile. "I'll see you tomorrow. Oh, don't forget your book." He pointed to the fairy tale, which was barely poking out from under the hem of my skirt.

"Oh. Right. I won't forget it." I picked up the book and stuffed it in my satchel before he could ask me any more questions about it.

Without saying a word, Alexander gave me a final smile and headed back to the palace.

As I called out a goodbye and watched him walk away, the sudden image of him dancing with Lady Cressida pierced my mind. An unsettling feeling swept over me.

There might not be much underneath those silky curls, but Lady Cressida wasn't a complete dunce. She knew she was beautiful, and she would try to capture Alexander's attention. After all, he was the prince and someday that prince would need to find a princess. She was probably picking out the perfect tiara to wear to their wedding this very moment.

I looked down at my satchel and the fairy tale, with the title *Cinderella* emblazoned across the spine, peeked through the opening. That's when it hit me. For someone who professed to be an intelligent girl, I almost missed what was right in front of me.

Alexander couldn't marry any of those girls because it would ruin the fairy tale, and the fairy tale said *Cinderella* had to marry him.

What if Lady Cressida succeeded in making Alexander fall in love with her?

Fear of the unknown seeped through my veins, spurring me into action. I couldn't let one of the courtiers marry Alexander—he had to marry the girl from the fairy tale. The monarchy might topple and Valencia could perish if I let Cressida have her way.

I had to start looking for a girl named Cinderella.

CHAPTER 4

I read *Cinderella* by candlelight that night and woke up the next morning before dawn. I dressed in haste, dashing down the stairs before Max was even awake. I left a note saying I'd be back by nine o'clock for our morning lessons.

My uncle and I lived above the library in a separate wing that was reserved for the librarians. It was a quaint living space with a cozy kitchen and an inviting sitting room. Every space that wasn't occupied by furniture was piled with Max's personal books or stacks of parchment containing whatever research he was working on next. Neither of us cared very much for cleaning up after ourselves, so half empty tea cups on saucers littered the end tables on either side of the settee, several of his tunics hung across chairs because he was too distracted to hang them up and I was too indifferent, and my various attempts at embroidery, a ladylike pastime I was trying to find the excitement to pursue, were scattered around the room. It was complete chaos when you looked at the way we lived, but there was familiarity in the chaos, so I didn't mind it too much.

Meow.

Muse, the well-fed tabby cat that Mother had bestowed to me on my thirteenth birthday, ambled over to me, *purring* as she rubbed against my legs in an uncharacteristic attempt to be affectionate. She was usually completely standoffish, so she was most likely telling me she was hungry.

I patted her on the head. "Sorry, girl. I can't feed you right now. I'm in a rush. Go be a cat and catch some mice until I get back."

Muse, who was chronically lazy and more likely to invite a mouse into our home than chase one away, gave me a cold stare with her amber eyes as I shut the door in her face. I figured she'd probably go knock all the trinkets off my dresser or hide my stockings while I was gone for revenge.

There was a hush that fell over the morning as the sun began to make its appearance. Dew clung to my skirt and dampened my slippers. A chill swept over me and I tugged my shawl tighter around my shoulders. After reading the fairy tale, I discovered that I'd find Cinderella at her stepmother's house somewhere on the outskirts of the village. I wasn't exactly sure where it was, and by the time I had walked the muddy roads for almost an hour, I was regretting not wearing boots because my slippers were soaked through.

"Cinderella," I whispered her name, "where do you live? How do I find you?"

Almost minutes later, I came upon a house that seemed to answer my questions.

The manor was tall and elegant, but I couldn't shake the gloomy feeling I had when I stepped onto the property. Vines ran rampant alongside the walls, wrapping around windowpanes like menacing claws. The hem of my skirt caught on a weed. As I yanked it free, I noticed the lawn was too overrun with weeds and rocks to allow any actual grass to grow. The glass windows were covered with thick black curtains to keep the sunlight out.

I got the distinct sense that I would not be welcome here, which was why I hesitated before knocking on the front door. I raised my hand to knock anyway. Even if this wasn't Cinderella's home, I could at least stop and ask if the owner knew where she lived. I hadn't seen another home and it was futile to keep wandering around.

"Can I help you?"

I turned around and met the gaze of girl dressed in a homespun dress with a tattered apron tied twice around her waist. She held a large stack of firewood in her arms that looked like it would topple to the ground at any moment. Her blond hair was piled on top of her head beneath a stained kerchief, but wisps of hair had escaped her bun and fallen to frame her face. Even though dirt and ash were smeared across her cheeks and forehead, she was lovely. It was the type of beauty your eyes couldn't believe the first time they saw it, so you were inclined to take a second look.

She had to be Cinderella.

"Hello. I'm Felicity." I stepped away from the door. I hastened to think up an excuse that was different from the real reason I was on her doorstep. "I came out to the country to take a morning walk, but I must have gotten lost. I can't seem to find my way back to the village."

The girl clutched the firewood to her chest like it was a shield. "I'm Cinderella. The village is about two miles that way." She jerked her head slightly in the direction from which I came. "It's just straight ahead. If you follow the road, it'll lead you to the heart of the village. Is that where you live?"

"I actually live in the palace."

"You are a courtier?" She started to curtsy. "I had no idea you were nobility."

"No, no." I stopped her before she could finish her curtsy and the firewood fell from her arms. "I'm not nobility. I'm a palace librarian."

"Oh. I didn't know there was a library at the palace."

She didn't know there was a library at the palace? Valencia's library was renowned for its collection of books and inspiring architecture. People traveled from miles around to see its splendor. Did this girl live under a rock?

I stood on her porch, shifting awkwardly from foot to foot. I couldn't leave yet. I had to learn more about her. "Um, thank you. I'll just head that way then..."

She shifted the firewood in her arms, almost dropping the entire bundle.

"Here," I said, latching onto an idea. "Let me help you carry those inside. They look heavy." I pulled off a few logs and tucked them under the crook of my arm.

Her mouth hung open slightly at the offer of assistance. "You don't have to help me," she whispered. Her eyes darted from side to side and she looked over her shoulder. It was as if she was waiting for a reprimand of some sort. "I can get them. I'm used to it."

"You were kind enough to give me directions. Let me return the favor."

After a moment of consideration, Cinderella nodded. "Thank you. Follow me."

I followed her in through a side door off the porch. I had to duck my head as I entered the low servants' entrance and skirt around the narrow doorway carefully, so the frame wouldn't knock the firewood from my arms. The kitchen welcomed me with the scent of freshly baked bread that made my mouth water. It was a cozy kitchen. Brass pots and cast-iron skillets hung over a red brick fireplace. Inside, a fire sparked and crackled from underneath a large pot with boiling water. The warmth brought a tingle back to my numb cheeks. As Cinderella added wood to the flames, a hiss of smoke curled up around her and spat cinders onto her apron.

"Just set those other logs over there," she said, pointing to a spot by the door. "I'll need to take them up to my stepmother's room when she awakens, but that won't be for a few more hours. She'll want a roaring fire in her bedroom to ease the frostiness in this house." Cinderella glanced outside the one window in the kitchen. She took in the gray, misty morning with a grimace. "Summer cannot get here soon enough," she said, more to herself than to me.

"I agree," I replied, rubbing the chill from my arms.

"How rude of me," Cinderella said. "You must be cold. Take a seat by the fire and rest from your walk. I'll find you something warm to drink."

"Please don't go to any trouble on my account."

"Nonsense." She waved away my protest. "You are a guest, Felicity. It's not often that I have a guest to take care of these days."

As I sat down next to the fire, I peeled off my slippers and set them down in front of the flames to dry. She handed me a cup of tea after I hung my satchel over the back of a chair.

I sipped the tea. "This is very good. Thank you."

Cinderella eased the teakettle back over the stove after pouring a cup for herself. She then sliced two pieces of bread and spread a generous amount of butter onto each before setting one in front of me. "You helped me carry in those dirty logs, a task that often requires two trips because they are so heavy. My father always said any kindness done to you, no matter how small, should always be repaid."

"He sounds like a wise man."

31

"He was."

In the glow from the fire, Cinderella looked like an angel basking in light from the heavens. I couldn't help but notice we were opposites as far as appearances go. She had deep blue eyes that set off a skin tone that absorbed the sun easily and fair hair that would only grow lighter in the summer months. Whereas my skin was excruciatingly pale, eyes a light green, and curly hair darker than Max's inkbottles.

"You said you work in the palace library, right?" she asked after taking a sip of tea.

"Yes, with my uncle."

"I'd love to the see the library someday."

I had another idea. "You should come by and—"

"*Cinderella!*"

We both jumped at the loud roar of her name, and Cinderella knocked over the teacup that was perched on her knee. It seeped through her apron and dress. I stood up to fetch her a napkin, but she pushed me back down.

"Stay here," she whispered.

"CINDERELLA!" I heard the piercing voice again. It was closer this time.

Cinderella stood up and scurried across the kitchen like a frightened mouse. She pulled the door shut behind her, but it creaked back open on its rusty hinges anyway, giving me a view of the hallway on the other side.

"Why didn't you answer when I first called?" a voice from the other side of the door. "I've been waiting for you in my bedroom for the past twenty minutes."

"I didn't hear you, Stepmother. I wasn't expecting you to call for me this early in the morning."

Cinderella's stepmother stood with her profile to me, but I could see her sharp, angular cheekbones and long, whip-thin frame. And I certainly didn't need to see her face to know it was twisted into a grimace.

"How dare you contradict me! You ungrateful brat."

"I didn't contradict you, ma'am. I only answered your question."

Thwack! I heard the thick sound of flesh slapping flesh, and the echo of the impact resounded in my ears. Cinderella tumbled back a few paces and hit the wall, her thin body falling into it with a thud.

I was on my feet in an instant. I took three long strides to the door, ready to intervene. Cinderella saw me coming and something in her eyes steadied my steps.

No, they pleaded. There were no signs of a desperate *help me* or a reassuring *don't worry.* They simply told me to stay put and not interfere. Whatever her reasons, Cinderella was more afraid of me intervening than not intervening at all.

Her stepmother's venomous voice filled my ears once more. "That will teach you to be disrespectful. You better get back to work. If I catch you slacking off again, you'll be sleeping in the cellar with the mice."

"I gather they are better company," I grumbled under my breath.

I heard the stepmother's footsteps strut away as the wooden floorboards groaned. I rushed over to Cinderella as she floundered back into the kitchen. Her hand was pressed against her mouth.

"Are you all right?" I asked her.

"You had better go, Felicity," she said in a voice a notch below a whisper. She pulled her hand away from her face and a trickle of blood escaped the corner of her mouth and ran down her chin. A tear or two leaked out of her beautiful eyes and fell through the soot on her face to mingle with the blood.

"That *horrible* woman," I spat. I gestured wildly at her face. "Why would she do this to you? You did nothing wrong."

"I have work to do," Cinderella insisted. "Please, just leave."

I pulled a handkerchief out of my satchel and tried to offer it to her, but she shook her head. "I want to help," I said.

"*Help?*" Cinderella broke into a dismal laugh. "There's nothing you or anyone else can do."

"You don't have to stay with someone who—"

Her back straightened and her eyes flashed. "You are a stranger. I shouldn't have invited you into this house."

A moment of silence passed between us before I nodded, understanding why she wanted me to leave so desperately. If Cinderella's stepmother caught her talking to me, a literal stranger off the street, she would be severely punished. Her face was mixed with fear and the apprehension of being caught, while I was certain mine betrayed my horror and anger at what I'd witnessed.

None of this should have surprised me. I'd read the fairy tale, after all.

But it *did* surprise me.

"You should go," Cinderella said, glancing over her shoulder at the door. "Now."

I couldn't just leave, though. Not without the possibility of seeing her again in the near future. I needed her in my life if I was ever going to get Alexander to fall in love with her. I had to befriend her, and, truth be told, she seemed like she really needed a friend.

In a desperate last-minute attempt to see her again, I left my satchel hanging over the chair. She'd have to return it to me or I'd have to come back and get it from her. Either way, it assured me at least one more meeting.

I slipped my shoes back on and left, shutting the door with more force than necessary. The chill greeted me once more. It was a stark contrast to the rage that burned inside my belly. Suddenly, I *wanted* the fairy tale to be true. It had to be true. If not for the sake of Valencia, for the sake of a young girl who desperately needed rescuing. I had to get her away from this manor, this prison.

My mind raced through the story I had read the previous night. The tale of a handsome prince with a courageous heart, the beautiful servant girl with a heart of gold, and the wicked stepmother with no heart whatsoever was coming to life right in front of me.

I pulled my shawl tighter around my shoulders as the ends of it snapped in the wind. I headed back to the palace with determination that pounded through my blood like the beat of a drum. I was going to save Valencia from destruction, I was going to save Alexander from marrying the wrong girl, and I was going to save Cinderella from her stepmother.

CHAPTER 5

The sun sat a little higher in the sky on my return to the palace. I longed for the warmth of the library as I sloshed through misty grass and sodden roads, dragging my hem through the mud. I sprinted up the steps of the palace, taking them two at a time. I was breathing heavily when I rounded the corner to the library and smacked into someone.

"Alexander!" I cried.

He set his hand on my shoulder to steady me.

"I didn't see you there," I said through another heaving gasp of breath.

"I can tell. I should have been watching where I was going, though. I was in a hurry to get to class on time. I told Father I would sit in on an early morning meeting with his advisors today. Thankfully, I was able to escape just before the High Chancellor droned on about foreign diplomacy." He eyed my wind-swept hair and my flushed cheeks. "And why are you late?"

"I went for a walk," I replied, tugging him into the library after me. Max couldn't scold me for being late if the prince of the realm walked in late with me. "I believe there's nothing like a brisk morning walk to get the blood pumping."

His forehead crinkled. "Since when?"

"Since this morning."

I turned to look at him and couldn't help but smile. The sunlight streaming in through a nearby window shone across his face, giving him a glow to his already vibrant aura. There was an ache in my chest and I realized how good it felt to have him home. He'd been gone from the palace or attending to his many duties so often lately. Our mothers had been the best of friends and that friendship had carried over onto their children. There weren't very many memories of my childhood that didn't come without a memory of Alexander as well.

He caught me staring at him and raised an eyebrow in question. I shook myself out of my stupor and started to ask him if he had time to finish the reading or if he'd spent all of the previous evening with Lady Cressida when I heard a loud *crash*. A large sphere hurtled in our direction from the other side of the room.

Alexander and I ducked. We exchanged glances and turned around to find where the commotion was coming from. It was no surprise that the disturbance came from Max.

My uncle was hovering over a large contraption that had multiple arms hanging from it like a spider with more painted spheres dangling from each arm. Max pushed his spectacles farther down his nose as he surveyed the damage. He gave the contraption a not-so-gentle kick, which did nothing but cause another sphere to break off and roll across the floor.

"There you two are. I was getting worried I'd have to calm Max down on my own."

Alexander's cousin, Jack, sauntered over to us. His copper curls flew aimlessly about his face and his hazel eyes missed nothing. The two boys were opposites in both appearance and personality. While Alexander's charisma and confidence were forces to be reckoned with, Jack's milder manners and pensive ways usually got brushed over.

"How long has he been like this?" I asked, pointing to Max as he circled the contraption like a rabid animal and continued to mutter.

"Since I showed up," Jack said, lounging against one of the library's tables in the common area. He eased his hands into his trouser pockets. "Max was telling me that thing is a model of the planets in our solar system. Apparently, the planets are supposed to orbit each other when you pull a lever on the model, but it isn't working. So Max thought if he kicked it and shouted some obscenities that would help, which is what you walked in on."

"The sun!" Max cried. "The planets are supposed to orbit around the *sun*, not each other!" My uncle pushed up the sleeves of his long burgundy jacket and loosened the strings that tied the collar of his tunic together. "Did any of you actually do the reading?"

When none of us answered, Max *huffed* dramatically. "I thought as much. And, Felicity, you are late. That means I want you to copy the notes from today's lesson twice."

"I'm not the only one who was late!" I pointed an accusatory finger in Alexander's direction.

Alexander shot me a look and whispered something about a traitor under his breath.

Max glanced at Alexander and nodded. "Ah, yes. Good morning, Your Highness. I'm glad to see you and Jack made it safely back from your patrol."

I rolled my eyes. I started to offer Max an excuse for my tardiness, but he had already turned his back to us and was ranting at the bizarre contraption again.

I sighed and stepped forward, placing my hand gently on Max's arm. "Max, we'll fix the lever on the model later.

Perhaps we can talk about something else today and save the astronomy lesson for tomorrow?"

Max looked like he wanted to protest, and I was relieved when he finally nodded his consent. "We'll do the astronomy lesson tomorrow. I'll show you three some of the maps I found preserved in the archives yesterday. We can practice our cartography skills today."

"Sorry, Max," Alexander said. "I can't make it to the lesson tomorrow. I have to meet the captain of the guards first thing in the morning. It's our weekly fencing lesson."

"We'll still have time in the afternoon for our studies."

"And I'll be training in the weapons room all afternoon," Jack commented. He straightened himself off the table and shrugged apologetically. "I meant to tell you earlier."

Max nodded briskly, but none of us missed the disappointment flickering in his eyes. "Then we should make the most of today. I'll go retrieve the maps."

After he was out of earshot, I turned on my heel to face the boys. "What is all of this about? Why have you two missing more and more of your lessons lately?"

They exchanged knowing glances. "Do you want to tell her?" Alexander asked.

Jack shrugged his shoulders.

"Tell me what?" I demanded.

"Uncle Frederic sat us down and said that we had certain responsibilities we needed to start attending to, Fliss. Alex has more court obligations he needs to fulfill, and I'm going to have more assignments after I'm knighted," Jack explained in a calm voice, like he was explaining a simple concept, not breaking apart my childhood. He ran a hand through his hair, tousling it further. "We are both nearly eighteen. At some point we have to stop educating ourselves about maps and astronomy and start educating ourselves on matters of the kingdom."

I turned to Alexander. "So after your eighteenth birthday your schooling is done?"

He nodded. "I'm sorry, Fliss. I think my father spoke to Max about it already, but I forgot to tell you."

"*You forgot to tell me?*"

I took a faltering step back. These lessons with Jack and Alexander had meant a lot to me over the years. When my mother died four years earlier, everything in my world was shaken up. Things I should have been familiar with felt foreign. Food tasted bland, days seemed empty without her laughter ringing through the library, and my spirit had suffered a crushing blow.

The one thing that remained the same was the time I spent with Alexander and Jack during our daily lessons with Max. They made sure I didn't fall apart or lose my mind to grief. Their presence in the library was a consistency I had come to count on, and now I was going to lose my time with them sooner than anticipated.

"Why didn't you two tell me?"

Jack started to speak up, but Alexander beat him to it.

"Felicity," he said gently. I looked up to see his eyes filled with sympathy, which irritated me for some unexplainable reason. "You had to know that this was going to happen eventually. Surely you can see that the three of us are growing up. Jack is going to be a knight someday, and I'm going to be—"

"King," I cut in. The energy I had felt coming back from Cinderella's manor was gone and replaced by something that left a strange, bitter taste in my mouth. I heard the truth in his words though—Valencia held claim to Alexander, this library did not. "I understand perfectly, Alexander. You can't spend as much time in the library."

"Like Jack said, at some point we've got to take what we've learned and test it out on the world."

I glanced at the bookshelves around me. This library was my world, but it seemed so narrowly small when compared to theirs. The reply on my lips was cut off when Max hurried back into the room with rolls of maps tucked underneath both arms. He called for us to take our seats, but as the lesson started, my mind wandered to what my own future plans would hold.

An hour into the lesson, Max was explaining one of the maps to Jack. He was enjoying himself so much that his nose was pressed up against the canvas and he was throwing his hands around so animatedly that Jack had to duck out of the way more than once. Upon hearing the clock strike a new hour, Alexander had to return to his meeting with the advisors and he offered his apologies for leaving so soon, Max waved him away and told him we'd pick up with the astronomy lesson next time.

Alexander caught my stare as I watched him turn to leave. He smiled, but it wasn't the familiar smile that reached his eyes. "If there's time in my schedule, I'll stop by later tonight. Maybe we can go over the chapter in our astronomy book together. Better yet, we could meet in the weapons room and continue your fencing lessons. I hope you've been working on your form while I've been gone. It was a little sloppy before I left." He said the last part teasingly, thinking it might get a smile out of me.

Instead, I stiffened. "I don't want to be forced into your schedule." I glanced back down at my map and feigned great interest in marking coordinates. "I will not fall apart because our time together is cut short. For that matter, neither will my fencing form."

I bit my lip, immediately regretting the tone in my voice. I could feel Alexander's frown without looking up to have it confirmed. When I did finally look up to apologize, he was gone.

The lesson proceeded without Max breaking anything else or another disruption, until a few minutes before noon when the library's door creaked open. Max asked me to go see if someone needed help. My eyes were thankful for a reprieve from looking at old maps, so I willingly hurried to the library's entrance.

The visitor was staring up at the sparkling constellations painted on the ceiling as I approached her. The sudden sight of soft blond hair and a dull gray dress slightly stained with ash and cinders made me pause.

"Cinderella?"

She jumped at the sound of my voice and turned quickly. "Oh, Felicity!"

"You are here... in the library," I said, blinking in surprise. I noticed the cut next to the corner of her mouth had stopped bleeding but was slightly swollen. There would be a bright purple bruise there tomorrow. "I wasn't expecting you to stop by today."

"You left your satchel in my kitchen," she explained. She held out the bag, and I reached to take it from her. "I didn't know if there was anything important in there. Just in case there was, I wanted to return it right away."

"Thank you. I would have come for it eventually."

Cinderella clasped her hands in front of her. "Your library is very impressive. I must say I'm ashamed I haven't visited before today. I wasn't even sure if I would be able to find it, but something this grand is hard to miss."

"Let me introduce you to my uncle and give you a tour."

She followed me deeper into the library and glanced around with awe and curiosity as she took in the magnificent displays of books and the architecture. I even saw her reach out and trace the spine of a book lovingly with her finger.

"I've never seen so many books in all my life." She reached to pull the book off the shelf but hesitated, as if trying to decide if she was allowed to handle the books.

"You can look at it," I said, holding back a grin. "You can even take it home to read if you want."

Her eyes widened. "I can take it home and read it?"

I pulled it off the shelf for her. "That's the very definition of a library."

"This is the royal family's library, though," she said. She jumped a little when I put the book in her hands, as though it contained some mysterious power. She caressed the cover reverently. Max would have approved of her reaction. He thought books should always be held with a certain amount of respect.

"I'm a commoner. I can't take the king's books."

"The royal family likes to share. They won't mind. The people of this kingdom have been borrowing their books for centuries." I peered at the title. "Plus, I doubt the king will stop by the library any time soon and demand this particular book of romantic poems. I could be wrong, though. Stranger things have happened lately..."

"Well... I would like to have something to read in the evenings after I finish my chores." She shrugged her delicate shoulders, which shifted the waves falling around her face just an inch or so. "At the very least, it's something my stepmother won't care to take from me. I doubt she even knows the front end of a book from the back end."

Impressed by her sudden pluck of courage I cried, "Brava, Cinderella!"

My cheer must have made her realize how fearless her words sounded. "I shouldn't have said that. You probably think I'm horribly rude."

"Quite the opposite."

We found Max and Jack where I had left them earlier, huddled over a map and discussing where Valencia's outlying defenses might be strengthened. Both of them looked up when they noticed us approaching.

"Max, this is my friend Cinderella. Cinderella, this is my Uncle Max, head librarian of this *impressive* establishment, as you called it."

Max came around and shook her hand. His eyes found mine over the top of Cinderella's head. I saw the question in his eyes. *This is the future Queen of Valencia?* Cinderella, despite her lovely features and genuine kindness, was dressed as a commoner, and not one of the more prosperous ones, either. Max wasn't being judgmental, simply curious.

I turned to Jack, who had stopped marking coordinates on his map and came forward to meet the library's newest guest.

"Hello, I'm Jack."

"I'm Cinderella," she replied. "I'm Felicity's friend."

I warmed at the word *friend.* I liked the way it sounded.

His brow furrowed. "I've known Felicity for some time now, and she never told me about you."

"In all fairness, we only just met," I explained. "But, yes, Cinderella is a friend." I turned to my uncle. "Max, if we are done with lessons for the day, I was going to give Cinderella a tour."

"We can be done." Max started gathering up maps. "I have some work I need to complete anyway."

I gestured for Cinderella to follow me. "Come on, I'll show you around the library and the upstairs portion. Max and I live above the library."

"You *live* in this wonderful place?" Cinderella made another sweeping turn around as she gazed at the domed ceiling and rows of bookshelves.

"We even have a cat. I'll let you meet her. Are you coming with us, Jack?"

Cinderella turned to follow me up the stairs, but Jack cut us off before my hand could touch the banister.

"As tempting as Muse is, and she isn't because I've met snakes cuddlier than that cat, I have to go check my traps in the forest." Jack glanced between the two of us. "Would you ladies like to come with me? It's too beautiful outside to stay indoors all day."

"Well..." I glanced at Cinderella, who nodded eagerly. "Sure," I replied. "I guess I could use some fresh air."

"Do you want to come with us, Max?" Jack called over his shoulder.

Max wrinkled his nose at the suggestion. He usually didn't leave the library unless it was a life or death situation. Apparently, traipsing through the forest with three teenagers was not a life or death situation.

"It's just the three of us then."

Jack, whose nonchalant manner and quiet spirit usually dominated his personality, seemed different. His step was lighter and his eyes more animated. For one small moment the way he was taking charge reminded me of Alexander.

He guided us to the exit. "Let's have an adventure, girls."

Cinderella and I exchanged glances and a certain wild excitement filled her eyes. That's when I realized we *would* make good friends, because maybe she craved adventure as much as I did.

CHAPTER 6

Jack escorted us outside the palace walls, and I sprang away from him and Cinderella when the cool air of early afternoon hit my face. Jack had been right, the day, which had started off with a dismal morning, had turned into the beginnings of true springtime weather. The sun shone like a bright beacon over our heads. The first traces of wildflowers erupted around the sloping hills, beckoning us outside into the rolling grass that swept over the landscape. Every blade of grass waved to us as it danced in the breeze. Spring, for all of its wretchedly chilly mornings and evenings, knew how to deliver a proper midday.

Jack took us to the outskirts of the palace grounds that fed off into a woodland area. There were trees as far as the eyes could see and the distinct smell of pine and sunshine swept over me, playing with my senses. The birds chirped happily in the trees, singing back and forth to each other. I watched as a chipmunk dashed across the forest floor, rustling leaves and stirring up pine needles as it ran.

I hoisted my skirts above my ankles and climbed over a log. "Why exactly are you setting traps, Jack?"

"It's a survival skill that I have to learn during my knighthood training. I have to check them every so often."

I turned to Cinderella. "Do you need to be home at any certain time?" I didn't want her to get into more trouble today because she stayed out too late.

She shook her head and her golden tendrils danced around her face. "My stepmother will be in the village shopping for most of the day, so it's fine if I'm gone a little longer. I could use the fresh air. The woods remind me of my father. We used to go on long walks around our property when he was alive. We would be gone for hours some days because we got so caught up in exploring, or fishing at the nearby pond, or climbing the hills that surround the manor."

"You speak of him with such fondness. He must have been a good man."

"The very best man I've ever known," she corrected me. She reached out to run her hand over the rough bark of a tree trunk. "He died a few years ago. My mother died a few days after I was born. He loved her so. I tell myself he missed her so much that he wanted to be with her again in the next life sooner rather than later." She glanced over her shoulder and caught Jack's stare. She offered him a forced, practiced smile.

As a fellow orphan, I knew that smile well. It said a lot of things you don't say out loud.

"I guess that's something we all unfortunately have in common," Jack said with a too light tone. When Cinderella looked at him questioningly, he explained, "My parents died in an accident when I was ten, and my Uncle Frederic and Aunt Briar took me in and raised me as their own."

"Uncle Frederic and Aunt Briar?" Cinderella blinked once, twice, and then once more. She looked up at him with wide, curious eyes. "You mean *King* Frederic and *Queen* Briar?"

The corner of Jack's mouth tugged upward. "Yes. I believe those are their official titles."

Cinderella plopped to the ground and leaned back against the tree. "Jack, you are *royalty*?"

"In a way."

A brief flash of worry crossed her face. "Do you have a title? Should I be calling you Lord Jack or something?"

I snorted at the idea of calling Jack anything but Jack, especially *Lord* Jack. It was preposterous. I already knew I'd have a hard time calling him *Sir* Jack at court functions after he was knighted.

Jack shot me an annoyed glance as I continued to stifle my laughter. He turned his attention back to Cinderella. "I didn't inherit a title from my father's side of the family. Father was a lowly, albeit brave, knight that just happened to steal the heart of King Frederic's sister, my mother, Princess Liana. It was quite a scandal in court when the two of them married in secret. My mother was set to marry a prince in another kingdom before she eloped with my father."

"She gave up marriage to a prince?"

"I think it worked out for the better." Jack leaned against the tree next to Cinderella. "Aunt Briar said my mother's betrothed was an arrogant, brutish prince who would have been impossible to live with."

Cinderella shook her head, as if she couldn't believe her surroundings. "My stepsisters would be so jealous to know that I was speaking to *The* Prince Alexander's cousin. They'd turn pure green with envy."

I sat down next to her and exchanged a quick look with Jack, whose face had turned unreadable with the mention of Alexander. "Maybe we won't tell Alexander people are calling him *The* Prince Alexander nowadays. It would go straight to his head."

"You know the prince, too?"

I nodded. "He's one of my best friends. I'll introduce you next time you come by the library."

I laughed at the genuine terror on her face. The poor girl was petrified of the very idea of speaking to a prince. If she reacted this way when merely being introduce to Alexander, what would she do when he got down on one knee and proposed someday?

I stopped laughing when I felt something strange sweep over me. An unexplained sense of foreboding rang loudly in my ear, and I noticed the forest had turned eerily quiet. The chatter of birds ceased, the hum of bees buzzing and crickets chirping fell to a hush, and even the rustle of leaves in the trees grew silent. Cinderella didn't seem to notice, but Jack and I exchanged a sudden glance.

He straightened himself off the tree, and I stood up half a second later, following his lead. He must have sensed something unfamiliar, too. My skin prickled with anxiety as I turned to look over my shoulder. Jack unsheathed his sword, and the slash of his blade swiping against the sheath echoed across the forest.

"What's wrong?" Cinderella asked. She eyed Jack's sword warily. "Am I missing something? I thought—"

"Shhh."

Jack tilted his head to the side, listening intently to the sounds, or lack of sounds, in the forest. His eyes scanned the line of shadowy trees. It wasn't the strange atmosphere that frightened me the most. It was his unwavering alertness and suspicion. He was suddenly not the familiar boy I studied arithmetic and geography with as a child. He had transformed into a knight trained to notice danger, to sense its very presence.

"*Jack*," Cinderella breathed. Her voice was a notch below a choppy whisper, barely audible even in complete silence. She raised her hand and pointed into a section of the trees.

Jack turned, presumably to tell her to *shhh* once more, but his eyes followed her outstretched hand. He almost dropped his sword when he registered what was before us.

Out of the shadows appeared three looming figures. Their bodies were lean and angular. Their faces were shrouded by black hoods and flowing capes that swished against the forest floor. An inky black mist swirled around them, rising like menacing tendrils of smoke from the ground. The mist seemed to slowly propel them forward, pushing them towards us.

Jack grasped his sword tighter, his knuckles whitening. "Felicity...*run*," he ordered through clenched teeth.

"Perhaps they mean us no harm," I whispered.

The figures brandished their own swords, which were stained with blood from previous victims that had rusted over, and the metal glinted in a small ray of sunlight falling through the treetops, blinding me momentarily.

I gulped. "Then again, perhaps not."

Jack placed a hand on my shoulder and pushed me toward Cinderella. "Take her and run," he ordered again.

Surprised, I stumbled toward Cinderella. My sudden movement made the creatures spring into action. Their once slow movements dissolved into lightning fast reflexes. They closed the distance between us, and Jack stepped forward to meet their swords.

Clang!

I winced as the clash of metal rang out like the toll of a bell. Jack grunted as he blocked a blow. I raced towards Cinderella but yelped as a bony set of fingers grabbed my wrist and black ooze seeped onto my skin. As I turned to look at the creature, it hurtled me down to the ground with such force I feared my shoulder had been torn from its socket.

I twisted my ankle and landed face first on the ground, barreling into a pile of prickly pine needles that stabbed at my cheeks. Stunned, I turned over to meet the eyes of whatever had thrown me. The face before me was hollow and menacing, the figure more skeleton than human. Black mist rolled out like waves from a pair of empty eye sockets, and its mouth formed a ghoulish sneer as dark liquid dripped from the cracks of sharpened teeth.

"Felicity!" Cinderella's voice called out a warning.

The creature's jagged sword came down swiftly, and I rolled away just in time to hear the tip of the blade sink into the soft earth instead of my flesh. I ignored the pain in my shoulder and foot, springing to my feet. After momentarily cursing myself for not carrying a sword, I reached for the nearest weapon I could find: a thick tree branch. I swung the branch like a club with my good arm, and it smacked into the side of the ghoul's face. Instead of the satisfying crack of bones there was only a mildly loud *thwack*. The creature brandished its sword again, an evil grin spread across its sickly face. It moved toward me with slow, deliberate intention, as if it relished the prospect of killing me. I took a few clumsy steps back and my backside collided into a tree trunk. My sole weapon, the tree branch, shook in my hands.

I looked for Jack, who just at that moment thrust his sword into the shoulder of the monster he'd been battling. The monster collapsed in a heap of mist onto the ground. Jack's eyes widened with alarm when he looked over and saw me trapped.

"Fliss!" he hollered, barreling forward. Before I knew what was happening, he rushed the creature, tackling it. As they tumbled to the forest floor, the monster lost his grip and the sword clattered to the ground.

I threw my branch aside and reached for the sword, wielding it wildly as I watched Jack wrestle with the creature. The monster's pointed teeth snapped at Jack, who lay trapped under the beast, his hands wrapped around the creature's neck to hold the sharp teeth away.

In a flash of black smoke and tingling mist that made my eyes water, Jack and the creature vanished under the dark silk fabric of the shadowy cloak. I frantically scanned the scene in front of me. I didn't dare thrust the sword into cape for fear of stabbing Jack.

A flash of red hair popped up over the black fabric, and Jack shouted, "Now, Felicity!"

"But—"

"NOW!"

I lunged forward to thrust my sword in the body behind the cape, praying I didn't spear Jack by mistake. A foul cry of pain pierced the air around us, and a horrible black liquid that must have been its blood seeped from the monster's body and mingled with the darkness of the cape. I pulled the sword from the creature's back, and Jack jumped to his feet and kicked the creature away.

I stared at the thing lying on the ground in front of me, writhing with pain as it took its last breath.

"I killed it," I murmured, dropping the blood-stained sword quickly as if it would singe my hands. The blade bounced away out of my reach. I shrunk back, colliding once more into the tree trunk behind me. "I killed that... monster... that horrible creature."

"It wasn't human, Fliss."

A tremble ran up my spine and ricocheted through my body. "Still, I've never killed anything before."

Jack's eyes were filled with venom as they watched the creature struggle to die. "It would have killed you," he whispered. "It would have killed me, too. It would have killed Cinderella if it had gotten the chance."

Our heads jerked up at the same time.

"*Cinderella!*" we said in unison.

She was gone. Nothing but a trail of footprints that had been dragged through the moistened earth remained. A gust of wind stirred the fallen leaves on the ground where she once stood. We heard Cinderella's cry in the distance, calling our names frantically.

"There were three of those things," I whispered. My breath quickened and I started after her. I stumbled as a flash of pain traveled up my leg.

Jack caught me before I fell to the ground. "Wait. You are hurt."

"We have to go after her!"

"I'll go after her," he said. "You can't even walk."

I nodded, conceding to his suggestion. "Then I'll head back to the palace and get help."

Jack took off and followed the tracks the monster left behind. I watched him disappear into the line of trees that were scattered densely around the forest and soon I was left alone with only the bodies of two fallen monsters and my wildly racing thoughts for company.

My foot throbbed and the pain in my shoulder was almost unbearable. I limped over to the sword I had dropped earlier, wincing as I reached down to pick it up. I bit my lip to keep a few tears from falling. After I retrieved the sword, I turned to begin the long walk back to the palace. I had to get to Alexander and King Fredric.

I stepped off to begin the journey to the palace when a familiar bony hand reached out and closed around my neck. My surprise attacker, the first monster Jack had run his sword through, had its fingers wrapped around my throat. Instinctively, I kicked and gasped and launched my fists toward its unholy face. The creature threw me hard and fast to the ground. My head smacked into the nearby tree and my body suddenly felt weightless.

My mind urged me to get up and run or fight back or do anything other than lay there helplessly, yet my body rebelled and my battered limbs refused to work. The shrouded figure hovered over me in a haze of darkness, and I was too weak and dazed to move away.

It's going to kill me, I thought.

I could feel the sheer hate and rage radiating off of it. The creature's eyeless sockets spilled black liquid over hollow cheeks as it lifted a sword above its head. This horrible face would be the last one I saw before I died. The blade glinted in the sunlight, and the light shined off the metal like a sparkling beam of magic. I expected the light to fade as the blade came down upon me, giving away to the darkness of the next life.

Yet the darkness never came, if anything the light before my eyes grew brighter and brighter still as it enveloped the space around me. Instead of giving away to the darkness, as I always thought a person would do when they died, I gave away to the light. If this was death, it was already not what I expected.

CHAPTER 7

I woke slowly and groggily. My muscles screamed in fury. I shifted uncomfortably in my sleepy state, and a swift bolt of pain in my head forced my eyes open. Temple throbbing, I looked at my surroundings through half open eyes. Instead of lying dead on the forest floor like I should have been, I was lying in a small bed in a tiny one-room cottage. The ceiling was low, so low that I wasn't sure I could stand without ducking my head. The bed was tucked safely away in the corner next to a writing desk and a small bookcase. I scanned the bookcase, looking for familiar titles, but all of them were in a foreign language.

"You finally woke up."

A petite woman with fiery orange hair seemed to magically appear at my side, and I jumped back in surprise, banging my already pounding head against the wooden headboard behind me.

"Ow!" I cried. I rubbed my scalp as the pain in my head intensified, squinting at the woman, leery of her sudden presence. As if it were a shield, I clutched the quilted blanket closer to my chest. "Who are you? Where am I? What happened?"

A smile peeled across the woman's face. She had luminous silver eyes that shimmered in the glow from the nearby fire. Her hair was essentially long pieces of bright, rust colored corkscrews that flew aimlessly about her head. She brushed one of her curls behind her ear before moving to the fireplace to pick up a teakettle that sat hovering over the flames on a hook. As she moved, her tiny frame wandered airily around the cottage. The woman couldn't have been more than five feet tall and her waist looked tiny enough to wrap my hands around. When she turned back around to face me, she said, "Which of those questions should I answer first?"

Pain thundered ferociously in my head, but the panic I felt stirring my heartbeat dominated my senses. "Where am I?"

She poured the liquid from the kettle into two cups. It smelled strongly of ginger. "My cottage in the forest."

"And how did I get here?"

She handed me one of the cups. "I brought you here."

"Did you stop that monster from killing me?"

A whimsical laugh bubbled over her lips and floated around the room. "You sure do ask a lot of questions."

I raised an eyebrow. "So that's a *yes*?"

"Yes."

"And my friends?" I asked quickly. "I was with a boy and another girl. They are about my age. Do you know if they are all right?"

"Trust me, your friends are fine. They escaped unscathed. They are probably even out looking for you right now."

"*Trust you?*" I questioned, my voice cracking. "I don't even know you. Why would you save me? Why did you interfere? That thing could have killed you."

"You ask foolish questions. I'm not some evil beast who gets twisted pleasure by watching an innocent girl die at the hands of a monster." She sighed wearily as she placed her own teacup on a table next to the bed. "I've never died before, but I imagine being run through with a sword would not be the most pleasant of ways to go. I had to do something."

"The last thing I remember was a bright light. Was that you, too?"

"Yes." As she pulled her hand back from the teacup, the flame from a candle cast a glow across her skin, causing it to shimmer like it had been sprinkled with stardust. She noticed my stare and shrugged.

"You are shimmering." I pointed to her skin. "You are practically glowing."

"Ah. Yes. It's part of the curse of being a fairy."

"Wait a second," I said, twisting my legs out from under the covers. My feet hit the cold floor with a *thunk*, and another jolt of pain flew up my right leg. "Ouch!"

"Oh yes," she said with a *tsk*. "Mind your foot. You twisted your ankle. I took the liberty of wrapping it for you. I also fixed your arm, so you are welcome for that, too."

I stared at her, my mind hovering between disbelief and delusion. "Did you say *fairy*?"

"I can see you are skeptical," she said. "You should drink your tea. You'll feel better."

"Tea? *Tea?*" I almost laughed at the suggestion. I set the teacup down on a nightstand with more force than necessary. The china rattled when it contacted the hard surface. "You tell me you are a fairy and then you expect me to drink tea? Like there's nothing out of the ordinary?"

"Given all that's happened, I'd think your interpretation of *ordinary* would be a little more open."

I crumpled the blanket on the bed between my fists. "I don't understand."

The young woman looked to be in her mid-twenties, but her eyes made me believe she was much wiser than her years. "No," she said softly. "I expect you wouldn't understand. You are, after all, only human, and humans have the narrowest minds of all the species I've ever encountered."

I wasn't sure how to respond to that statement, so I settled on saying, "My uncle told me once that fairy tales were written by actual fairies. Did you write *Cinderella*?"

"Ah-ha. Now you are asking the right questions. Maxwell would be so proud." Her silver eyes shined with excitement and playfulness. She repositioned herself in the chair and tucked her small legs underneath her flowing skirt. "What else has your uncle been telling you?"

"You know Max? And you didn't answer my question."

"Of course, I know Maxwell. I knew your mother, too. We all sort of... grew up together."

"Sort of?"

"That's another story for another day." Almost an instant later, her head snapped up firmly, as if she had an idea, and she pushed my cup closer to me once more. "You should drink your tea. It'll help with the pain in your head."

I eyed the drink with suspicion. "My mother told me to never accept food or drink from strangers."

"Your mother was wise. However, if I wanted to harm you, I wouldn't have saved your life." The fairy rolled her eyes. "Are you always this skeptical? You must get that from Maxwell."

"Who knows if you are even a fairy? You could just be an eccentric looking human."

She flicked her dainty wrist, and a sudden bright fire roared to life in the fireplace, spitting embers onto the hearth. Startled once more, I gasped. To add to my bewilderment, the teacup and saucer appeared in my hands again. I almost spilled the contents on my lap.

Magic.

"Not a fairy, you say?" she said with a wink. "Go on. Drink your tea."

I took the proffered tea from her, eager to gulp anything down so long as it stopped the pounding in my temple. The drink filled me with the sensation of floating on clouds.

"Hmm. I can't believe it. I'm drinking tea with a *fairy*." I put my cup back down on the nightstand. My eyelids grew heavy and I had to blink several times to keep them open. "You must be Cinderella's fairy godmother. I read about you."

She raised an eyebrow. "Did you now?"

"You turn a pumpkin into a carriage fit for a queen. That's what the fairy tale says at least."

"Then it must be true."

"By the way, what's your name?"

"Katrina. You may call me Katrina."

I felt the urge to snuggle deeper into the covers. The warmth in my belly from the tea was making me drowsy, and I wanted nothing more than to drift into a peaceful slumber and forget how exhausted my bruised, battered body actually was.

"Katrina..." I tested her name on my lips. She pulled the covers over my shoulders, tucking me in like a small child. "That doesn't sound like a fairy's name."

"Did you think I was called something ridiculous like Pixie or Blossom or Moonbeam? Hmm?" I couldn't see her face. I was too far under the covers and too tired to turn my head, but I could hear laughter in her voice.

Somewhere in the back of my mind, I battled the urge to sleep. I had questions to ask her, answers to discover. Yet my body fought me, and I was in no condition to fight back. But one question in my brain stood out bold enough to merit just a few more moments of consciousness.

"Katrina?" I whispered through a small yawn.

"Yes?"

"If you knew my mother and my uncle, did you ever meet my father?"

I never heard her reply, if she gave me one at all, for I was already being welcomed back into the open arms of sleep.

CHAPTER 8

Felicity!"

A familiar voice called my name from somewhere in the recesses of my mind, awakening me.

"*Felicity!*" The voice was closer now, more urgent.

I stirred in my sleepy state and rolled over onto something hard and wet. There was a terrible pain in my head, a dull ache in my shoulder, and my ankle throbbed vehemently. The smell of pine needles and damp earth roused my senses. When I finally opened my eyes, my palms reached out and grasped the cold ground underneath them, and I noticed my fingers were caked with mud.

I gazed at my surroundings in wonder, half dumbfounded and half relieved, for I was not in Katrina's cottage anymore. I was in the forest again. Long, thin beams of light peeked through the splayed branches of the trees hanging over me and prickled my face with warmth.

"FELICITY!"

This time I jumped at the sound of my own name. "I'm here!" I replied, slightly annoyed. Whoever was yelling my name was not helping the pounding headache in my skull settle down. I clamped my hands over my ears. "For goodness' sake, please just stop yelling."

"Felicity?"

I turned my head, but even the slightest movement made me wince.

The commanding voice wavered with breathless relief. "Fliss..."

I knew that voice. "Alexander?"

Alexander dropped to his knees next to me, reaching out to slowly tilt my chin up to meet his gaze. His eyes looked like thunder as they inspected my face and traveled down my body, looking for injuries. "Oh, Fliss..." And in the span of a one more heartbeat, he reached out and wrapped his arms around me. "I found you."

I gave a hiss of pain as I pushed his crushing arms away from me. "No offense, Alexander, it's really good to see you too, but maybe it would be better if you didn't touch me right now. I'm not feeling so great."

"Of course. I'm sorry. I wasn't thinking. I was just glad to find you..."

"Alive?" I ventured. I winced as I tried to move my head again.

His eyes narrowed. "What hurts?"

"In a word; everything." I rubbed my hand across my face wearily. "My head and ankle seem to have taken the brunt of it though."

"Can you stand?"

"I think so."

He reached out and pulled me to my aching feet. A rush of dizziness made my head spin and I leaned against a tree trunk for support.

Alexander hovered next to me. "We need to get you to a healer soon."

I tested putting some weight on my ankle. After I was satisfied that it wasn't going to completely collapse underneath me, I said, "I'm not going back to the palace just yet."

He stared at me for a long minute, like I might have hit my head harder than he thought. "I'm sorry. I must have misunderstood you. I could've sworn you said you weren't going back to the palace."

"Correct. Don't give me that look. I'm not crazy." I scanned the forest, eyeing the shadows. "I'm looking for someone."

"Pray tell, who?"

"There's a young woman who rescued me. She lives in the forest. She was a—" I stopped to consider that if I told him Katrina was a fairy, my words would not help my plea against insanity. In fact, they would do more harm than good. "She was a young woman with silver eyes, wild orange hair, and shimmery skin like it was dusted with diamond powder."

"Right. Okay. Shimmery skin." Alexander ran a hand through his hair. "Well, we'll sort it all out after you've seen the healer. Priority one is getting you to the palace. There's a search party looking for you. Max is beside himself."

"In all fairness, Max is, at any given moment, beside himself about something. You should have seen him last week when he found Muse scratching the spine of one of his books."

"I think nearly losing his niece is slightly different—"

The brush behind us rustled and the sound of cracking twigs echoed across the forest, and our attention snapped toward the noise. Alexander reached for his sword. I held my breath.

"Fliss!" Jack cried, emerging from the shadows. A look of relief swept across his face. "Thank goodness!" He rushed toward me. "We've been so worried."

Alexander sighed, sheathing his sword.

I clasped Jack's hand. "You are all right? What about Cinder—"

"We're both fine," he assured me quickly. "I was able to find her. She's home right now." Jack squeezed my hand gently. "The search party has been looking for you for hours. Let's get you home."

I tugged my hand out of his. "Not yet."

Jack exchanged a look with Alexander, who merely shrugged his shoulders. "Why not?"

Alexander cleared his throat. "She's *looking* for someone. Someone with sparkly skin."

"I said *shimmery* skin. If you are going to be condescending, at least get my words right." I snagged a fallen tree branch to use as a makeshift walking stick. I hobbled forward a few steps, leaning harder than I cared to admit on my cane for support. The wood was rough and scratched at the tender skin on my palm. "I have to find her."

"Who?" Jack questioned.

"Katrina. The young woman who lives in the forest."

Alexander frowned at my teetering cane. "That's enough. You aren't going off to look for some fictional, *shimmery* person after being attacked in this very forest only a few hours ago. It's not safe."

"It's perfectly safe. The creatures that attacked us are dead."

"There might be more we don't know about. You are coming back to the palace."

I planted my feet firmly on the ground. Well, as firmly as I could without doing further injury to myself. "I have questions to ask Katrina."

"What questions are so important that you need to go in search of some girl you conjured up in your delusional mind?" Alexander asked.

"*Delusional?* I am not making this up!"

Alexander opened his mouth to reply, but he snapped it shut, biting off whatever retort he had resting on the tip of his tongue. With a sigh that sounded more like a groan, he swept his arm out in a forward gesture.

"Lead the way, Fliss."

I lifted my chin, suspicious. "You aren't going to stop me?"

"I learned a long time ago that I can't stop you from doing anything you set your mind on doing. So, since I can't beat you, I might as well join you in your search and keep an eye on you." He turned to Jack. "Alert the search party that she's been found; make sure Max knows. We'll be back as soon as possible." Alexander watched me take a few hobbling steps with my cane. "From the looks of it, that won't be long."

Jack reluctantly agreed. We watched him disappear into the forest, calling out for the search party.

Alexander swept his arm out once more in a grand, dramatic gesture. "After you."

I straightened my spine, squared my shoulders to the best of my ability, and took off.

It wasn't long before I felt the pressure in my head pulse wildly and the swelling in my foot increase. My steps were less certain and my shoulders drooped as I fought exhaustion. I winced and bit back a hiss of pain. Alexander, who had kept quiet about my injuries for far longer than I expected him to, came to a halt, looked down at me, and frowned.

"Enough, Fliss. Come home with me," he said. His words intermingled with the rustling leaves. "I can tell you are tired."

"I just... I thought perhaps, if I found Katrina, she might have answers for me..."

"You don't have to find the answers you are looking for today."

I said nothing.

"Let me take you home. *Please.*"

"Fine," I relented, too weary to argue anymore.

"Do you... um... need me to carry you?"

"Of course not."

Ever persistent, he offered me his arm. "Care to lean on me then?"

I conceded to my exhaustion and wrapped my arm around his. "It wouldn't be the first time."

"I daresay it won't be the last, either."

We trudged toward the palace quietly and slowly, each lost in separate thoughts. Halfway home, Alexander cleared his throat. "My mother and father are giving a dinner party next week."

The wind swiped at my face, swirling around us with gusto as it listened in on our conversation. "Oh?"

Alexander noticed my struggling steps, so he took care to slow down our turtle's pace even more. "Mother said Jack and I should add a few of our own friends to the guest list."

I paused to catch my breath. "Is this an invitation to dine with the royal family of Valencia?"

He stopped next to my side. "It's an invitation to dine with me and my parents."

"Who happen to be the royal family," I pointed out. I started walking again, pressing on against the pain. "You know I don't do well at formal gatherings. I'm not a courtier. And if I'm being honest, courtiers intimidate me."

An obnoxious laugh escaped from Alexander. His head tossed back, he laughed so loudly a group of birds flew from a nearby tree. "Says the girl who slayed a so-called monster only hours ago and is now trekking all over the forest where she was attacked. You, my dear, are not afraid of anything."

My stomach fluttered involuntarily at his gentle *my dear*, and I tried not to read too much into his words. I barreled on ahead, but this time Alexander stopped walking, and I was forced to slow down next to him.

He turned slightly to face me, the merriment dimming from his eyes. "I'm leaving again, Felicity. I volunteered to go to the Avondale court to meet with their king, King Bram, for a few weeks. There's much unrest within Brittolia right now. If a war breaks out in Brittolia and finds its way to Valencia, Father wants to make sure Avondale stands with us, as an ally."

"Is there a chance Avondale wouldn't stand with Valencia?"

"With these matters, there's a chance that anything could happen."

I faltered slightly, and not only because of my ankle. "Why can't one of your father's ambassadors go?"

"I told you, I volunteered. It's my duty to see to the needs of this kingdom." His voice was weary and contrasted sharply against the laughter from earlier. "I have to go. I dare not leave the future of Valencia up to something so fickle as chance."

"Of course you wouldn't," I agreed, thinking more of the fairy tale and not a war with a neighboring kingdom.

"I leave the morning after the dinner party. I want to say goodbye to you at the dinner party before I leave."

"It would be easier to say goodbye without having half the court standing over my shoulder."

"It's just a dinner." When I didn't respond right away, he went on to say, "What I'm trying and failing to say is, I *really* want to see you before I leave."

"Is that a command from a prince?"

"No." His smile resurfaced. "It's a request from a friend."

His smile had a way of making me agree to almost anything, so I replied, "In that case, I'll see you there."

He stood close to me and his dark hair fell forward in an attractive way. I felt a prickle of something strange inside my chest, which caught me off guard. I stepped away too quickly and my ankle gave away underneath me. Before I could smash into the ground, his hand reached out and snaked around my waist, pulling me even closer to him than before.

His face was inches from mine. I held my breath for a moment.

"Hey, go slow. It's not a race," he whispered.

I exhaled, breaking our eye contact. "If it was, I'd still beat you. Bum ankle and all."

Alexander looked down at my battered ankle and a dark shadow crossed his face. Anyone else could look at him and see a calm, controlled prince, but I was familiar with his masquerade. There was always something brimming under the surface of Alexander, something waiting to shatter the control he sought after so ardently. That's when I felt his hold on me tighten; like he was afraid I would fall out of his reach.

"You are angry," I stated.

His eyes flashed with surprise. "What makes you say that?"

"I'm good at reading people, even princes who think they don't deserve to show emotion."

His grip loosened. "I'm angry at whoever attacked you and Jack. I vow I will find them."

"I think all the creatures who did this are dead," I whispered. The mental image of me running a blade through the heart of one made me grimace.

"Then I will make sure no more ever return to Valencia." His voice lowered drastically and those familiar blue eyes darkened into a shade more dangerous than I'd ever seen them.

"I'm not so sure. These creatures seemed almost... magical." I let the last word fall loosely from my lips. "I don't know how else to explain it. They were unlike anything I've ever seen."

"*Magical?* First, you speak of a mysterious, shimmery young woman living in the forest. Then, you tell me there are magical monsters. What's next? A fire-breathing dragon?" He looked down at me peculiarly. "Magic isn't real, you know. Perhaps what you saw was a new breed of wild animals?"

"That walked on two feet and wielded swords?"

He sighed. "Well, if there are more of these *monsters*, I will find them, and they will answer for what they've done. Being the prince has some advantages, especially when it comes to dealing out swift justice."

I shuddered at the thought of him seeking out those horrible, frightening creatures just for my sake. They wouldn't hesitate to kill him. Their image and that terrible black mist would haunt my dreams for many nights to come. I certainly didn't want Alexander subjected to that kind of horror... or danger.

"Spare me your vows of justice," I pleaded softly. "Right now, I just want to go home."

And so we hobbled, one measly, painstakingly slow step at a time back to the palace.

CHAPTER 9

We arrived just as the sun began to set after the long day and immediately went to the infirmary, where Max was waiting for us. Max looked as though he'd aged ten years in the last ten hours, and Alexander smiled to himself as my uncle danced back and forth across the room trying to "help" the healers and recited every possible internal injury I might have.

"I have to go," Alexander said after a few minutes. "I'm meeting with Jack and the captain of the guards to discuss the attack and what measures need to be taken next."

I grasped his hand, pulling him down next to me on the bed I had been forced onto when I arrived. "Don't leave me here with Max," I whispered. "He's driving everyone mad. You've got to help me control him." Alexander and I watched an apprentice healer roll his eyes as Max dictated instructions behind his back.

"We both know there's no controlling Max. Besides, it just means he cares." Alexander winked as he got up to leave. "He's your uncle; let him worry over you."

So I did, to a certain degree. When it was time for him to leave at the end of the day, Max insisted on staying the night with me. Though the healers and myself protested, he planted himself firmly on the seat of an uncomfortable looking chair and promptly fell asleep.

I woke up the next morning to the sound of his gentle snoring with a monstrous headache and a still slightly swollen ankle. I nudged Max's shoulder, stirring him from his sleep.

"Fliss," he mumbled, sitting up quickly. His neck popped several times from sleeping in an unusual position and he fumbled for his glasses on the bedside table. "How are you feeling this morning?"

"Better," I replied. "My head still hurts, but the healer said that's expected. My ankle looks a lot better though." I poked my foot out from under the covers and showed him how much the swelling had gone down. "Though I won't be sprinting across a field of wildflowers any time soon."

Max frowned as he assessed my ankle, reaching back to pat down his mussed-up hair at the same time. I held back a grin. I might have been the one lying in a bed with bandages wrapped around various parts of my body, but he looked utterly ridiculous with his bedhead hair, crooked glasses, and still sleepy eyes.

He sighed, a steady release. His eyes met mine and seriousness filled them. "You are to never, ever leave my sight again. Do you understand?"

"It wasn't my idea to be attacked, you know. Take that up with those creatures."

"I intend to," he said, leaning forward, probably for dramatic effect, "once I know what they are. Jack gave me a thorough description of what they look like, and I will begin doing research as soon as we are back in the library."

"Alexander said he has the palace guards looking into what happened."

"I trust my books more than I trust the bumbling oafs dressed as palace guards." Max searched my face and winced at the purple and blue knot on my forehead. "You look terrible."

"You know how to make a girl's self-confidence soar. By the way, you don't look so great yourself right now."

It was true. He did look paler than normal and fine beads of sweat were pooling on his forehead.

"I blame you. I'm exhausted from worrying about you, thank you very much. What would Rosalind say if she could see you right now? She'd say I was a failure as a guardian that's what she'd say."

"Speaking of..." I pulled away from my pillows and leaned forward. "I met a fairy named Katrina in the forest. She saved me and helped patch me up after the attack. She said she knew you and Mother."

Surprise flitted across his features, giving away to a slight look of wonder, and then turning to an emotion I couldn't find a name for because it was too deeply masked to see. He cleared his throat once and then once more before he softly said, "You met Katrina? She revealed herself to you?"

"Petite, short fairy with wild orange curls and silver eyes? Yeah, I met her. Frankly, I'm just glad you know who I'm talking about. I was almost convinced I'd imagined her." I quickly told him about waking up in her cottage and how she had saved my life. "She was certainly... interesting."

"That's putting it lightly."

"Why didn't you ever tell me that you knew a fairy? How in all of my seventeen and a half years of life did that not once pop up in conversation?"

"I didn't think she was still living in Valencia," he whispered. He turned to look out the window, his eyes scanning the forest as if he was looking for the very fairy that hid in her small cottage. "All this time, she was right here. She never left." There was a depth in his voice that startled me, and I could tell he was speaking more to himself than to me.

"I don't understand what she is doing here."

"Felicity, there is more magic in this world than you can comprehend, than any of us can comprehend. There is magic we miss completely because we can't see it, and then there is magic we miss because we choose not to see it."

He turned and softly rested his eyes on mine, and I caught another glimpse of the mask Max was trying so hard to hide behind. "Then there is also the magic we see but mistake it for something else entirely. If Katrina chose to reveal herself to you, you can be assured it was for a greater purpose."

I clasped my hands together, ignoring the cuts and bruises on my palms, and twisted them together excitedly. "What greater purpose?"

His face softened, my eagerness amusing him. "How do the fairy tales put it? Oh, yes. *Once upon a time*, there was a world with seven realms. One of the realms was the human realm, which consisted of five kingdoms: Valencia, Avondale, Brittolia, Aurum, and—"

"Camelot," I interjected impatiently. "Yes, yes, I know all about the five kingdoms. I did, after all, sit through your countless geography lessons."

"You didn't let me finish." Max gave me the same sharp look he relied upon when I interrupted him during his lessons. "There are five kingdoms in the human realm, which you are obviously familiar with, and six other realms that make—*made*—up our world. The realm of enchantment belonged to the sorcerers, the realm of harvest belonged to the giants, the realm of craftsmanship belonged to the elves, the realm of mining belonged to the dwarfs, the realm of fire belonged to the dragons, and the realm of dreams belonged to the fairies."

I counted the number of realms in my head as he recited the names off. There were seven realms in total.

"The sorcerers conjured spells, the elves were exceptional builders and crafters, the dwarfs mined minerals in the mountains, the giants worked the land, the humans governed the land, the dragons protected the kingdoms, and the fairies divided their magic between the seven realms to help each one flourish individually."

"Sounds picturesque."

Max laughed at my dry tone. "I suppose it was, for a while. But the sorcerers' magic became very powerful, even greater than the fairies' magical abilities, and the other realms were either frightened or jealous. Fear spread like wildfire through the other six realms, giving the sorcerers an upper hand. The humans were the most worried. They thought the sorcerers would try to control all the realms. If that happened, it was assumed humans would be the first to be destroyed or made into slaves, considering humans are absolutely ordinary with no magical qualities whatsoever."

"So what happened?" I moved to sit on the edge of the bed, taking in all the details with wide eyes. "Did the sorcerers take over?"

"No. By the time the sorcerers had garnered enough support in their own realm, the humans had conquered all the others. The leaders of the five human kingdoms coerced the other realms into fighting against the sorcerers, tricking them into war with twisted lies and empty promises. The sorcerers were overpowered. During this war, the dragons almost became extinct, the giants dwindled considerably, the proud races of the dwarfs and elves felt defiled because their craftsmanship was used for killing. But the fairies..."

"Yes?" I prompted. "What happened to the fairies?"

"The fairies, besides the sorcerers, were the only beings left able to conjure magic, and that frightened the humans."

"The fairies must have been very powerful."

"Oh, yes. Though fairy magic is different from sorcerer magic. It is simpler in a way, but infinitely more complex in another, and it can play on emotions and dreams rather than solely enchanting objects and elements like sorcerer magic."

I opened my mouth to ask a question, but Max continued on.

"As the human realm came to power, our kings and queens were somewhat lenient with the other realms, but with the fairies they were much harsher. If a fairy didn't submit to our realm's wishes, they were destroyed. The humans feared any being that could be more powerful than them. The giants they could outsmart, the elves and dwarfs they could bribe, and the dragons they could slay... but the fairies were resilient. Many fairies were killed because they would not yield to the commands of humans."

A beat of silence filled the room as I stared at Max in horror. "Your story makes humans out to sound awful! Why were we so brutal to the fairies?"

"It wasn't all humans, Fliss. It was mostly the past kings and queens of our realm. They were already in a powerful position and had the most to lose. They let power overrule their good sense and the fear of the unknown creep into their hearts. As a result, the remaining fairies wielded their powers together and cast a curse over all the royal families in our realm, a curse that has haunted our monarchs for centuries. The human realm was forced to live a life of seclusion amongst themselves, never to intermingle with the other six realms again. The fairies repaid the kings and queens with the same ultimatum they were given by the humans: Obey or be destroyed."

"The fairy tales," I said softly.

"Precisely."

I looked over at him, continuing to twist my hands together until I was sure I was going to shred the bandages. "Why does no one in Valencia talk about what happened in the past? It seems like humans don't even realize the mistakes their ancestors made centuries ago."

"Only the people directly involved with the fairy tale, such as the librarian and the royal family, are made aware of what happened in the past."

"Is that how Katrina and Mother met?"

Max's shoulders sagged, as if this entire story from his past was weighing on him. "Katrina was sent from the fairy realm to deliver King Frederic's fairy tale to your mother. Rosalind felt it was wrong to coerce someone into a destiny that they didn't get to choose. She told King Frederic, he was Prince Frederic at the time, about his fairy tale—she gave him the choice to decide whether or not he wanted to follow it."

"And what did he choose?" I asked in a whisper, though I was almost certain I knew the answer.

"King Frederic chose to pave his own destiny. In his youth he had great plans of making Valencia the most dominant and powerful kingdom in all the land. He wanted the kingdom to grow and prosper, to flourish under his reign. He was headstrong and rash, much unlike the monarch he is today. When young Prince Frederic found out his future was to be another complacent, peaceful king and that he had to marry a girl he'd never met, he rebelled as most teenagers do. He didn't like the idea of a group of fairies controlling his kingdom.

"The fairies couldn't bear to lose any more of their kind again to a war against Valencia, so they formed an alliance with a powerful sorceress named Bruna, who was more than happy to fight against the humans who had dethroned her realm from power centuries ago. The fairies promised Bruna that she could rule Valencia as queen if she would punish King Frederic and his kingdom for his rebellion. Bruna attacked the palace and ransacked the homes of citizens in Valencia, killing hundreds of humans. Bruna didn't want King Frederic to come to his senses and follow the fairy tale, so she placed a curse on Queen Briar, who was still only a peasant girl at this time, and the curse made her fall into a deep, death-like sleep. The king wouldn't be able to complete the fairy tale without a queen."

"What did King Frederic do?" I whispered. My hands clasped the cool cotton sheets on top of me, kneading the fabric with tension. "How did he stop Bruna from taking over the kingdom?"

Max looked like he wanted to smile at my question, but he held it back. "*He* didn't stop Bruna, your mother did. Rosalind felt responsible for the terror being wrought on Valencia since she gave King Frederic a choice in his destiny. She was the one who needed to destroy Bruna." This time he did smile. "It was quite a feat, and a battle that none of us saw coming."

"What do you mean Mother destroyed Bruna? Like she *killed* her?" I asked.

Max nodded.

I slumped down into my pillows. I couldn't imagine my mother, who had possessed the sweetest laugh and kindest soul I'd ever met, killing anyone, even an evil sorceress who had cursed her best friend and was bent on destroying the people in this kingdom.

"After Bruna was destroyed, King Frederic dared not anger the fairies again by continuing to refuse the fairy tale, so he broke the curse that kept Queen Briar asleep and married her, despite hardly knowing her or loving her," he explained.

"How did King Fredric break the curse?"

"You've read *Sleeping Beauty*, Fliss. You tell me."

"True love's kiss, or so the story goes. But is that even possible?"

Max shrugged. "That is something you'll have to ask the king and queen."

"This is all so strange." I rubbed my temples, scrunching up my face in thought. "How does nobody seem to remember this? I get not telling people about the fairy tales, but surely somebody in this kingdom remembers when Bruna tried to control it. I have not heard talk of sorcerers, fairies, or curses until now."

"Rosalind asked Katrina, whom we had become close friends with during all of this, to place a spell over Valencia so the people in our kingdom would forget about the war with Bruna and be able to live in peace. That's why no one but the royal family and the librarians know what happened, nobody else remembers. It's easier to have the people forget than to live in fear."

"Why would Katrina help humans? She's a fairy. Isn't she supposed to hate us?"

"As you said earlier, Katrina is *interesting*. She doesn't see in black and white like others do. She doesn't agree with everything the humans have done in the past, but she also doesn't agree with what the fairies did in retaliation to the humans when they involved Bruna. She refused to fight hate with more hate. The other fairies called her a traitor for helping us. She wasn't exactly welcomed back home with open arms."

The room fell silent once more, and I felt a pang of sympathy for Katrina. All these years she'd been living alone, ostracized by her own realm for helping humans, but still not welcome in ours.

Max found his voice again. "If you are curious about what Rosalind did after all of this, she was so shaken by the ordeal with Bruna that she left Valencia and vowed never to return. She was gone for almost three years before she came back."

My brow crinkled. "I never knew she left Valencia. Why did she return?"

"To have you, of course. One day she showed up heavily pregnant on the library's doorstep. She told me she had fallen in love and married a man, but that he had died suddenly and she had nowhere else to go."

It was my turn to face the window and look out into the forest. My eyes traced the tops of the trees, searching for answers to questions that raced through my head. I wondered...

"Do you think Katrina would know who my father was?" I asked, still facing the window.

I watched as Max shook his head in the reflection of the windowpane. "I doubt it. Rosalind was very secretive about his identity."

All the same, I was going to find that fairy someday and ask her again.

CHAPTER 10

Unfortunately, I had little time to investigate Katrina's whereabouts the next week. The unusual weariness Max had been feeling after my visit to the infirmary turned into a horrendous stomachache. The sudden illness left him either in bed or doubled over the chamber pot heaving up the contents of his stomach. That left me hobbling around the library on my good foot trying to do both of our jobs. My own weary bones and body screeched in protest every time I made any unnecessary movement.

I found myself looking longingly at the library's door on more than one occasion, wishing for an escape, or at least a revival of energy. After a particularly busy day at the end of a busy week, the library's doors did, in fact, burst open with an unexpected visitor. I was shelving books when I heard someone call out my name.

"Felicity!"

My head shot up. A familiar blue-eyed girl with curls like golden ribbons came into my view. Her smile, which was even brighter than her eyes, filled the library with energy.

"Cinderella, what a surprise!" I sat the books down and met her halfway across the room.

Jack entered the library a second after Cinderella did, and I waved to him excitedly. "Jack, it's good to see you, too!"

"Oh Felicity," Cinderella said, wrapping me in a great hug before I could utter another word. "I was so worried about you! Jack told me you were injured in the attack. I tried to get away all week to come see you, but my stepmother's been watching me like a hawk."

"Worried about *me*?" I laughed at her concern and returned her hug. "I wasn't the one who was carried off by those creatures—you were! Thankfully, Jack ended up helping you escape."

"Yes... *Jack*," Cinderella whispered his name with airy sweetness. She eyed him pointedly. "It was very brave of him."

At her praise, Jack's cheeks turned the color of his hair. "It was nothing," he mumbled.

"I meant to come see you myself, but Max took ill this week. I haven't had a moment to spare."

I glanced down for the first time at Cinderella's dress and was surprised to find it wasn't her gray one with cinders and soot lining the hem. Instead, it was a lovely shade of violet with a sweeping organza skirt and dark purple sash. She looked radiant with her perfect hair and flowing dress. Not to mention a smile hadn't left her face since she entered the library.

"What are you so dressed up for?" I questioned, suddenly feeling self-conscious standing next to her in my simple attire with a limp, frizzy braid hanging down my back. "You look marvelous, by the way. That dress is beautiful."

"Thank you. It was my mother's dress. I'm going to the party," Cinderella breathed excitedly as she clasped my hands. When I blinked uncertainly, she hastened to say,

"Queen Briar's dinner party? Jack invited me. He told me you were going and that we could all arrive together."

I covered my face and groaned. "The dinner party is today?"

Cinderella looked to Jack for confirmation.

"Come on, Fliss. Don't tell me you forgot." When I said nothing, Jack rolled his eyes. "You *did* forget, didn't you?"

"In my defense, it's been a hectic week."

I leaned back against a desk, my tired body ready to sit back down. I wanted to go to the party, truly I did. I wanted to see Alexander and tell him goodbye before he left for Avondale. I wanted to give his mother, Queen Briar, a long overdue hug, sneak a handful of pastries from the dessert table to bring back to Max, and stand next to Jack in the corner of the room while we laughed at the other courtiers who were too pompous for their own good. I did not, however, want to watch Alexander be accosted by every young lady of marriageable age, which is what usually went on at these events.

"Alexander will be disappointed if you don't show up," Jack said, breaking into my thoughts.

"Alexander will survive. There's so much to do here in the library and Max is still sick. You two go on without me."

Cinderella's sudden frown looked out of place on her lovely face. "I can't face an entire room of courtiers without you by my side. They'll all take one look at me, immediately discern that I'm a commoner, and laugh in my face. I need your courage."

"Alexander would never allow that to happen, and neither would the king and queen," I assured her.

"*I* would never allow that to happen," Jack clarified.

Cinderella still looked doubtful.

I winked playfully at her. "Go to the party and give the courtiers something to talk about, Cinderella. Goodness knows this court could use some shaking up."

CRASH!

A loud noise sounded from Max's study, and Cinderella and I exchanged surprised looks.

I shook my head with half exasperation and half amusement. "There's no telling what Max has done this time. I'd better go check on him." I gestured to the door. "You two go on to the dinner party."

Before they could protest, I took off towards the study and swung open the door so roughly I feared pulling my shoulder out of socket again. Immediately, I spotted my uncle's form sprawled out, face down, and across the floor in a puddle of ink and a pile of broken glass.

"Max!" I cried, running to his side. "What are you doing out of bed?"

"Nuh eed tuh wuhee," Max mumbled into the rug.

"What?"

Max pulled his head up. "No need to worry," he assured me.

"No need to worry?" I echoed in disbelief. I helped him to his feet. "Look where I found you; passed out on the floor." Max swayed slightly, and my hands clutched the fabric of his tunic to keep him upright. "Honestly, you are no better than a wayward toddler. You are supposed to be in bed."

"I came in here for my good quill pen and a bout of dizziness overtook me. Where's my decanter?" His eyes skimmed the top of his desk. "I'll feel better after a drink."

I forced him, none too gently, into a chair. "You are sick," I reminded him. "You should be resting, not climbing up and down stairs to find some silly pen."

Since Max's glasses had come off in the fall and he had not yet bothered to put them back on, he squinted up at me. "If you had just brought me the pen earlier when I asked, this wouldn't have been a problem."

"I told you there would be no working until you rest," I snapped. "And if you don't rest, you won't get better."

"I am not a child."

"I didn't compare you to a child. It was a toddler, I believe."

Max huffed as he placed his skewed glasses atop his nose. He settled back into the chair, clutching the arms tightly. His colorless cheeks made me suspect he was fighting another wave of dizziness. "I'm not sick. Perhaps tired, but I never get sick."

I leaned forward to feel his forehead and the warmth of a fever seared my palm. "You are lying. This sickness is a lot worse than you've let me believe."

"It will pass, Felicity."

I wanted to shake him. If he weren't feeling so terrible, I would have. "You are in pain."

Max closed his eyes and said nothing.

"Maxwell!" I snapped. "Tell me what's wrong!"

"You've done enough this week trying to pick up my slack since I've been ill. I didn't want you to worry on top of everything else you are doing. Now have you found my decanter?"

"Forget about the decanter!" I stood up quickly, determined to find a palace healer and have them assess Max's condition. "To think I almost left you here alone so I could go to some dinner party with Alexander and Cinderella."

"What?" Max asked, his lethargic demeanor was gone, replaced with seriousness. "Cinderella is meeting Alexander tonight?"

"Yes."

"And this setting is where they meet in the fairy tale?" Max probed in a hushed whisper.

I cocked my head slightly, confused by his ominous tone. "No... they meet at a ball in the fairy tale."

"Goodness, Felicity!" Max pushed up off of his chair with a fierceness that made me stumble back a few steps. "They are supposed to meet each other like they do in the fairy tale! This evening could upset everything. You must stop Cinderella from going to the party. Events in real life must coincide *exactly* as they do in the story."

I blinked as a hush fell over the room. "I didn't realize the danger..."

"Obviously not," Max retorted. He plucked his glasses from his nose and rubbed his eyes roughly. "You have to stop her from going. Make up an excuse, any excuse. Alexander and Cinderella cannot meet each other tonight."

"Yes, yes..." I straightened my back, ready to chase after Jack and Cinderella. "I'll fix things. I promise." I exhaled sharply as I remembered how ill Max was. "Will you be all right if I leave you alone for a while? I have to find Cinderella."

"Go." He pointed to the door. "The fairy tale takes precedence."

I eyed him warily. "Are you sure you'll be okay by yourself?"

"If it makes you feel better, I'll go to the infirmary right now to see if there's anything the healer can give me for the pain."

His reassurance was all I needed to hear before I turned on my heel to sprint towards the door.

"Do you have a plan?" Max called after me. "How are you going to stop this?"

I didn't bother answering. Of course I didn't have a plan.

* * *

It took me less than five minutes to race upstairs, throw on a suitable dress, drag a brush through my tangled waves, which only succeeded in making my hair frizz more, and head downstairs to the dinner party. I zigzagged in and out of hallways, up and down corridors until I found the royal family's wing of the palace. My journey to the other side of the palace was a familiar one. If I hadn't been so consumed with worry about the fairy tale, I would have stopped to smile faintly at all the memories I had from this place. It would have been impossible to count all the afternoon teas my mother and I had taken in Queen Briar's sitting room over the years. Tea time usually involved palace gossip and painful attempts at embroidery, but Alexander would often rescue me by swooping in to challenge me with a game of chess.

As a servant opened the door to the king's personal dining room, I felt a sweep of nostalgia pass over me. How long had it been since Alexander and I had done anything that involved just the two of us? Bickering and searching for obscure fairies together didn't count.

"Felicity, dear!" a melodic voice rang out. "You were able to make it after all."

I looked up to find Queen Briar gliding over to me like some airy, ethereal creature of elegance. The queen's honey colored hair was piled intricately on of her head with a silver crown perched on top, a chain of dainty diamonds dipped onto her neckline, and she wore an enchanting dark blue dress that made her ivory skin look more like a moonbeam than actual flesh. But for all of her beauty, the feature I liked most about the queen were her blue eyes, like Alexander's.

Queen Briar placed her hand lovingly on my shoulder in a welcoming gesture. I dropped into a curtsy. "Your Majesty, I hope I haven't offended anyone by arriving later than expected."

"Not at all! Not at all!" The queen beckoned me inside. "People are still trickling in. It's a rather large gathering, and we've only just begun the party. We won't sit down to dinner for another half hour."

I tried to glance discreetly around the large room, looking for Alexander, Jack, or Cinderella. An obscenely long mahogany table with sparkling china and silver platters caught my eye. The grandiose room, opulent furnishings, and the other guests' fancy attire made me wish I had put a little more thought into my appearance before showing up.

Queen Briar's eyes held an unusual amount of warmth as she smiled down at me. "Alexander said you were coming tonight. I'm so glad that you did."

"I wanted to make sure I got a chance to say goodbye to him before he left in the morning," I explained.

Aha! I had finally spotted Alexander on the other side of the room, slumped up against the wall, completely cornered by Lady Cressida and a gaggle of her friends. I almost chuckled at the sight of his face as Lady Cressida recounted what I assumed was court gossip. He was a mask of politeness, but underneath the surface I could see the boredom radiating from within him. Lady Alana stood on his other side. She caught my stare, discreetly pointed to Cressida, and rolled her eyes as the young noblewoman droned on with her story. This time I did chuckle, and Lady Alana covered her mouth with a gloved hand as she joined in.

Queen Briar's smile softened as she delicately reached out to smooth a crease on my sleeve, like a mother would. "I haven't seen you in some time, Felicity. I'm afraid my duties have kept me busy. You've grown into quite a lovely young woman. Rosalind would be proud."

Lovely? Had she taken a good look at my unruly hair? Nevertheless, I took a brief moment to bask in her thoughtful compliment.

"Thank you, Your Majesty," I replied.

Guests mingled around us, still buzzing like bees from a safe distance. They glanced curiously at the conversation we were having, probably wondering why the queen was speaking to a lowly librarian. Queen Briar gave no indication of the other courtiers' glances. She steered me over to the side of the room and then beckoned a servant to bring us goblets with some unknown beverage.

"Here," she said kindly. "Have a refreshment before dinner starts." We casually sipped our drinks, some crimson-colored, fruit-flavored cider, and Queen Briar waited to speak until some of the eyes around the room had lost interest and averted away from us.

"So," the queen said lightly. "My husband tells me you have big responsibilities regarding Alexander's future. I could think of no other girl I'd trust with Alexander's fairy tale."

Her pointed comment made me choke on my cider. I coughed loudly while some of the drink dribbled down my chin. I wiped my chin while the queen patted my back like she hadn't said anything out of the ordinary. I looked up at her with wild eyes. Was she seriously bringing up the fairy tale here? *While half the court stood in our presence?*

"I-I, um..." I spluttered over my words, which only seemed to amuse the queen. "You see, Your Majesty, I can't really talk about it. I promised Max, and your husband for that matter, that I wouldn't—"

"Shhh." The queen placed her hand once more on my shoulder. "I know Alexander is in good hands, as is my kingdom. If there is anything I can do to help, please let me know."

I laughed nervously. "Thank you for your faith in me."

"Have some faith in yourself, dear girl." Queen Briar squeezed my shoulder reassuringly. "I've always trusted the librarians in your family."

"*Actually*," I spoke up, a little too loudly since several heads swiveled our direction once more. I tried again, this time in a lower voice. "Actually, there is something you can do to help."

Her eyebrows arched upward. "Name it."

"A ball," I whispered. From the corner of my eye I caught a flash of violet. Cinderella entered the room with a graceful stride. She was perched on Jack's arm already looking like the queen she would be someday. They headed toward the far corner of the room, the one furthest away from prying eyes after snagging a goblet of cider from a servant. "I need you to hold a ball in honor of Alexander's birthday."

"A ball?" the queen repeated. She tilted her head ever so slightly, causing a few loose curls to tip over the edge of her shoulder. "In Alexander's honor?"

I nodded briskly. "Yes. Also, it needs to be a masquerade."

"And who exactly should I invite to this ball for my son?"

Before I could answer, I saw Alexander detach himself methodically from Lady Cressida's attention and step lightly around her silk skirts and those of her friends. He paused to offer an excuse, which was probably polite but fictional, and began to slowly back away from the pack of ravenous, crown hungry women. Lady Cressida looked petulant, Alexander looked relieved, and I felt certain I looked sick to my stomach because he was no longer staying put, he was striding across the dining room headed straight for the corner where Jack and Cinderella were.

"No! Stop!" My cry was soft enough to not draw attention to myself, but loud enough to make Queen Briar jump in surprise. "If you don't mind, Your Majesty, I'll have to get back to you about the guest list. There's, um, something I need to attend to before dinner."

I didn't wait for a response and a second later I was darting across the floor, praying I got to Cinderella before Alexander did or at least that some other maiden swooped in and claimed his attention. My steps were a staccato *tap tap* across the polished marble tiles, and I sloshed cider out of my goblet as I scurried over to Cinderella.

"Felicity!" Cinderella looked up and saw me coming, smiling as she waved me toward her corner.

Jack straightened as I approached them. "Fliss..." He took in my wrinkled dress, riotous long curls, and my hand dripping with cider. A few drops fell from the side of the goblet and splashed onto the floor. "You look..."

"Ravishing?"

I glanced over my shoulder to find Alexander. As I did, his gaze caught mine. His eyes sparked with eagerness and he offered me a wave. His steps picked up speed, propelling him faster towards the group. Thankfully, one of his father's advisors cut him off before he could reach us. I watched Alexander's face once more form a mask of politeness as he exchanged greetings and formalities.

I breathed a sigh of relief.

"Disheveled," Jack amended bluntly.

"Well, I think she looks lovely," Cinderella said. She nudged Jack playfully in the ribs. "I'm so glad you decided to come, Felicity. Jack just promised me an introduction to his cousin, Prince Alexander."

Jack looked past me and saw Alexander trying to subtly inch his way closer to us and end whatever conversation he was currently having. "Speaking of the prince, it looks like he's on his way to grace us with his presence," he said, taking a swig of his drink.

I clutched the goblet in my hand fiercely, eyeing the remaining contents. There was enough to do some damage. I could only hope Cinderella would forgive me someday.

I pretended to trip over my dress and lurched forward dramatically, spilling cider down the front of Cinderella's beautiful violet skirt.

"Argh!" I cried gutturally, sounding more like a wild animal than a girl.

The liquid seeped through the pale organza and marred the lovely fabric like a pool of blood. The accident was met with a gasp from Cinderella, a creative curse from Jack, and another very theatrical groan from me.

"I am so sorry!" I cried, stepping in front of Cinderella to block her from the view of prying courtier eyes. "I should have watched where I was going."

"No, no, it's fine," Cinderella assured me. However, I could see thick tears form in her eyes. She bravely brushed them away. "It's just a dress..."

Except it wasn't just a dress—not to her. It was her mother's dress, her *deceased* mother's dress. This was a girl who dressed in rags most of the time and braved a crowd of unknown elitists, and I had ruined her beloved dress. I suddenly felt no more than ten inches tall. I hadn't expected her tears, but I *did* expect her next reaction.

Cinderella turned to Jack. "I can't meet the prince like this."

"He won't care about your dress," Jack insisted. "Anyway, it's Felicity's fault, not yours. If anything, Alexander will have anticipated her clumsiness."

Cinderella's lower lip trembled. "I didn't want this to be my first impression."

"It will be okay," he promised. "Alexander doesn't care about—"

"Oh no!" Cinderella gasped. The pink color in her cheeks drained to a chalky white. For a moment, she looked almost as ill as Max. She blinked and shook her head fiercely, as if she couldn't believe what she was seeing.

"What's wrong?" Jack asked, concern marring his features.

"My stepsister is here," she whispered.

"Who?"

"C-C-Cressida," she stammered.

"Wait a second." My stomach dropped. "*Lady Cressida* is your stepsister?"

Cinderella nodded slightly. "I've got to go. Now. It was foolish of me to come tonight. If Cressida tells my stepmother that I was here..." Before I knew what was happening, she took off, darting towards the door.

"Hey wait!" Jack called after her. He shoved his cup in my hand. "Hold this. I'm going to check on her."

I stared after them stupidly, still not believing that Lady Cressida and Cinderella, two girls who were as opposite in personality as possible, were related to each other. Jack followed her swiftly and deftly to the exit, and I finally shook off my befuddlement and took off to find Alexander, who was once again headed in my direction.

I met him in the middle of the room.

"Finally. There you are," he said.

"Yes, um, here I am." My eyes were still focused on Cinderella and Jack as they swept past the servants at the doorway, effectively escaping.

Alexander followed my stare and his brows furrowed. "Why is Jack leaving so soon?" he asked.

"Jack's guest spilt something on her dress," I explained, hoping he didn't have any intentions of going after Jack. "He was going to help her."

"Oh." Alexander looked back at me and smiled. It was *my* smile. I had seen that smile a thousand times over the past seventeen years and it never once got old. It spread wryly across his face. "You are late. I thought you might not come."

"I almost didn't."

"What changed your mind?"

"I wanted to say goodbye to my friend."

He raised an eyebrow at my statement.

"Your Highness!" A voice sang loudly from behind us, breaking into our conversation.

I peeked over Alexander's shoulder to find Lady Cressida slithering over to us with purpose. She flashed me a wide smile as she stopped to stand between us, and I dismally noticed that even her teeth were perfect.

"Cressida." Alexander looked surprised to see her, like he hadn't expected her to follow him. But he should have known a snake always stalks its prey before striking. "Is everything all right?"

"Of course," she replied, holding out the *s* in a dreamy hiss. She placed her small hand on his broad shoulder. "I wasn't finished telling you the story about how Lady Delilah wore her apricot gown to two consecutive balls last winter. Can you believe it? How tacky."

Alexander frowned at her words. Whether from the fact that she was criticizing another woman or because he wondered why she would think he cared about the color of some lady's gown I could not say.

I started to say something about how a tacky dress was more attractive than spreading tacky gossip when Alexander clamped a hand down on my wrist, a warning.

"Oh, look! There's Lady Alana." He waved over Alana, who had been passing by us on her way to the refreshment table. Perhaps he hoped her calm and controlled poise would have a positive effect on the conversation.

"Honestly," Cressida continued on, "and tonight she's wearing that atrocious blue gown with the horrid ruffles. I just know it was her mother's gown that she remade over."

Alana approached the group with a curtsy, grimacing as she overheard Cressida's callous words.

Alexander cleared his throat. "I'm sure her gown is perfectly fine." He looked relieved when the newcomer joined our group, because anyone was a welcome distraction from Cressida. "Lady Alana, nice of you to join us. I was just telling Felicity here—"

"Your Highness," Cressida interrupted. She cast a cold glance at Alana, probably upset that she had stolen the attention away from her for even the briefest of moments. "Did you hear what I was saying?"

Alexander looked taken aback, for it wasn't many people who had the audacity to interrupt a prince. "I think we all heard what you are saying," he replied. His jerked his head to the left. "Even Lady Delilah. She's heard every word you've said about her gown."

Sure enough, we all turned slightly and found Lady Delilah staring at the group, her face crumpled into despair and shame. A moment later the poor girl whirled around and fled the room.

Cressida stiffened. "She's been a bit touchy lately."

My ears buzzed loudly and refused to focus on another word uttered from *Lady* Cressida's overly pink lips. Ha. Lady, indeed. She didn't deserve the title if she couldn't act the part. I couldn't stomach the thought of having to stand here and listen to her gossip about Lady Delilah, whose father had recently passed away and finances were too tight to allow her family to buy new dresses.

Alana stepped forward. "Cressida, you should not be so harsh on the poor girl. I thought Delilah was your friend."

"She *was* my friend—"

Alana looked directly at me, then at the cup in my hand, and finally at Cressida. She raised an eyebrow, practically daring me.

I ignored the buzzing in my ears and accepted Alana's dare by unceremoniously dumping the contents of Jack's drink down the front of Cressida's dress. I didn't even bother to pretend my clumsiness was an accident this time.

"Ah!" Cressida screeched. She darted away a moment too late. The red liquid seeped through her bodice and made the silky material stick to her skin. Her eyes snapped to mine, and a spark of dangerous anger seemed to light them on fire.

I didn't back away from her though. Instead, I righted myself and bit back a grin as half of the guests in the room swiveled their heads around to stare at her shrill outburst.

"This was a new dress," Cressida whispered fiercely but with a forced smile, so as not to attract more unwanted attention. "Now it's ruined for good."

I swept my hand across my chest to gesture to the door. "Oh? Well, then perhaps you could ask Lady Delilah if you might borrow her apricot dress?"

Alexander made a choking noise in his throat as he held back surprised laughter.

"You are going to regret that, librarian," Cressida spat. She turned on her heel and made a dramatic exit from the dinner party, her soaked skirts twirling behind her as she left.

Alexander turned to me. "That was bold, even for you, Fliss."

"You should give Lady Alana some of the credit," I said, raising my glass a little in a mock toast. "I merely executed her idea."

"Lady Alana was a part of the scheme? I must say that surprises me," Alexander said with a laugh.

"Are you going to reprimand me, Your Highness?" she asked.

His features turned serious. "I'm more likely to commend you. "

Alana's shoulders straightened a little at the compliment. "She should not have said those things about Delilah. Speaking of, I'd better go make sure the poor girl isn't completely distraught."

Lady Alana curtsied once more before she glided away.

Alexander turned his attention back to me. "Now back to the conversation I've wanted to have all night." He took my hand, in front of too many witnesses to count, and grinned down at me. "I'm glad you came tonight."

I tugged my hand from his. "Your Highness," I whispered. "You can't do that."

"Do what?"

I felt a warm blush creep up my neck, which was ridiculous. This was Alexander for crying out loud. I had nothing to be embarrassed about. "Take my hand in public."

"Why not?"

"People might talk."

Amusement sparkled in his eyes. "What would they say?"

"You know very well what they would say. Anyway, you should be mingling with your guests, not wasting time with the palace librarian."

He did look handsome tonight in his formal dinner attire. Even if he weren't a prince, young women would still flock to him, and he looked at me with such care, all of the air in my lungs fought to escape as I held my breath. He reached for my hand again, and this time I let him keep it. "A moment spent with the palace librarian is never a wasted moment."

"Felicity!"

We broke apart, and I turned at the sound of my name. Jack tore through the crowd, rushing toward us.

"What's wrong?" Alexander and I chorused at the same time.

"*Max*," he whispered.

Something in my heart dropped at the mention of my uncle's name and the hushed tone of Jack's voice. Fear paralyzed me, striking hard and fast through the tips of my toes and ricocheting up my body like tiny bolts of lightning. I swallowed dry lumps of anxiety while exchanging a look of worry with Alexander. His face mirrored my own apprehension.

"What happened?" I managed to croak out.

Jack took a deep breath and pity lined his features. "The healer is looking for you, Fliss. Max is unconscious."

CHAPTER 11

That night was somehow simultaneously the longest and shortest night of my life. I immediately fled the dinner party, with Alexander and Jack close on my heels, and raced toward the infirmary only to find Max's unconscious body wracking with tremors. The healers couldn't subdue the tremors or combat his raging fever no matter what they tried, and I made sure they tried it all. Hours later, his body finally stilled before the sun rose, but the fever inside his body waged on. His forehead was blistering to the touch. I could only imagine what it was doing to him on the inside.

The worst part of it all was that I had seen this sickness before. It was the same illness that had plagued my mother and eventually led to her death. I was reliving my most horrific and terrifying memory over again.

The healers had no answers then for Mother's sickness, just as they had no answers now.

The splash of raindrops filled my ears as a rain shower tapped soothingly on the windowpane. It sounded like the overture of a grand production, hinting that this was only the prelude of something more grandiose to come.

I took a deep breath, inhaling the scent of rain and damp earth that had seeped through the windows.

"Felicity."

I was sitting by Max's bedside when I heard a gentle voice call out my name. I looked up to find Alexander hovering in the doorway, deep lines of concern etched across his face.

I nodded absentmindedly towards him and then turned my attention back to Max. Alexander's boots scraped quietly against the floor as he made his way over. When he reached my side, he tentatively kneeled down.

My eyes didn't meet his. They stayed locked on Max's unconscious form, willing him to live. My hands twisted nervously together as I knotted my fingers into balls. "I thought you were leaving for Avondale at sunrise," I whispered.

I could feel his eyes on me. "There's still a little time before daybreak."

My mind raced back to hours before this moment when Alexander had traveled down to the infirmary with me. Since the healers said there could only be one visitor with Max during the night, Alexander had promised he would wait outside the room until morning.

"You've been here all night, haven't you?" I looked over at him. The faint shadows from the candle next to the bed flickered across his face. He looked how I felt: exhausted. I couldn't fathom how he was going to complete the journey to Avondale with little to no sleep.

"I couldn't leave. I wanted to stay and see how Max was doing."

"You should have gone to bed and gotten some sleep. It'll do no one any good if you fall out of your saddle and break your neck because you can't stay awake."

My hands wrung together, faster and more furious with each second that passed as anxiety, fear, and desperation welled up within me. "Now I will worry about Max *and* you."

"Felicity."

"Honestly, you should have thought about that before you decided to sleep in a chilly corridor all night long."

He reached out to grasp my hands. "*Felicity.*"

His voice was close, but it still sounded a million miles away. His hand slipped into mine, stilling the nervous fidgeting that would have driven Max crazy if he were conscious.

At his touch, something inside me broke apart, shattering like tiny shards of glass into every direction. I had held on to the potential agony of losing Max all night, and my desperation surged forth in a tidal wave of emotion. I uttered a soft cry and turned toward Alexander, who seemed to anticipate this reaction, because his arms were already open, waiting for me.

Alexander said nothing while I cried. He didn't offer me empty reassurances or half-hearted promises that Max would be all right. Instead, he simply held me, which was more reassurance in that moment than a thousand useless words from his lips ever could have been. When I finally pulled away, he brushed a fallen tear from my chin.

"What can I do for you?" Alexander asked. His own face was twisted with worry, as if he too were fighting back emotion. "What can I do to make things easier for you and Max?"

I shook my head. "There's nothing to do." My hands went back to wringing themselves together, clawing at each other carelessly. "The healers have no answers for me."

"There must be something. Perhaps I can—"

"No," I said sharply. "There's nothing."

"You didn't let me finish."

My fear dissolved into anger, not at Alexander, but at the situation. "What are you going to do, *Your Highness*?

Command the sickness to leave Max's body? I'm afraid it doesn't answer to other people—not even a prince."

I rose to my feet, my stiff joints protesting as I did, and realized how furious, how bitter I sounded even to my own ears. I turned my back to Alexander, lacking the courage to face him for fear I would burst into tears once more.

I took a deep breath and counted the seconds it took for me to inhale and exhale until my breathing returned to normal. *One. Two. Three.* I gazed out the window into the ebony sky that would soon turn into morning. Time would move forward, the world would keep spinning, and people would go on with their lives while mine got ripped to shreds and changed forever. It didn't seem fair. Tragedy was never fair.

"There's nothing that can be done," I finally said, more calmly this time. "I've seen this before. I've seen this exact sickness once before—it killed my mother. It claws away at the body it dwells in until there's nothing left and it robs that person of life."

Alexander rose and came to stand behind me. If he was insulted by my harsh words from earlier, he didn't show it. "I can ride to Avondale and seek out answers from their healers," he insisted. "Perhaps they know something about this malady that our healers do not."

I shook my head.

Not one to take *no* for an answer, Alexander pressed on, relentless, "Then I'll go to Brittolia or Camelot or Aurum. There must be *someone* in another kingdom who knows of a cure or treatment."

I shook my head again, harder this time. "You don't understand. If this is like my mother's illness, at this stage Max has hours to live, if that. You wouldn't even make it to one of the other kingdoms before he..."

I couldn't allow myself to finish the thought.

My heart crashed into my chest and tangible fear swept over me. "Oh, Alexander—I'm going to lose him, just like I lost my mother," I whispered hoarsely. Thick tears welled up in my eyes and sobs threatened to choke me. I made half-hearted attempts to push down hysteria as I turned to face Alexander, who stood tall and stoic like a pillar of strength. It dawned on me that for the first time I was getting a glimpse of the man he was evolving into and the king he would be someday. I was so used to the boundless energy and charisma of the boy I knew in my childhood that this new, indomitable Alexander caught me off guard.

"Did the healers not give you any hope for recovery?"

"*Hope?*" The word tasted foul and bitter in my mouth. "It is pointless to hope. Unless you believe in miracles or magic then I suggest you..." My voice trailed off as my mind wandered to a new place. Half a heartbeat later, I spun around to look out the rain-streaked window at the forest beyond the palace grounds once more.

Hope. Miracles. Magic.

I *did* have reason to hope.

"Alexander!" I shouted his name with sudden urgency and excitement. "There *is* something you can do to help me."

"Anything."

I took off towards the door. "Stay here with Max while I'm gone."

"Stay with him?" Alexander's face contorted in confusion. He stepped in front of me and blocked my path to the door. "Where exactly are you going?"

I grasped his forearms and attempted to push him out of the way.

He didn't budge.

I threw my hands up in exasperation. "There's no time for an explanation! Just promise me you will stay with Max. I'll feel better knowing that you are here with him."

"But—"

"Promise me!"

He quickly blinked, caught off guard by my outburst. "I promise."

At the last minute, I turned to Max and kissed him lightly on the forehead. "I'll come back," I whispered in his ear. "And I'll bring *her* with me this time. Just stay alive until I get back. Please. *Please.* Stay alive." I brushed another tear off my cheek. I had one chance to tempt fate, one chance to help Max, and that one chance lay in the hands of a fairy that lived in the forest.

And this time, I was going to find her.

* * *

I ran.

My feet made quick *thump thumps* on the dewy earth and the clouds above me drizzled and spat tiny raindrops onto my face. My slippers got stuck in the mud, causing me to trip and fall head first into the cold, wet ground. When I rose to my feet, I saw my dress was covered in mud and my body was shaking from the early morning chill. My ankle, still not completely healed from the sprain, throbbed.

It didn't matter. I pressed on.

The stitch in my side swelled to the size of an apple long before I reached the lining of pine trees. The thick, coarse adrenaline that pumped through my veins propelled me farther away from Max and closer to Katrina—closer to hope.

When I entered the forest, I hunched over to place my hands on my knees, gasping for breath. I gulped air like someone lost in the desert might gulp water from an oasis. As my heaving breaths subsided, rain continued to trickle down through tree branches and landed on my back. I straightened to a standing position and the smell of wet pine and damp leaves and soggy grass overtook my senses.

"Katrina!" I bellowed. My voice carried through the trees. I picked up my skirts and continued onward, praying I wouldn't get lost.

"Katrina!" I called out again. "I know you can hear me. I need your help!"

The wind whistled in my ears, thrusting another wave of rainwater at my face. I spluttered and pushed the liquid from my eyes. I took a few steps but sunk into the muddy ground.

I cupped my hands around my mouth. "*Katrina!*"

"Stop yelling."

I turned at the sound of a voice, tripping once again because my feet were submerged in a puddle. An instant later, a pale hand appeared before me, and I gratefully reached out and accepted it.

For such a tiny fairy, Katrina hauled me to my feet with relative ease. Once both feet were firmly on the ground, I looked down at her with desperation. "I need your help. I've been looking for you."

"I gathered. You were bellowing loud enough to wake the dead. I'll just tell you right now though, if you've come for information about your father, I don't have any to share with you."

"This isn't about my father!" I grasped her arm and started back to the palace, pulling her after me. Katrina, who was probably more intrigued by my peculiar behavior than upset, let me drag her along. "This is about Max!" I shouted to her over my shoulder. "He's in trouble!"

Katrina came to a halt. I tugged her arm, but she only stared at me with an expression mixed with wonder, shock, and fear.

"*Maxwell?*" she whispered. The rain was coming down harder and harder. It soaked her vibrant orange hair and made her corkscrew curls stick to her cheeks.

"Yes. Max. He's sick—dying, in fact." Like a petulant child I stomped my foot. "I need your help."

Her lips trembled. "*Dying?*"

"Yes. Dying. You are a fairy. I need you to fix him or heal him or restore his health or do something with your magic."

"*You need my magic?*"

My nostrils flared in annoyance. "Are you going to repeat everything I say? This is a crisis, and you are standing around like you haven't half a thought in your brain."

Katrina snapped back to life, the daze left her eyes and she centered on me. "I can't help you, Felicity. If it's Maxwell's time to go, I dare not interfere with Death. That is something I learned long ago as an immortal. Death comes for all humans."

I clenched her arm harder. "Well, *Death* is not coming for Max today! I won't allow it. You must come and stop him from dying."

"You cannot stop Death. Delay it, perhaps. But you cannot stop it."

I had the urge to pick her up, throw her over my shoulder, and force her to come with me. Whatever small amount of control I held onto split apart.

"I. DON'T. CARE." I raised my chin in defiance and looked at her, eyes wild with emotion. "Do you hear me? I don't care what you say about life or death. This world will not take Max from me today."

Katrina reached for me. "Felicity..."

I batted her hand away. "You said you were my mother's friend. You said you were *Max's* friend!"

Her eyes were gentle, pitying almost. "You don't understand."

"Yes. I do." I reared back on her, furious at her refusal to help me, furious at the world in general, too. "You are a coward. You hide in the forest, disdained by your own realm but too afraid to join the human world."

"What do you know about that?"

"Max told me about how the last fairy tale almost brought about the destruction of Valencia, and how you are trapped between two worlds for betraying the fairies and helping humans. And to think he felt pity for you, to think he spoke of you with fondness!"

"I know you are in pain right now."

I wanted to shake her, make her see reason. "You stupid fairy! What does an immortal know of pain or death or loss? You know *nothing*!"

"Felicity!" Instead of being angered by my words, she reached for me again, holding on tightly to my wrists while I tried to push her away and worm from her grasp. "Felicity! Felicity, stop it! *I said stop it!*" I quit flailing, the edge in her voice quelling me. "You don't know what you are saying. You don't know what you are asking me to do. I cannot save Maxwell, not if it is his time to go. If you steal a life from Death now, Death will certainly steal from you later. It will steal from you when the loss will be even harder to bear."

I forced a deep breath down my throat. "That's a chance I'm willing to take. This is Max, my uncle, my only family. He's all I have left. Please, please..." My words turned to sobs, and I dropped to my knees, clutching the hem of her damp skirt, begging unashamedly for help. "I cannot lose him. It would be like losing the last piece of myself. He has to live. He is too young, much too young, to come to this end."

Katrina reached down, pushing dark, damp curls from my face. Her hands were soft and gentle, like my mother's had been. Her eyes filled with sadness. It was an impenetrable sadness that came from centuries of living in a world where Death claimed those you love while you had to stand back silently, helplessly. In that moment, I wasn't sure which one of us had the harder burden to bear.

"Katrina, please. Max is dying."

She looked off into the forest, her silver eyes stormy like the clouds hovering over us. Her voice came out in an even whisper as she said, "I loved him once, you know."

"*Max?*"

"Yes. Maxwell." Water ran down her face, and I was unable to tell if it was the rain or tears. "I was sent by my realm to Valencia to deliver King Frederic's fairy tale to your mother, but I met Maxwell first. He didn't know I was a fairy then. He thought I was just another visitor in the library. He began to tell me all about the library, all about the power in the books on the shelves."

Hope swelled within me. "Yes. That sounds like him."

"I asked him if he truly thought power was hidden within books, or if it was librarian prattle. Maxwell looked at me oddly and replied that power isn't *hidden* in books; it's always in plain sight. You merely have to open the book to see it." Katrina gave a painful laugh at the memory. "In hundreds of years of living, I had never heard someone speak with such passion as Maxwell did that day."

Katrina reached down and squeezed my shoulder. "Disastrous things could happen if I save him. I could unleash a chain of events that ultimately would do more harm than good. I am not supposed to stop Death, Felicity.

Fairies are warned against interfering with human lives. I've already done it once in my life, which is why I am disdained, as you so eloquently put it, by my own realm."

"You are already living alone. What else can you lose?"

"That's not the point I'm trying to make. To save Maxwell's life might mean that someone else loses theirs later on."

"You can't interfere? Even if it is someone you love?" I asked her.

"Especially then."

I opened my mouth to argue with her, but she *shushed* me. "However, for Maxwell's sake, perhaps I could trifle with Fate just one more time."

CHAPTER 12

Katrina and I ran back to the palace together, and I clutched her hand like it was a lifeline. The storm didn't slow us down. If anything, the rain fell around us like a symphony's crescendo, urging us faster and faster to Max. When we reached the infirmary, I didn't bother to wipe my muddied shoes on a rug, wring out my wet skirt, or swipe the water from my cheeks. I strode past the healers and into the room where Max was without bothering to explain my sodden appearance or my unknown guest to them.

I halted only when I came to the doorway and saw Alexander sitting next to a very still, very pale Max.

Katrina bumped into me, knocking me forward.

"Fliss?" Alexander looked up, just in time to see me come crashing into the room.

I righted myself. "How is he?" I whispered, cautiously stepping forward. "Is he...?"

Alexander's face took on a pained expression, one that hurt him to make almost as much as it hurt me to see. "I think..."

Katrina peeked around my shoulder and gasped when she saw Max.

I clenched my fists. I would not let this world take Max away the same way it took my mother. "I won't let him die, Alexander."

"I am so sorry…"

"I will not let him just die." I looked to Katrina, whose eyes were glazed over as she stared at Max. "Go on," I urged her. "Save him."

"Oh, Fliss," Alexander whispered.

"No, she has to save him."

He searched the room and then his eyes found me. "Who are you talking about? Who is saving Max?"

"Katrina!" I glanced over my shoulder once more at the obvious fairy in our presence, but when I noticed Alexander's gaze staring blankly behind me, I knew he couldn't see her. Max had told me once she didn't reveal herself to everybody.

Alexander shook his head pityingly and reached for me. "Felicity, I think you should sit down. I'll call for the healer to see to Max."

"NO!" I wrenched away from him. "Leave us, Alexander."

"Leave you? But I want to—"

"I said leave!" I swept past him.

Alexander's brow furrowed as he nodded, thinking my reaction was out of grief and not determination. The door clicked quietly behind him. After he left, I knelt next to Max's bed and pulled a still dumbfounded Katrina down next to me.

I rested my hands on his chest and uttered a gargled cry of happiness as I felt the slightest rise and fall. It was faint, but it was still there. "He's still alive! He's not gone yet."

Katrina, upon hearing my declaration, pushed me aside and began running her hands over Max's body, chanting foreign words over him. Her hands glowed with a dim white light as magic entered into her body through the breathless words on her lips and flowed out through her fingertips. Her words were low and soft, and they warmed the air around me. My body reacted to Katrina's words. All the way down to the tips of my toes I felt the tingling presence of something unknown, something *magical*.

I jumped in surprise as a deep burst of air escaped from Max. His chest soon rose and fell as if there was a strong pendulum inside it pushing it back and forth. Katrina stopped chanting and gently rested her hand over Max's heart.

"Max?" I called his name tentatively. I leaned over Katrina's shoulder, peering at my uncle. When he didn't respond, I tried again. "Max?"

Max's eyes slowly opened, and the sight of his familiar brown eyes looking at me made my heart soar wildly inside my chest. "Max!" I cried. I practically leapt over Katrina and wrapped my arms around my uncle's shoulders. I buried my head in the crook of his neck. I was getting Max wet, what with my dripping hair and damp dress and all, but he didn't seem to care. And if he didn't care, I didn't care.

"Felicity," he whispered in my ear.

"Max. Oh, Max." My body shook and my hands trembled as I clutched him tighter. I felt his hand reach out and pat me lightly on the back. "I thought I had lost you forever."

His thumb brushed away a tear that fell down my face. "I felt your presence earlier. I heard you tell me you were going to get *her*."

"Oh, yes!" I backed away from the bed and made room for Katrina. "Katrina saved you! You should have seen her magic. It was amazing!" I motioned to the fairy to join me. "Katrina, come here. Look at what you've done. Max is alive!"

Max's eyes tried to look past me to find Katrina, but he wasn't wearing his glasses so I knew he couldn't see very far. Katrina, who was standing on the other side of the room now, would only be a blobby shape to him.

Katrina stood silently, staring at Max in the same bewildered manner as she had when she first entered the room and found him on Death's door.

I beckoned her once more. "Come on. Max wants to see you."

She shook her head, fiercely. It was if a sudden chill swept through the room and her tiny body began to wrack with shivers. She backed away. And where I expected to see joy fill her eyes at Max's restored health, only fear filled them.

I tilted my head, confused by her reaction. I straightened and walked toward her. "Katrina, my uncle wants to see you."

"I can't," she whispered, so only I could hear. She took a deep breath to calm her nerves. "I can't face him. You are right, Felicity. I'd rather hide in the forest like a coward."

She turned to flee.

"Stay." The command came from Max. His voice was warm but firm.

A sob escaped Katrina and she hastily covered her mouth to hide it.

Max set up straighter in the bed. "Katrina."

"Maxwell, don't be mad at me," she pleaded softly. She turned around slowly to face him. "I wanted to come back to you, so many times. I felt awful about leaving you the way I did, without warning, without letting you know where I was going."

Max reached for his glasses sitting on the nightstand next to the bed. He plopped them onto his nose. When he got the chance to see Katrina clearly for the first time, he shook his head, as if perhaps he didn't believe he was seeing her clearly.

"Katrina." He said her name softer this time and a fraction of a smile lifted the corner of his lips. "Come here."

Katrina took two steps forward. "I can explain."

Max shook his head again. "I don't want an explanation. I want you to come here."

I was certain she would ignore his command and flee. Instead, she surprised me by scuttling across the floor with a look of pure guilt etched across her face. "I can explain," she said again. "I have a very good explanation for leaving you."

"You don't have to explain things to me."

"But I do! You have to let me explain. You have to let me apologize."

"It doesn't matter." Max took her hand. "I forgive you."

"I don't deserve..." She took in a shaky breath.

"That's the thing about forgiveness; no one deserves it, but we give it anyway." He ran his fingers across the back of her knuckles, swiping over the shimmery ridges, as the look on his face grew tender. "I forgive you. I forgave you for leaving me a long time ago."

Katrina fell to her knees and threw her arms around his neck, much in the same manner I had earlier. She began crying. "I loved you." Her words came out short and choppy between sobs. "I loved you so very much. I was afraid if I didn't leave you I would lose you. The fairy elders were already so unhappy with me for helping Valencia. They called me a traitor. They branded me as an outcast. I feared their increasing wrath if they found out I wanted to be with a mortal, a human. If they had discovered us, they would have killed you."

Max had almost married Katrina?

"I know," he said lightly. "I was willing to take that chance."

He continued to stroke her hand. It was the calmest I had ever seen him. Gone was the eccentric uncle of mine that filled up any room with his energy. He was replaced by a more tranquil Max, who looked younger than he had in years. Even moments after being on the brink of death, Max looked at Katrina with such serenity in his eyes that I longed to feel about someone the way he obviously felt about her.

Katrina hiccupped as she raised her head to look at him. "If I had told you I wanted to separate us to spare your life, you never would have let me. You would have persuaded me to stay. And I, being so enraptured with you that I was, would have let you. Don't you see? It was easier to say goodbye to each other without actually having to say goodbye."

Max leaned forward, his forehead almost touching hers. "I never said goodbye to you, though." His other hand covered his heart. "At least not in here. I want to be with you, Katrina. Even after all these years, that has never changed."

A fresh trail of tears fell from Katrina's silver eyes. "What kind of life would a mortal human and an immortal fairy have lived together anyway?"

"A very good one, I imagine." A beat of silence passed between them. "You broke my heart, you know. First, Rosalind left Valencia mysteriously. Then, you decided to vanish. I found myself in the midst of a very lonely life inside my library and I feared my heart would never recover. For all I knew, you could've been dead."

She brushed a tear away and shook her head, tossing her curls back as she did. "You know perfectly well that fairies can't die from natural causes."

"But fairies can die from *un*natural causes. I was afraid for you. I was afraid the fairy elders had punished you for aiding Valencia, sentenced you to death or something else tragic. I had no way of finding you or helping you. I never heard from you again."

"I left you a note."

"You mean the note you left on my doorstep three years later the night after Felicity was born? The one that was tucked inside Prince Alexander's fairy tale with instructions to give the book to Felicity before the prince's eighteenth birthday? You mean that note? That was hardly an indication that you were alive and well."

"I signed my name at the end of the note. Obviously, I was alive." Katrina looked out the window for a moment and then at Max. Her voice softened. "Your heart must have mended a little, because Rosalind eventually came back. She brought Felicity with her, too. Surely you were not so alone then?"

"Their arrival was like a breath of fresh air." Max glanced at me thoughtfully. "Felicity's existence has saved me on more than one occasion."

Katrina pulled her hand from out of Max's. "When I first came to Valencia to tell Rosalind about her role in King Frederic's fairy tale, I never imagined that I would fall in love with her twin brother."

He nodded solemnly. "I know."

"I never could really separate myself from you, though. As I'm sure you now know, I hid in the woods outside this palace. Close enough to keep an eye on you, Rosalind, and Felicity, but never close enough to allow myself to enter into your lives once more."

"Until now."

"I couldn't just let you die." Katrina huffed and shot a pointed glance in my direction. "And your niece can be very stubborn."

"She's a lot like Rosalind in that way."

"She shares that trait with her uncle, too."

I was so enthralled with their exchange and their story that it took me a moment to remember my voice. I cleared my throat loudly. "I, um, I should go..." I took a few steps back, edging closer to the door. "You two obviously have things to discuss, and I need to go tell Alexander that Max isn't dead. He's probably pacing the floor like a madman right about now."

"You don't have to go," Max said.

"I think it's best if I give you two time alone. I'll be back later." I hurried toward the doorway, but I turned around to look at them one last time before I left. "By the way, Katrina, whatever your reasons for leaving were, they aren't nearly as good as your reasons for returning."

"It's not like you gave me much of a choice."

The fearful, bewildered fairy from a few moments ago was gone, and the faint traces of the original fairy I had encountered in the forest shone back at me. I could easily see why Max fell in love with her.

I turned and shut the door behind me.

CHAPTER 13

As expected, I found Alexander pacing up and down the length of the hallway outside the infirmary. His back was to me, but I could see that his dark brown hair was falling wildly around his face, his rumpled shirt had long ago come untucked, and his pants were haphazardly shoved into his riding boots. If I hadn't been so drained from sprinting to the forest and worrying about Max, I might have laughed at his disheveled, unprincely appearance. Instead, I merely smiled.

"Alexander."

His head popped up and turned over his shoulder when I spoke his name. "Fliss!" he answered back, jogging over to where I stood. "What happened? Is Max...?"

"He's alive. He's going to survive."

Alexander let out an immense sigh of relief that mirrored the way I felt. He slouched against the wall, as if all the events that had happened during the night had suddenly sapped the last of his energy and he couldn't hold himself up without support. It was in that moment, with the exhaustion brimming from his eyes and his unkempt appearance, that I was never more grateful to have Alexander as my friend.

His blue eyes flitted anxiously to mine. "You sure?"

"Positive."

"How can you be certain?"

How did I explain Katrina's magic had saved my uncle? Wouldn't that lead to more questions I was forbidden to answer?

I took an unsteady breath. "Just trust me. Max is going to be fine. He's made a full recovery."

Alexander raised an eyebrow in question. "So you are telling me, in the ten minutes since I've left the infirmary, Max's health has been completely restored?"

I nodded mutely.

"And there's no proper explanation for it?"

I said nothing.

He looked purposefully down at the floor, shook his head, and released another sigh, only this one was a huff of frustration. "I shall never understand why you are keeping secrets from me."

"I'm not keeping secrets—"

His head snapped up. "Come now, Fliss. I'm not a fool. I know you better than almost anyone else, and I know when you are hiding things from me."

I swallowed a lump of tension building up in my throat.

"But I also know that you'll tell me the truth in your own time," he said quietly. "I am a patient person. Well, relatively patient at least."

I could feel the weight of his questioning stare, and I found a sudden interest in the floral design on a nearby rug.

A grandfather clock in the hallway chimed loudly as its hands struck a new hour. My eyes darted to the clock, eager for somewhere else to look besides Alexander. A faint trickle of sunlight was starting to shine through the row of windows lining the hallway, drawing the previous night's cold away with a new sense of warmth. The morning's rays seeped over onto the carpeted floor and cast boxes of square shadows from the windowpanes.

"I guess this is goodbye," I whispered. "You must be off to Avondale. If you don't leave soon, you'll miss leaving with your company of knights."

"I doubt they'll leave without me. I am, you know, a prince." I heard the good-natured humor in his voice. "Besides I still have to wait for Jack. I suspect he's taking his time saying goodbye to that girl right now. We can catch up to everyone else together."

"That girl?" I frowned, bringing my head up to look at his face. "What girl?"

"He rushed off this morning to say his goodbyes to the blond girl he brought to the dinner party. Pity I didn't get to meet her. It would seem Jack has a certain fondness for this mystery girl."

The shock from Alexander's statement could have hit me no harder than if I had run into a wall made of stone. "What do you mean he's fond of her? Did he say that?" I demanded. My tone was sharper than I had intended it to be.

Alexander tilted his head, confusion spreading across his face. "What's got you so upset?"

I wanted to scream that Jack *couldn't* be fond of Cinderella. What's more, Cinderella certainly couldn't be fond of him. She was destined to marry the prince standing before me, not his cousin. I couldn't let Jack ruin the fairy tale—the one thing I was supposed to get right.

I turned on my heel, determined to find Jack and put an end to whatever was going on between him and Cinderella. "He can't do this!" I muttered fiercely.

Alexander quickly stepped in front of me, blocking me from taking off down the hallway. "Where are you going?" I tried to sidestep around him, but he remained firmly in my way. "Wait a second."

"I have to find Jack!"

Alexander reached out, hooked a finger underneath my chin, and leveled my gaze to his. I sucked in a quick breath. There was something in his eyes that calmed me and startled me all at once. It suddenly didn't feel so important to go chasing after Jack and Cinderella in that moment, not when Alexander was looking at me that way.

"Can you spare a moment of this definitely surprising and probably uncalled for outrage against Jack so can I speak with you?" he asked.

"We are speaking."

"No, I meant..." His words trailed off, and his hand strayed from the tip of my chin to lightly brush across my neck. "There's something I need to say. If I don't say it now, I may never find the courage, and I've been trying to say it for a while."

Alexander's touch had a peculiar effect on my body. I felt like I was being consumed by fire and ice all at once. Half of my mind pleaded with me to turn and run, while the other half urged me to stay. I listened, somewhat reluctantly, to the half that beckoned me to stay.

"The Alexander I know is never without an ample amount of courage."

"The Alexander you know is quaking in his boots at this very moment."

"What do you have to fear? It's only me."

"Exactly."

As he edged closer, my heart hammered so violently in my chest I was sure he could count along to the beat if he chose to do so.

"Your Highness."

Alexander released me as we both turned to find one of his knights standing a few feet away from us. He swallowed another sigh as the knight offered him a bow. "Yes?"

"We are ready to move out. I was instructed to come find you when it was time to go."

"Well, your timing is impeccable."

The knight dipped his head once more and left us.

We were alone once more in the corridor. There was a quick pang in my chest as I realized he was about to leave again. I wouldn't see him for several weeks. The notion left me feeling slightly empty inside.

"It seems you were right. I guess they won't leave without their prince after all." I smiled up at him, taking advantage of the last few moments I had with him. "Thank you," I whispered.

"For what?"

"For what you did last night."

"I didn't do anything."

"Yes, you did. You stayed with Max," I looked down the corridor, my voice lowering to a whisper, "and with me."

I don't know why I did what I did next. Maybe it was because my mind was still foggy with exhaustion and clouded with the exhilaration of Max being alive, but before I knew what I was doing, I was on the tips of my toes, leaning forward to kiss him on the cheek. It was a quick, harmless kiss, yet it took us both by surprise.

Alexander's eyes widened as I pulled away. "*Felicity.*"

I blinked, suddenly realizing my error. "I shouldn't have—I just got caught up with gratitude. You are such a good friend, you see."

"Felicity—"

"The best one I've ever had," I rambled on. "I hope you know how much our friendship means to me."

I couldn't read his emotions. His eyes were still wide, searching my face. I wasn't sure what he was looking for, though.

He stared at me questioningly while clearing his throat awkwardly. "Friendship. Ah. Yes. Well, that is important."

My stomach twisted and embarrassment crept up my spine. I had crossed some invisible border between us and made myself look like a fool in the process. The last thing Alexander needed was for me to behave like the simpering, moonstruck damsels at court he tried so hard to keep his distance from. "Alexander, I didn't mean anything—"

He held up a hand to silence me, disappointment flashing in his eyes. "Of course you didn't. I think this is where I should leave you, though. I'll see you when I return. Do be careful. I'd like to find my *friend* in one piece when I return."

I watched him walk away, the sword at his hip tapping against him to the beat of his determined stride. He didn't look back.

CHAPTER 14

My stomach was still in knots when I made my way back to Max's sickroom. I waited an extra five minutes in the hallway to make sure the heat from my cheeks had disappeared and my hands had stopped shaking.

Once I was certain I had my wits about me, I rounded the corner into Max's room and paused mid-step in the doorway. I expected to find Katrina and my uncle in the midst of a heartfelt discussion about their future. Instead, one of the apprentice healers was putting a stack of books the size of a small child on the edge of the bed, and my uncle's nose was buried deep inside a thick book.

The apprentice glanced over at me sheepishly, looking as uncertain as I was about what he was doing here.

"Where's Katrina?" I asked. "And where did all these books come from?"

Max looked up. "No!" he shouted, causing the apprentice to jump. "Place the books on the nightstand. They'll topple over if you put them on the bed. Felicity, don't stand there like a simpleton, help the lad before he drops the books and creases their pages."

I leapt forward to rescue the books, catching them before they plummeted to the floor. "Max? Where is Katrina?"

"And don't rub your hands all over the pages," Max ordered the apprentice. "You'll smear the ink. Some of these books are older than your grandfather, so mind that you handle them with caution."

"Maxwell!" I plopped the books down harder than necessary on the nightstand. "Where is Katrina?"

"She left." Max skimmed his book without looking up at me. He dismissed the apprentice. "The healers insisted I stay in the infirmary this morning to observe me, so I made one of those bothersome apprentices retrieve a few of my books from the library." He patted the stack of books on his nightstand. "If I must remain in bed, I'm going to get some work done."

"I don't care about your reading. Where did you say Katrina went?"

"She left," he repeated. Although he still looked a little gray in the face, everything else about him was back to normal from the skewed glasses perched on his nose to his furrowed brow that always made him look like he was lost in thought.

"Why?"

"Why do you think?" Max pushed up his glasses unnecessarily, a tale tell sign he was distracted. "There's no reason for her to stay."

"Unbelievable." I snatched the book from his hands. I shut it with a decisive *snap*. "You two were reunited after almost two decades apart, and now you let her go again?"

"I never let her go in the first place." His eyes flashed with annoyance, but it didn't seem directed towards me. He sighed wearily after realizing I was not likely to drop the subject. "Our circumstances haven't changed, Felicity. Just because she saved my life doesn't mean we can be together. Things had to go back to the way they were before."

"But-but you love her." My words came out like a choppy accusation. "You can't deny it. I saw it on your face."

"I'm not denying it."

I made a big show of pointing dramatically to the doorway. "Then, go after her!" I cried.

"She doesn't want me to."

"Maybe she doesn't know what she wants?"

"Katrina is a centuries old fairy who's had multiple lifetimes to decide what she wants. I must respect her wishes."

"You are content with being alone forever?"

"I'm not alone."

"Yes, yes." I waved away what I knew would come next. "You aren't alone because you have your books and studies and your precious library to keep you company."

"No, I'm not alone because I have *you*."

I bit back the retort on my tongue. Leave it to Max to say something uncommonly sentimental when I least expected it. I half suspected him of saying it because he wanted me to stop hounding him about Katrina, but the other half of me loved him all the more for it.

I turned to the window, thinking about that mysterious fairy. The sun was gradually soaring over the horizon and I could see the lining of trees clearly. It would be easier to find her cottage in the daytime. I wondered what would happen if I...

"Don't even think about it," Max said.

My attention snapped back to him. "Think about what?"

"Going after Katrina. She made up her mind years ago, and it hasn't changed."

"Did you tell her you still love her?"

"Of course. I'd be a fool to have her in my presence again and not say anything." He leaned his head back and massaged his temples. "Alas, as I said earlier, it changes nothing. We have other things to worry about now."

"Like?"

"The sickness that plagued me."

I stood up straighter, remembering the seriousness of the situation at hand after having been blinded momentarily by Alexander's departure. "It was the same sickness that killed Mother, and now it targeted you. There's something that doesn't add up. Two perfectly healthy people, sound in mind and body, contracting the same mysterious illness that our healers have never seen before?" I shook my head. "Are you convinced there was something unordinary about her death? I certainly am."

"Me too."

"But who would want to harm you two?" I sank down on the edge of the bed next to Max. "There's got to be some link between her death and your sickness."

"I've always suspected dark magic."

I sucked in a deep, startled breath. "Truly?"

A wind of eeriness swept through my body. I had come to terms with my mother's death long ago, but if the possibility of foul play were involved, everything would change. It would make her death a *murder*. Which was something I was *not* willing to come to terms with just yet.

"There's no evidence right now," Max assured me quickly, seeing where my mind was wandering to next. "We'll figure out what's going on, but, until we do, I don't want you to stray too far from the palace on your own. There have been too many close calls lately. I will accompany you if you need to go somewhere outside the palace walls."

I balked. "I don't think—"

"Felicity, I know I don't often act like a proper guardian, but you *will* listen to me when I tell you not to put yourself at unnecessary risk." Before I could protest again, he continued on. "Now are you going to tell me why you arrived so flustered a few moments ago? Or shall I have to use my imagination?"

"Flustered?" My eyes widened at the abrupt topic change. "What-what makes you say that?"

Max narrowed his eyes. "Your face is completely flushed. Either you just ran ten laps around the palace or something happened between you and Alexander while you were gone."

"No!" My reply was too hasty, which only served to add further proof that something *did* happen. My cheeks felt like they were going to light on fire they were so warm. I silently cursed my fair skin. I took a deep breath and tried again. "No," I said with forced calmness. "We just said goodbye."

"Come now," he said softly. "I've always been able to see the effect you have on him." He studied me closely for a moment. "And now I'm starting to see the effect he has on you."

I tugged absentmindedly at the remains of my braid. I shuddered inwardly as I thought of how I must have looked when I said goodbye to Alexander—like a wet, ruffled crow. "It doesn't matter. I've got bigger problems right now. I think there's something going on between Cinderella and Jack." I fell face first against a pillow on the bed and groaned into it loudly. "Why can't everyone fall in love with the person they are supposed to fall in love with?"

"There would be very few happy couples if everyone fell in love with the person they were *supposed* to fall in love with."

"Said the eternal bachelor."

"Goodness." Max scratched the dark stubble on his chin. "Look at us, two people pining over lost love because our circumstances got the best of us."

I stood up abruptly, knocking the pillow off the bed as I did. "I have *never* pined over a boy in my entire life. And I will not start now, thank you very much."

"Very well." Max looked as if he was struggling to bite back a grin. "Since you obviously don't have feelings for a certain prince—"

"Obviously," I chimed in.

"What are you going to do about him and Cinderella?"

"I have some matchmaking to do and a ball to plan. What's more, I have to find some glass slippers."

* * *

When the healers came in one last time to examine Max, I made up a quick excuse to leave.

"Where are you going?" he asked.

"I need to change out of this muddy dress and I'm sorely in need of a bath." The lie rolled too easily off my tongue. Despite Max's wishes, I was going to leave the palace alone. I needed to speak with Cinderella privately, but I couldn't do that with my uncle hovering over me. "I'm going home."

He squinted curiously at me over the rim of his glasses but eventually waved me away.

I headed straight for the countryside to Cinderella's manor. The ground was still muddy and damp from the thunderstorm, so by the time I reached the manor I looked like a swamp creature. My hair, which had officially come out of its braid, hung in tangles down my back, my filthy dress looked worse than I remembered in the light of day, and my hem was soaked from wading through mud puddles.

A grand carriage, one with glinting gold trim and mother of pearl door handles, was parked in the driveway led by four black stallions, a coachman, and a footman waiting like statues for their master to return. My eyes widened at the impressive display of wealth, for the carriage surely did not belong to Cinderella or her stepfamily. Curiosity filled me as I wandered past the carriage and onto the landing of the front porch.

"I wouldn't do that if I were you," the footman called out. His voice was soft but held a hint of warning. I glanced over my shoulder, surprised by his statement. I was even more surprised to see the coachman nod in agreement.

Ignoring the stares from the coachman and footman behind me, I knocked three times on the door and waited.

Seconds trickled by into minutes. I heard a faint commotion inside, the slamming of a door and the shout of an unfamiliar name, and just when I had given up hope of anyone answering, the door flung open.

I jumped back, startled.

A young girl with mousy brown hair, rogued cheeks, and a pink dress that was too tight over her generous bosom frowned at me. "What?" she snapped.

Her waspish tone caught me off guard. "Oh. Hello. I am looking for—"

"A washroom perhaps?" she offered dryly while surveying my dress. "If you are here for an interview, you'll have to go through the servants' entrance."

"Interview?" I questioned. "No, you don't understand. I'm here to see Cinderella—"

The girl huffed. "I don't care who you are here to see. You'll not be allowed through the front door dressed like a scullery maid, especially today." The girl rolled her eyes heavenward, as if this conversation had sapped the last of her willpower. "You'll find the servants' entrance around back."

I stepped back just in time to avoid being crushed by the weight of her impressive door slamming skills.

Shocked, I stared at the closed door for a moment, grounded my teeth together, and turned on my heel to find the servants' entrance, hoping that would lead me to Cinderella. The footman and coachman snickered as I stormed past the carriage.

I stopped to glare at them. I had just been insulted and had a door slammed in my face. I was in no mood for their mockery, too.

"What's so funny?"

"Easy there," the young footman chided. "It was a mighty bold move for the help to waltz right up to the front door. I admire that kind of spirit."

"Help?" I echoed.

"Bold?" The older coachman repeated. He raised an eyebrow from atop the box seat. "Her actions were foolish." He shared a laugh with his friend, and the blood in my veins boiled at the sound of it.

"Now don't sour your face with that expression," the young footman said through a chuckle. His blue-gray eyes sparkled with mischief and his sandy hair blew over his face in the breeze. With his charming smile and light-hearted attitude, he seemed the type of person who would always act like a boy no matter how old he actually was. "You couldn't have expected your actions, amusing though they were, to end well. It is best you learn your place now if you ever want to work for nobility."

"No, you don't understand. I'm not a servant. I'm a palace librarian."

Just then a girl, no older than myself, came around the corner from the servants' entrance. "Thomas!" she called out, smiling towards the footman. "Wasn't expecting to see you here."

"Hello, Mary girl." Thomas tipped his hat in her direction. "Me and Harold's only waiting for the master to finish paying a call on the lady of the house."

Mary had a rosy complexion and bright eyes, which made her already lovely face all the more appealing. I couldn't help but notice Thomas seemed to think Mary's features were lovely too, for he purposely leaned closer to her with the same moonstruck expression Max had used on Katrina earlier this morning.

"I was just finishing up interviewing for the new maid position here," Mary explained. "Though I've heard the mistress is a hardened shrew, I'm in need of work. Papa lost his job at the milliner's last week, and we've got too many mouths to feed." She shrugged. "No matter. It is better to work for a dragon than to go hungry."

Harold and Thomas nodded understandingly.

Mary turned to me. "And who might you be, miss? Come to interview for the position yourself?"

"I'm Felicity. I've not come for a job, though. Besides this home already has a maid. Her name is Cinderella. That's who I've come to see."

"Aye, yes. The pretty girl with blond hair?"

I nodded.

"Just had the pleasure of meeting her. She's the one finding a replacement maid. You'll find her in the kitchen." Mary nodded to Thomas and Harold, her eyes staying on Thomas a moment longer than necessary. "Well, I must be off. See you gents around."

Thomas brought Mary's hand to his lips and made a great show of kissing the tips of her fingers. "Until we meet again, fair lady."

"Thomas, you cad. I bet you sweet talk all the ladies in the village."

"Only the ones named Mary."

She smiled, satisfied with his response, and turned to flounce away.

"You like her," I stated after Mary was out of sight.

"Who?" Thomas's head swiveled back to me. "*Mary?* Nah."

My anger from his teasing earlier had evaporated, only to be replaced with amusement. "You admire her," I confirmed.

His mouth drooped open like a codfish. "But—"

"You admire not only her lovely features, but you admire her strength and determination to help provide for her family."

Thomas's cheeks reddened as Harold tossed back his head of gray hair and roared with enough laughter to make his eyes water. The old man slapped his knee with enthusiasm. "She's right lad. I've seen the way you look at that girl."

"You should tell her," I said.

Thomas scratched his head. "Tell her?"

"Yes." I looked up to find Harold nodding in agreement. His smile deepened the wrinkles on his weathered face. "Tell her."

I nodded to them, turned to find Cinderella, and, perhaps, interview for a position as a maid.

CHAPTER 15

I tapped lightly on the door leading into the kitchen.

"Come in!" Cinderella called out. She stood up quickly from the table when I pushed the door open. "Felicity? What are you doing here?" She crossed the room to usher me in.

"I wanted to apologize for ruining your mother's dress last night."

Her brow furrowed. "There's no need to apologize. I know it was an accident. You shouldn't have trekked all the way out here in this weather. You'll likely catch your death."

"I'm fine." I waved away her concern. "I wanted to see you. I also wanted to discuss the dinner party."

"I should not have gone. If Cressida saw me..."

"She didn't. She was more concerned about the bright splash of red cider on her dress."

"Yes, I know. Just this morning she sent the dress over from the palace and I was tasked with trying to get that stain out. Please don't tell me you had a part in ruining her dress? She'll never forgive you and she's not someone you want as an enemy."

"Cressida does not scare me in the least." I hung my satchel over the back of a chair. "Enough about her. Let's speak of things that don't leave a sour taste in my mouth."

Cinderella slumped back down into one of the chairs. "I'm afraid today is not a good day for idle conversation. I've been tasked with trying to find a new maid to help around the manor, and my stepmother has a very important guest that's caused an uproar amongst my stepfamily."

I joined her at the table. "Uproar?"

"Apparently some wealthy lord has come to ask for permission to marry one of my stepsisters, probably Cressida. My stepmother's been in quite a tizzy trying to keep up appearances and impress him."

"Ah." I settled back into my seat with a new understanding. "That's why I wasn't allowed through the front entrance. A girl slammed the door in my face and told me if I wanted to interview for the new maid's position I'd have to go around back. I should have told her if she wanted to impress a man, she ought not to wear so much rouge she looks like a court jester. While she's at it, she should loosen the stays in her corset before the contents inside it spill out. Though I suppose that might tip the odds in her favor depending on how Lord What's-His-Name sees it."

Cinderella's eyes widened to the size of the teacup saucers. Finally, as if contemplating whether it was allowed or not, she giggled. "That one would be Agatha. She does wear a rather impressive amount of rouge, doesn't she? Agatha's a bit younger than Cressida. Though she's not as cruel, she can be just as demanding. I'm actually surprised she even opened the door for you."

"In all fairness, no matter which one answered the door, they probably would've both been equally capable of insulting me."

"I'm sorry Agatha insulted you. You won't have to worry about Cressida answering the door though. She lives at the palace when court is in session. She wants to be close to the prince. She's set her sights on marrying him, along with every other female in the kingdom."

"Well, perhaps Alexander will get lucky and Lord What's-His-Name will propose to Cressida and take one of his admirers off of his hands. By the way, I wasn't insulted Agatha thought I was a maid. With the dress I'm wearing, I'm surprised she didn't think I was here to muck out the stables. No, I was insulted she treated me like less than a human being, which I imagine is what you face on a daily basis."

"I've gotten used to it."

"You should never get used to being treated less than you deserve."

The door from the house to the kitchen burst open, and a horrible voice that was more like a banshee screech yelled, "*Cinderella!*"

Cinderella's stepmother, with her wide set eyes and even wider set cheekbones, strode into the kitchen unannounced. Her perpetual frown deepened when she saw us sitting casually at the table.

"What is going on in here?" she barked.

Cinderella leapt from her chair. "We were just, um, just—"

"Interviewing me for the new maid position," I finished.

The stepmother wrinkled her nose. "You are a maid?"

"Yes, ma'am."

"Yes, *Lady Maura*," she corrected me. "You will use my title when addressing me." She eyed my dress suspiciously. Although it was filthy, it was still good quality, and servants didn't generally own good quality dresses. "Let me see your hands."

"Yes, *Lady Maura*," I replied. I held out my hands, which, thankfully, were still covered in grime and dirt and who knows what else from last night's escapades. They certainly did not look like a prim and proper librarian's hands. They looked like servant's hands that were used to dirty work.

"Hmm." Lady Maura batted my hands away. She ran her critical eyes up and down my person. "You seem strong enough and used to work." She spun around to face Cinderella. "Was this the girl you were going to recommend to replace you?"

"*Replace me?*" Cinderella squeaked. "You never said you were replacing me. You only said we were in need of more help around the manor." Her eyes welled with unshed tears and she gulped loudly. "You are tossing me out onto the streets, aren't you? You can't do that. This was my father's home, you know."

"I'm not tossing you anywhere except for into the sitting room to entertain Lord Reginald." She pushed Cinderella none too gently towards the door. "He's asked to see you."

"See *me?*" Cinderella's face paled. "What of Cressida and Agatha?"

Lady Maura smirked wickedly. "Lord Reginald has not offered to pay me an exorbitant amount of money in exchange for the privilege to marry them."

An icy wash of realization flooded my veins, and Cinderella gasped as her own realization sank in. "*That* is why you are replacing me with a new maid. You mean for me to marry him," she said with wide eyes. "He's at least thirty years older than I am!"

"He's suitable enough."

"You mean the gold he's lining your pockets with is suitable enough," Cinderella contradicted in a rare show of outrage. Her fists balled into the fabric of her skirt. "You cannot sell me off to the highest bidder. My father would not stand for it!"

"Your father is dead! And the dead have no opinions!" Lady Maura raised her hand to strike, and Cinderella, who seemed to anticipate the blow, flinched in fear.

"Stop!" I screamed. I jumped in between Cinderella and her stepmother just in time to receive the forceful blow. The back of Lady Maura's hand cracked across my face.

I uttered a gasp of pain and fell back, clutching my cheek.

"Felicity!" Cinderella cried, rushing towards me.

Lady Maura glowered at me. "Serves you right, brat. You shouldn't have interfered in family business."

Fresh tears fell from Cinderella's red-rimmed eyes. She turned to her stepmother. "We are *not* family!"

I winced as my finger trailed across the raised bump on my cheek, but my pain soon ebbed away into seething anger. If this woman knew what Alexander had taught me to do with a sword, she would not stand there crowing over me so triumphantly. "I'd interfere again if I could," I spat. "In the future, you should not strike your stepdaughter. I doubt Lord Reginald will pay for damaged goods."

Lady Maura raised an eyebrow. "If you want to work in this house," she said in a low, dangerous voice, "you will learn the proper amount of respect that a servant gives their master." She turned to Cinderella. "You have one minute to present yourself to His Lordship or I shall burn that confounded instrument you adore, do you understand? And dry your tears," she barked. "The wench is right. He will not pay for unsightly goods."

Cinderella nodded through a hiccup. Her compliance seemed to satisfy her stepmother, who stormed from the kitchen with as much commotion as when she had entered it.

As soon as Lady Maura was gone, I took Cinderella by the hand and ushered her to the back door. "That's it. We are leaving. Right this instant."

Cinderella skidded to a halt. "Felicity, your face. You'll have an ugly bruise come tomorrow." She bit her lip as more tears threatened to fall. "No one has stood up to Lady Maura for me before. Thank you—"

"I don't want your thanks. I want you to leave with me. I refuse to allow you to stay with that horrible woman or marry a wretched man old enough to be your father. You can stay with Max and myself at the library. I hope you like cats." My voice left no room for argument, but I should have anticipated one anyway.

She tugged her hand from my grasp. "I have to stay here, though."

I whirled around to face her. "Are you crazy?" I threw my hands up wildly in the air. "These people are abusing you! They are selling you to a man just to line their own pockets with gold! You said so yourself. What is so important about staying in this house that you would forfeit your freedom for it?"

"I can't explain," she whispered.

"Try."

She brushed away tears on her cheeks. "I know you think me weak. I don't have the courage you do to face all my fears. Every memory of my father is buried in this house and to leave... would be like losing him all over again."

"Your father wouldn't want you to live like this."

Cinderella rubbed her temple and looked out the window once more, the far-off distance of the horizon calling to her. "My father was a musician, a brilliant pianist and composer. His collection of instruments I'm sure rivals even that of the musicians at the palace." She paused as if trying to figure out what she wanted to say next. While I wondered where this story was going and why it was more important at the moment than leaving this place for good.

"Come on. Let's get out of here." I reached out to tug Cinderella's hand, much harder this time, but she refused to budge.

"This was not always such a dreadful place to live. There used to be laughter and love and music that filled the halls of this house. Father inhaled music as if it were air around him. His passion was such that he breathed in every note and piece he played through his very soul, and he passed that passion on to me." Cinderella grew silent but whether it was from thoughtfulness or sadness I could not say. "He died shortly after he married Lady Maura, who soon realized my father had very little in the way of worldly possessions or fortunes for us to live off of, and she became embittered at the thought of poverty. Lady Maura had only married him to escape the debts her former husband, a lord at the palace who I hear gambled away the family's fortune, had left behind after his own untimely death."

"Forgive me for bring frank, but what did your father see in her?"

"She portrayed herself as a desperate, weak lady in need of a husband to secure her future. Father was never able to resist someone in need and he longed for me to have a mother again and to have siblings to grow up with so I wouldn't be lonely. That's why he married Lady Maura. He didn't realize that I wasn't lonely though, not when I had him." She huffed out a bitter laugh. "Now I have a stepmother and stepsisters and I've never been lonelier in my entire life."

"I still don't understand why you stay here. Your father would probably be much more at ease knowing you weren't being treated like a slave in your own home, in *his* home."

"When Father died, my stepmother confiscated every piece of music he ever wrote and every instrument he owned. She threatened to destroy them all if I did not comply with her wishes. But every year I work for Lady Maura, she gives me back one of his compositions and one of his instruments. That is why I stay with her. The longer I stay, the more of my father I receive. Music was his life's work, Felicity. I won't rest until I have every piece he ever composed and every instrument he loved back in my possession. It's all I have left of him—his music. I owe it to him to stay and make sure it's kept safe. Once it is returned to me, somehow I will share his compositions and music with the world. The world needs his music."

I could feel my eyes widen at her story and form a few tears of my own. I stared at Cinderella in amazement, astonished by her sacrifice. She didn't stay because she was afraid of facing the world on her own. She stayed because there was something worth fighting for, something worth forfeiting her freedom for. That was not cowardice—that was courage beyond measure.

"How much of his music do you lack?" I asked quietly.

"One instrument and one piece of music," she replied. "The last instrument is a harp my father gave my mother as a wedding gift. She was harpist, a talented musician in her own right I was always told. He composed a duet that they played at their wedding. Lady Maura has been holding onto Mother's harp and my parents' duet for years, knowing it was what I wanted most."

"Do you think she will finally give it to you?"

"She will if she wants me to marry Lord Reginald," Cinderella replied. A gleam of defiance sparked in her eyes. "I'm going to offer to marry him in exchange for the last of my father's music and my mother's harp."

My heart dropped into my stomach. If she married someone besides Alexander, I'd have an even bigger predicament on my hands.

"Let's not be so hasty," I implored. "If you marry this man, you very well could be exchanging one form of slavery for another. Do you know if he will treat you any better than your stepfamily?"

"What do you suggest I do?" Cinderella shook her head and slumped against the wall like a ragdoll. "I am running out of options if I want my father's music back."

"We are going to pretend as if you are going to follow through with your stepmother's plan. I will come here for the next few weeks under the pretense you are training me to be the new household maid."

"What of Cressida? Won't she recognize you if she sees you at the manor? She'll know you aren't a maid."

"You said so yourself she lives at the palace while court is in the session. If she happens to come home while I'm here, I'll make myself scarce."

Cinderella bit her lip, still uncertain. "I don't know—"

I grasped her hands. "Come on. It will give us time to figure a way to get you out of this mess, but it'll give your stepmother the appearance that you are going along with her plan."

"I *was* going to go along with her plan."

"Don't," I commanded. "There's more to your life than being a misused servant in this house or the wife of a crotchety lord whose only hopes of marrying a woman lie in how much he can grease the palms of her family members."

"I fear you expect too much of my future."

I leaned against the wall next to her, realizing how personal this task was becoming. Cinderella was now an unexpected friend—someone I wanted to help not only because a fairy tale told me to but also because I cared about her. I took a deep breath and whispered, "What if I told you a future—a destiny—awaits you outside these walls that you can hardly fathom? If you trust me, I'll make sure you find it."

"I'm not sure I believe that. Though if I'm going to believe in anyone, it's going to be you."

CHAPTER 16

Max paced the length of our living room after I told him my plan. "No. Absolutely not. I won't allow it."

"It's not your call to make," I pointed out casually from the settee where I reclined. My eyes followed Max as he charged to and fro across the floor. "I'm doing it for the fairy tale. I can't have Cinderella marrying another man that isn't Alexander, and she would just to get her father's music back. I have to stall her—at least until Alexander returns home and there's a ball."

"That woman hit you!" Max pointed accusingly to my cheek, where a purple bruise was already threatening to deepen and linger.

"But—"

"*She hit you!*" His voice was higher now and a vein on his temple looked ready to burst at any moment. "I will not allow my niece—my sole living relative—to put herself in the clutches of that woman ever again."

I whipped my legs out from under me and strode over to him. "I understand your frustration. I am, after all, the person she hit, so nobody feels more strongly about hating Lady Maura than I do, except perhaps Cinderella. However, Cinderella needs me to be there for her right now, which means the fairy tale needs me to make a few sacrifices."

Max, despite my rational tone, continued to glower. "Tell Cinderella she can come live with us for the time being. When she is Alexander's wife, she can demand her music back from her stepmother without fear of endangering her life *or* yours, for that matter."

"I tried that already. She won't do it, and, now that I've calmed down a bit, I realized she *can't* come live with us."

"And why ever not?" Max sat down and took my place on the settee in a huff.

"You of all people know why. Because we have to follow the fairy tale," I explained. "The fairy tale doesn't say Cinderella lives out the remainder of her days in the library until she meets Prince Alexander. She has to stay with her stepfamily if we want to stay true to the original tale. Alexander has to be the one to convince her to leave."

Max made no arguments. We both knew the fairy tale came before everything else.

So, with the weight of Valencia's future and the fairy tale hanging delicately in the balance, Max reluctantly agreed to allow me to work for Lady Maura. The only stipulations he made were that he was allowed to escort me to and from her manor every day and that I carry my sword with me. He still wasn't keen on letting me leave the palace alone and unprotected.

Every morning we arose well before dawn to trek out to the country manor together. Max would stop a couple hundred yards away from the manor, so as not to be seen accompanying me, and every evening, just before sunset, I would return to find him sitting on a log in the same spot, waiting for me to finish my work. Max was always a welcome sight after the long, tiring days working alongside Cinderella.

And those days were surely long and tiring. I spent most of my time on my hands and knees washing baseboards, waxing marble floors, and scrubbing fireplaces. By the time I left the manor at the end of the day, every part of my body throbbed in pain and the cinders and ash from the fireplace had ruined most of my dresses and aprons. The worst part was the way Lady Maura and her cackling younger daughter treated me. In their eyes, I was no better than a poor servant, and I was subjected to the same treatment as Cinderella. I bit my lip and kept my mouth shut—for Cinderella's sake—when all I longed to do was strike back with my words or, preferably, my fists. Still, I was grateful Cressida had yet to make an appearance and, despite the way the family treated me, every morning I rose stiffly and served them all over again.

Lady Maura had agreed to postpone the wedding between Cinderella and Lord Reginald, only because it meant Cinderella would have time to "train" me to take over the household chores and upkeep of the manor. Apparently, the only thing that drove Lady Maura more than money was the fact that she might have to lift a lazy finger to do work if her stepdaughter left her without providing a proper replacement. My plan, as I had hoped, had bought us time.

The only good part about my servitude was I was often too busy or too exhausted to allow my thoughts to drift to Alexander. When I did find myself wondering what he was doing or what I was going to say to him when he returned, I went looking for baseboards to scrub.

One afternoon, almost two weeks into working at the manor, I was painstakingly mending the ruffles in one of the stepsister's gowns. There were still piles of clothing around me to be mended when Cinderella burst in through the kitchen. I was so surprised by her abrupt arrival that I accidentally stabbed my finger with the needle, not for the first time that day, causing three drops of blood to well up and fall onto a pristinely white ruffle.

I groaned. Now there were bloodstains I had to wash out too.

"Felicity!" Cinderella cried. Her eyes sparkled with brightness. "They are gone! For the entire day!" She clapped her hands and twirled around.

"Who's gone for the entire day?" I asked, setting my needle and thread gleefully down on the table next to me. I wrapped my finger in a handkerchief. "Lady Maura and Agatha?"

"Yes! They are spending the day shopping in the village and then they are going to see Cressida at the palace. Do you know how rare it is for all three of them to be gone?" Cinderella twirled around once more and her apron strings caught on the fire poker. She stumbled back toward the fireplace and an absentminded flame leapt forward, catching the material of her dress and singeing the backside of it.

"Gracious, Cinderella!" I beat out the sparks with her stepsister's dress, which was rumpled up in my hands.

Cinderella craned her neck to look at the damage done to her dress. "My entire backside could have been blackened. I really would have looked like a scullery maid then." She frowned at the sight of her stepsister's dress in my hands and bit her lip nervously. "And you burnt Agatha's favorite dress trying to save mine. She'll never forgive us."

"Her favorite, you say?" I paused for a moment and eyed the fire. I shrugged my shoulders and tossed the dress into the flames. The crackling fire sounded like sweet music to my ears. "You know, I can live without Agatha's forgiveness."

Cinderella gasped. "Felicity! No!" She leapt towards the flames to try to rescue the dress, but I held her back. Her mouth fell open. "Why would you do that?"

"She makes me empty her chamber pot. It takes every ounce of resolve I possess not to dump the contents over her head. This was almost as satisfactory."

"You should have exercised some of that resolve just now."

"If Agatha asks where it's gone, I'll just tell her she misplaced it somewhere in the piles of clothes she already has." I pulled Cinderella out of the kitchen before she could protest and into the main part of the house. "What shall we do with all this extra time to spare without one of those vultures looming over us, ordering us about?"

Cinderella smiled and pulled out a key from her apron pocket, turning to look over her shoulder, as if she feared someone else was watching us. "Would you like to see the music room?" she whispered. "I snuck the key out of my stepmother's bedroom."

"Yes!"

I followed her up the winding staircase near the entrance of the manor, down a long hallway with creaking floorboards, and around the corner to a wing of the house I had never been in. She stopped before a closed door. Cinderella's hand shook as she rested it on the doorknob, and she clenched the key tightly in her other hand.

"Maybe we shouldn't go in here. My stepmother despises it when I am in the music room or playing the instruments," she whispered. "She'd be furious if she knew that I took the key without her permission."

"That's not surprising; she despises most things that are good and pure. I don't see why music would be an exception."

"What if she knew we were neglecting our chores?"

"She's not here." I reached out, grabbed the key, shoved it inside the keyhole, and pushed down on the handle.

The door swung open to reveal a spectacular space with various instruments arranged throughout. It was airy and open. Windows wrapped around the room, letting in light and the smell of sunshine and happiness. I counted no less than two violins, three different wind instruments polished to perfection, an imposing piano, and a glinting horn that looked as if might belong to some celestial being. However, the most eye-catching of the instruments was an immense six-foot pedal harp with intricate floral designs etched onto the body. It stood in the middle of the room directly under a chandelier that cast rainbows across the surface when the sunlight hit the dangling prisms.

I strummed my fingers across the harp's strings, emitting a light, dulcet sound from the instrument that traveled over the stillness of the room. "It's beautiful," I whispered in a hushed, reverent tone. I ran my hand over the name carved on the base of the harp. "*Charlotte?* Was that your mother?"

"Yes. *Charlotte.*" Cinderella's eyes lit up as she whispered her mother's name. "Even though it wasn't his, this was always my father's favorite instrument. It reminded him of her and he always kept it right here—in the heart of the music room."

"Can you play it for me?" I asked her.

"Yes, but I'm not allowed—"

"She's not here." I turned to face Cinderella. "Don't let her control you even when she's not present. *Play for me*," I implored. "I want to witness firsthand the passion for music your father passed on to you. Any girl who is willing to part with her freedom in order to rescue this exquisite instrument must know how to play it and play it well."

Cinderella needed no further encouragement. She perched herself delicately on the stool before the harp, raised her arms to the strings, and soon music, lovelier than I could imagine, sprang from the instrument with the sweep of her fingers. Her movements were precise and graceful and mesmerizing all at once, and the gentle notes traveled like drops of rainwater across the room and washed over me. Cinderella might have played for one hour or one minute, I was so lost in the sweet-sounding notes and the feeling of floating on clouds that I almost didn't hear the rickety sound of a carriage pull up.

I raced to the window to see if Lady Maura and her daughter had arrived earlier than planned. Instead, I was greeted by a much grislier sight.

"Cinderella!"

The music stopped abruptly, and the last note echoed across the room. "What is it?" She scraped her stool against the floor, knocking it over as she rose with haste. "Are they back so soon?"

I pointed to the familiar carriage with Harold the driver reining in the team and Thomas the footman opening the carriage door for his portly, aging master. "No, it's that awful Lord Dunderhead come to pay you a visit."

Cinderella peered over my shoulder. "Oh, you mean Lord Reginald." She wrung her hands together. "I don't want to see him. Last time he was here he looked at me as if I were a pastry on the dessert tray waiting to be gobbled. He was getting too free with his hands as well, if you know what I mean."

"Horrid man! I'll go tell him you aren't here." I turned to dash down the stairs, but Cinderella pulled me back.

"Lady Maura will be furious if she finds out I sent him away."

"Then *I'll* send him away."

"She'll still take it out on me."

I opened my mouth to reply.

"I know, I know," Cinderella cut me off. "She's not here. Lord Reginald will tell her he came by to visit, though. She'll know I purposefully ignored him."

I watched the odious man climb out of his carriage; it lurched forward under his impressive weight and sprung backward when his feet hit the ground. Lord Reginald squinted up at the window, and Cinderella and I ducked out of sight.

A few moments later there came a distinct *tap* from the front door.

"I'm going to have to let him in," Cinderella sighed. "He'll just keep knocking until his fist wears a hole in the door. He's persistent that way."

"I've got a better idea. We let him come in for a cup of tea, but perhaps I can manage to spill a cup of piping hot tea on his trousers. He'll have to leave sooner than expected." I winked at her conspiratorially. "I *am* good at spilling drinks on unsuspecting people, you know."

Cinderella agreed to our plan, and I soon found myself rushing downstairs to greet our guest. Lord Reginald knocked again, louder and with more force this time. I pried the door open just in time to be greeted by a meaty fist poised to strike the door again, which I only narrowly managed to dodge at the last second. Max wouldn't be pleased if I came home with more bruises on my face.

"It's about time, girl," Lord Reginald barked. He stepped into the manor, his protruding gut leading the way, and brushed me aside. "A gentleman shouldn't be kept waiting out on the porch like a commoner. I shall have to speak to Lady Maura about her help."

I had all sorts of things to say about him being a *gentleman*. Instead, I dipped into a curtsy and mumbled, "I beg your pardon, milord."

I reached to close the door behind him and saw Thomas and Harold waiting with the carriage. Thomas tipped his hat in a debonair sort of fashion, and Harold waved from atop his perch. I returned the wave discreetly before shutting the door.

Lord Reginald reached into his pocket and pulled out a handkerchief to mop his moist brow. I nearly gagged when he ran the same handkerchief under his nose. As I offered him a chair in the sitting room, I couldn't help but wince as I took in his stern face, beady eyes, and, worst yet, his still damp forehead.

He plopped down into the seat like an overfull sack of potatoes. "Don't hover like an imbecile, girl! Get me Cinderella at once." There was a gleam in his eye that did, in fact, look like he was waiting to devour a tasty morsel on a dessert tray when he said her name.

I made no attempt to move.

"I have things to discuss with the wench. Hurry!"

I took my time exiting the room, not remotely eager to obey his command. I leisurely circled around furniture and stopped to replace the firewood in the fireplace, trying to keep my anger at bay. Lord Reginald's glower was palpable.

I glowered right back.

I found Cinderella in the kitchen trying in vain to wipe the dirt and cinders from her dress and apron.

"I don't know why I'm even bothering to clean up for that man." Frantic, she turned to me. "You promise to come quick? I can't stand to be alone with him longer than necessary."

I paused, thinking about the greedy gleam in his eye. "Actually, I don't think you should see him alone. It doesn't feel right."

"He'll pitch a fit if I don't. I'd rather not face my stepmother's wrath if she found out I ignored him."

"But—"

"He'd be suspicious. Let's stick to the original plan. I'll tell him I've sent for some *hot* tea. You will come to my rescue, won't you?"

"Of course," I replied. "As soon as I set up the tea tray, I'll be there."

She nodded weakly and headed out to receive our visitor. I hastily set about boiling water for tea—taking care to make it extra hot—just in case Lord Reginald forgot to act like the gentleman he claimed to be. The back door of the kitchen swung open. Startled, I almost dropped the teakettle as I turned to see who was at the door.

Thomas the footman was standing in the doorway with a foolish grin smeared across his face. His wispy blond hair danced around his face as a gust of wind blew past him. The breeze was strong enough to blow out the fire in the fireplace. I stifled a groan when I realized I'd be even longer saving Cinderella from Lord Reginald's company.

"Felicity! Remember me?" Thomas' voice and genial spirit lightened the otherwise tense mood. I couldn't help but smile. "It's Thomas. We met a few weeks ago."

"Shut that door, will you?" I hastily coaxed another fire to warm the teakettle. "Of course, I remember."

Thomas sauntered in after pushing the door closed with a *click*. "I was wondering which girl got the job here. It wasn't Mary, you know. She was quite broken up about it. Still hasn't found anything." He helped himself to a muffin on the counter, munching into it with enthusiasm. "You don't mind, do you?" he asked.

"Well, seeing how you already bit into it..."

"Right." He grabbed another muffin. "One for Harold too. Poor man's having to sit with the horses."

I turned to stoke the fire. "Was there anything else you needed? I really do have a lot of work to do." I hoped my gentle prod was enough to get him out of the kitchen. "Lord Reginald and Cinderella will be expecting their tea soon."

"Cinderella?" Thomas questioned. "Who is that?"

"My friend," I replied. "The girl Lord Reginald is supposedly going to marry."

"Marry?" Thomas blinked in confusion. "I didn't know the old taskmaster was considering marrying again."

I wheeled around to face him, sloshing water from the teakettle as I turned. "Again? Has he been married before?"

"Three times." Thomas took another enthusiastic bite of his muffin. A few crumbs fell and landed on his jacket. "The poor ladies never stood a chance. All of them wound up in an early grave."

"*What?* He killed them?"

"What? Oh no." Thomas shrugged, backing out of the kitchen. "He didn't kill them... all kinds of mysterious deaths, though. You know, accidents that were suspicious: a carriage ride gone awry, a fall down the stairs, a drowning in the lake." He paused. He must have seen the horror etched on my face. "Don't want to worry you. I shouldn't have said anything. If Lord Reginald found out I told you anything..."

"Thomas?" I questioned. "What aren't you saying? What do you mean by *accidents?*" I reached out and snatched the muffin out of his hands. I crumpled it in my fist, sending crumbs scattering to the floor. "My friend is up there with that man right now. Do you think he means to harm her?"

Thomas gulped. "Well, now..."

"Let me put it this way, if it were Mary, would you leave her alone with that man?"

"Never." His usually bright eyes darkened. "I wouldn't leave *any* woman alone with that man."

Not wasting another moment, I pushed Thomas towards the door. "Tell Harold to ready the carriage. Lord Reginald will be leaving shortly."

Thomas thankfully complied and dashed out of my sight. As soon as he was gone, I heard a loud *crash* of glass shattering on the floor echo from the other side of the manor. Next came a distinctly female scream and a resounding *thud*.

I grabbed my sword, silently thanking Max for forcing me to carry it, before sprinting across the manor to the sitting room.

"Cinderella!"

I pushed open the door to find Lord Reginald lying unconscious on the floor amidst a pile of shattered glass, a puddle of water, and several wilted flowers. I let out a little gasp and my eyes met Cinderella's, who hovered over his body. She had swollen lips, a torn bodice, and she was clutching the remains of a broken vase. Her face was stony and resilient, but her legs trembled as she sunk down into a nearby chair.

"What happened?" I whispered.

"I didn't have any hot tea. I had to improvise."

CHAPTER 17

I haven't killed him, have I?" Cinderella whispered into the palm of her hands.

I nudged Lord Reginald's body with my toe. He released a groan from deep in his throat but remained unconscious.

"Unfortunately, no. Are you okay?"

She nodded absentmindedly.

I leaned over to pick up several pieces of glass. When I reached for a particularly large piece, my hand slipped. I felt a slice of pain. A gash welled up across my palm with a bright red pool of blood. I pulled a handkerchief from my apron pocket and wrapped it clumsily around my hand.

"I am pleased to see that he is in a great deal of pain, though. However, your stepmother's vase didn't survive."

"I cracked it over his head." Cinderella groaned. "She'll never forgive me."

"For rendering your suitor unconscious or breaking the vase?"

"Both," she muttered.

I stepped over the glass and it crunched loudly under my boots as I made my way over to her. I pulled her hands away from her face. "This is not your fault." I pointed to the unconscious body next to us. "It's Lord Dunderhead's over here, him and his meaty paws."

"I just didn't know what else to do. He pressed his advances on me." Cinderella's fingers brushed across her

155

lips. "He kissed me. Tore at my dress. I told him to stop..."
Tears sprang to her eyes. "I reached for the vase. Before I
knew what was happening..."

"He's the lowest form of man." I took her hand in
mine. "Are you sure you aren't hurt?"

She shook her head. Her curls had been pulled from her
bun and they hung like tragic, limp waves around her
cheeks. "Only my pride."

I glanced at Lord Reginald's still form. "What should we
do with his body?"

"*We?*" Cinderella straightened. "I can't ask you to help.
You'll only implicate yourself."

"You aren't asking." I stood up, hauling Cinderella with
me. "I'm offering. Let's get him out of here before he
wakes up. Or worse, before Lady Maura gets back."

"Hello? Felicity?" Thomas appeared in the doorway. "I
heard a commotion and thought..." He noticed Lord
Reginald. "Good gracious! The man isn't dead, is he?"

A sob caught in Cinderella's throat. "What have I
done?"

"He's not dead," I snapped. "And he deserved what he
got."

Thomas glanced at Cinderella and back to his
unconscious master. A flash of sympathy filled his eyes.
"I'm sure he deserved what he got and more."

I stooped down to hoist Lord Reginald's arm over my
shoulder. The awkward position and weight made my body
fall forward, directly into his rounded gut that felt like a
mound of dough. Disgusted, I quickly pushed off him. My
hand connected with his face, which, to my dismay, was
still moist.

"Seriously?" I wiped my hand on my apron. "The man's
unconscious and he's still sweating like a hog?"

Thomas jumped forward to help me lift his master off the ground. "If you'll take this other side, we can transfer most of his weight over to me."

I slung Lord Reginald's arm over my shoulder again. His underarm reeked of body odor and his breath smelled like curdled milk. I coughed back a gag and resolved not to breathe through my nose. "We need to get him to the carriage before he wakes up."

Thomas and I half dragged and half hoisted the body to the carriage. It took us a few minutes to get him down the steps of the front porch without tripping over our own feet. Harold saw us coming and sprang forward to open the carriage door for us. Thomas tossed his master's body, much rougher than necessary, onto the carriage floor, and once my hands were ridden of the foul man, I felt immensely grateful to have discovered Thomas—an ally— in the midst of this crisis.

Harold slammed the carriage door shut.

"There." I wiped my own sweaty brow. "Let's hope he sleeps it off for days." I felt a prick of panic. "What will you tell him when he wakes up?"

"Don't worry about that. We'll take care of the explanation," Thomas assured me. He placed a hand gently on my shoulder and nodded to the house. "Go see to your friend."

"But—"

"Go. We've got this covered. This is not the first time we've brought the man home unconscious. Granted, he's usually had a bit too much to drink and not a wallop on the head, but we can think of some excuse."

I started to protest, but Thomas cut me off. "Harold and I will see the master home."

"Thank you," I breathed. "If I can ever repay you..."

"No thanks or repayment necessary. Though if you happen to know someone hiring a new maid, I'd be grateful if you mentioned Mary's name."

"Of course." I bobbed my head. "I'll keep my eyes open."

Thomas waved me away as he scrambled up the carriage. "Now go on."

I uttered another word of thanks and stumbled toward the house. I found Cinderella standing on the doorstep with her arms crossed and eyes red-rimmed, waiting for me and watching the carriage rumble down the driveway.

"Are they going to take him home?" she asked.

"Yes. Thomas, the footman, said he'd handle everything. We can trust him." I took a step forward. "Come on. Let's go clean up the mess in the sitting room."

Cinderella continued to stand in the doorway. "Go home, Felicity."

I tilted my head. "What?"

"Go home," she repeated. "This isn't your problem."

"But I want to help."

"I want to be alone right now." Cinderella tightened her arms over her chest, squeezing them securely around her middle. "Please. Just go. I need to sort things out on my own. I can't keep asking you to come here and clean up all of my messes for me."

I got the distinct feeling she wasn't talking solely about a broken vase. "I just wanted to—"

"Help," she finished for me. There was a caustic bite to the word that I had never encountered before. The bitterness was so foreign sounding in her voice that it made me pause. "I know. You have been a true friend these past few weeks. You've stood by me and worked alongside me as my stepfamily treated you like a servant. I will always appreciate your loyalty." She took a deep breath.

158

"But you being here, it doesn't really change anything. We aren't fixing anything, just prolonging the inevitable. So go home. Go live your life in the palace. Find joy and happiness where you can. You certainly can't find it here."

I took another step forward and she backed further into the house. "I don't understand," I said.

"I appreciate your friendship too much to allow you to keep coming here." Cinderella looked over my shoulder as the carriage turned the corner and rolled out of sight. Her eyes narrowed. "I've always known my lot in life, Felicity. It's to be somebody's maid, cook, wife, and mother. I can't change my life. *You* can't change it, despite all of your ideals about my destiny. I'm—" Her voice broke off. She reached out to swipe a tear away. "If you must know, I'm tired of fighting. I'm tired of looking for hope in an existence where there's no hope to be found. It's exhausting and disheartening. It is better to be plagued with misery than to suffer from false hope. The misery is bearable. It's the hope that crushes you."

I shook my head, baffled by what she was saying. "Wait a second. What are you talking about? You can't just give up. I don't accept that," I argued.

"No," she whispered with a sad smile. "I suspected that you wouldn't. But you don't have to be the one who accepts it—I do." She turned away slowly and trudged back into the house. She pulled the creaking door behind her. "I'm going to marry Lord Reginald. And I'm going to have to ask that you let me. It's the only way to escape this manor and get my father's music and my mother's harp back."

I threw my hands up wildly in the air. "*Marry him?* After what he just did to you? If you marry him, you are exchanging one life of slavery for another. As his wife you'll be subject to every whim that abominable man has."

Cinderella said nothing for a moment and her tears vanished. She shifted her feet, blocking me from getting into the manor. "Go home, Felicity. I've made my decision. There are some fates we cannot escape. Please do not come back to this manor."

Then she quietly, but resolutely, closed the door in my face.

CHAPTER 18

I stumbled onto the road, too shocked to coax my feet to move properly. Slouching down on a log, I waited for Max and forced an easy breath to calm my raging insides. Had I really managed to mess everything up so thoroughly? Thus far, everything that could go wrong had, and everyone that was supposed to cooperate wasn't.

I did what came naturally.

I brought my knees up to my chest, buried my head in my hands, and let myself have a well-deserved cry. It was an ugly cry—the kind with throaty sobs, sloppy sniffles, and shaking shoulders. I hated crying, but there was something cathartic about the idea of wallowing in misery for a moment when things were spiraling out of control.

A few minutes later I heard footsteps crunch over leaves and boots thudding across the earth.

Max.

Max had come to see me home and he arrived just in time to watch me turn into a watering pot.

I felt a pinprick of relief as I wiped my eyes on my apron. Yes, my uncle would know how to fix this. Max, with his brilliant mind and persistent ways, would know how to undo the mess I had made. When I lifted my apron from my eyes, I saw that streaks of soot and dirt and blood had marred the once pristine white fabric. If my apron was any indication of the rest of my person, I must have looked absolutely frightening. Absentmindedly, I reached up and felt my hair—limp and frizzy from the hours it had spent tucked under my kerchief. Max would be in a foul mood when he saw me disheveled, filthy, and bloody.

The footsteps came closer.

I sniffed loudly and unattractively. "Can you give me moment, Max? I'd like to wallow in my self-pity for a little longer."

The footsteps slowed, eventually coming to a complete halt.

I stared down at my bloody hand. "You know, Max, I tried. I really did. I thought I could change the circumstances, but I've concluded that you can't change how other people *feel* about the circumstances." A hiccup escaped and shook my shoulders. "I've muddled everything up and now all of Valencia is doomed."

"That's a bit melodramatic."

My head shot up. "Alexander?"

Sure enough, the prince of Valencia stood a few feet away, staring at me with his usual commanding presence. The sun was setting behind him, and the bright pinks and purples of dusk outlined Alexander's silhouette. I adjusted my eyes and saw that he wore a billowy white shirt open at the collar and tucked into black pants. His tall riding boots were still dusty from travel. The brightness of the white shirt contrasted nicely against his dark hair and blue eyes. As he closed the distance between us, it did not escape my notice that his steps were weary and there was an unusual shadow of worry cast over his features. He looked older than when I had seen him last, older and wiser.

"What are you doing here?" I asked.

"Why are you crying?" he asked.

Our questions collided into each other and we both chorused, "You first."

A half smile flickered on his lips. From the looks of him, it was probably the first one to have graced his face in days. "I stopped by the library to see you as soon as I got back from Avondale. Max told me I could find you here."

My pulse quickened as Alexander slowly lowered himself next to me on the log and I wondered if he'd bring up the quick kiss I'd given him before he left. I groaned inwardly, knowing I'd melt into a puddle of embarrassment if he did. His thigh bumped into mine, and the tingling sensation from the contact propelled me to scoot away. "No. That's not what I meant. What are you doing in Valencia? You weren't supposed to be back until next week."

"I was sent home early."

"Did Jack come with you?"

His sigh was long as he reached up to massage his temples. "No. He stayed in Avondale. He said he had other things to attend to there before he came home."

I frowned. That was unlike Jack. He was usually quick to follow wherever Alexander went. "Is everything all right in Avondale?"

He gave a noncommittal shrug.

"Well, then is everything all right with *you*?"

"Of course." His answer was short, pointed. There was a hollowness to his voice that surprised me. I craned my head to get a better look at him, but he wouldn't meet my eyes.

"What's the matter?" I asked, forgetting about my own problems for a moment.

"Nothing. I'm simply tired."

"Well, something is wrong. You aren't acting like yourself at all." When he didn't respond, I tried again. "Was your trip really all that bad?"

Still, he said nothing.

I swallowed a lump in my throat. I touched his arm, shaking him lightly. "You are scaring me. What's wrong?"

His eyes finally met mine. "Honestly, I'm scared myself."

His words caught me off guard. "You are not afraid of anything. You are..." I searched for a word. "Indomitable."

"Hardly." He moved and the log creaked under his shifting weight. "Things are spiraling out of control in our neighboring kingdoms. I fear that Valencia will get sucked into the madness. Brittolia's on the brink of war with Aurum, there's unrest amongst the nobles in Camelot, and the king of Avondale went missing during my stay."

My spine straightened. "How does a kingdom lose their king?"

"We believe he's been abducted. We waited for a ransom note, but nothing was ever delivered to us."

I gasped.

"The queen is inconsolable. Every able-bodied man in Avondale is searching for him. I was sent home early, though. My advisors thought if I stayed, there might be a threat on my life too."

"Then I am glad you left. It sounds as if Avondale is falling apart."

He let out a dry, clipped laugh. "The world is falling apart, and I'm an inadequate prince who is powerless to stop it."

"You are anything but inadequate."

"It's true," he said. "When I rise in the mornings, I look outside my window and I see all of Valencia staring back at me, pulling me in every possible direction. I have a destiny that I cannot outrun, one that pursues me relentlessly. I feel pressure rising up inside of me until I think I might burst from the fear of knowing that an entire kingdom will someday look to me to guide them. I wonder if I'm enough.

"For now, my father encourages me to travel to other kingdoms as a goodwill ambassador, fostering peace between our neighbors. That's his legacy—peace. But things are changing, Fliss. Deep in my bones I can feel Valencia changing. I fear war may seep over into Valencia, despite my father's precautions, and I will someday be in a position responsible for determining if my kingdom fights or if it flees. What if the power to send men to war, to break apart families, to potentially end lives rests on my shoulders? I hope I have the wisdom to pursue peace at all costs, but I also hope I have the courage to stand and fight if the time comes."

Neither of us said anything for several minutes. The silence hung thick and heavy like a curtain drawn between us.

"I—I had no idea you felt this way," I finally whispered when the silence became uneasy. "I wish you had said something sooner."

"I should've said nothing at all. This is not your burden to bear." Alexander nudged me with his elbow. "Forgive me? I did not seek you out to spill my concerns." He paused and then offered me a smile that accentuated the softness in his eyes. "Then again, maybe part of me did. Even princes need confidants."

"I want to help—"

"Enough about me; it's your turn. Why were you crying?"

I shook my head. "It's not important."

"Honestly, Fliss. Come out with it. There's something you've been keeping from me for the past few weeks; I can read you like one of those books in your library, you know. Just tell me the truth."

Tell him the truth? That wasn't likely. Instead, I grimaced at my dirty apron and skirt. "The truth is that you have caught me at my worst."

Alexander pursed his lips, like he wanted to protest my lack of a direct answer but thought better of it. "Max said you were helping a friend who recently found herself in trouble. It seems to me I've caught you at your best." He took my injured hand in his, and I trembled as his warm, calloused fingers held my hand with such easy care. "You are a little jumpy tonight. Something on your mind?"

I didn't respond right away. What would I say? *Yes, Alexander, your presence is unnerving me and every time you touch me it feels like a bolt of lightning strikes my chest.*

I thought not.

"Hmm?" I muttered, pretending I didn't hear him.

"I said," he traced the edge of my fingertips lazily with his and brushed his knuckles across the pulse in my wrist, "what's got you so jumpy tonight?"

You.

"Nothing. And give me back my hand."

He wouldn't release it though. Alexander leaned over, bringing our bodies even closer. Our heads huddled together, and I forced calming breaths into my lungs. My hand was cradled gently in his and our shoulders connected, sending that familiar spark directly to my heart once more.

I inhaled again, raggedly.

Alexander looked up. The weariness was gone from his eyes, replaced with distinct and pointed yearning. He was suddenly too close. He was always too close. But I leaned forward anyway, because, despite it all, he was still not close enough.

"You should get that cut looked at when we return to the palace." He carefully set my hand down on his lap.

"Didn't I tell you I wanted to find you in one piece when I got home?"

"If you had returned next week like you planned, you would have."

"Well, it's a good thing I came home early. Mother cornered me as soon as I got to the palace and told me all about some ball she's hosting for my birthday next weekend. It was meant to be a surprise, but I've ruined it by coming back sooner than planned."

"A ball?" My eyes widened. Since I had become preoccupied with helping Cinderella, I had forgotten my request to Queen Briar. If I couldn't convince Cinderella not to marry Lord Reginald, I might be able to at least convince her to go the ball. And when she was there if she just happened to run into a certain prince...

My breath caught in my throat.

Drat! When I had told Queen Briar to host a ball I had forgotten to mention that she needed to invite every single female in the kingdom—nobility *and* commoners. Cinderella wouldn't get an invitation to the ball if only courtiers were invited.

"Who is invited to your ball?" I asked.

"It's not *my* ball. I just didn't have the heart to tell my mother to cancel it."

"I think you should invite everyone in the kingdom. You should include commoners, too. At the very least, you should invite all the maidens in the kingdom. I doubt the young men will care as much if they don't receive an invitation."

Alexander looked at me as if I'd gone mad. I could tell he was half ready to dismiss my unusual request. "Invite *all* the maidens in the kingdom? Absolutely not, Fliss. That would be utter chaos. I don't mean to sound pompous, but you do realize who I am? I'd have every maiden in the kingdom vying for my attention at once."

Apparently, he was completely ready to dismiss my request.

I pressed on anyway. "It would show tact and thoughtfulness on your part. As the future king, it's important to show gestures of goodwill to your subjects. Even more so during these trying times." Mostly I just needed Cinderella to get an invitation. If Alexander had to invite every other girl in the kingdom, so be it. "It would improve everyone's spirits."

"You are aware if I invite every female in the kingdom, I'm making this ball an even bigger ordeal than it already is? It doesn't sound like an appealing way to spend my birthday."

"Do it for me. Please."

He raised an eyebrow. "Is it really so important to you?"

"I wouldn't be asking if it wasn't."

He shook his head, but not before sighing in defeat. "That's what I thought. Well, consider it done." Alexander leaned forward once more. "I'm tired of stalling and talking about invitations to balls, though. I sought you out today for a purpose. Can we be frank with each other?"

He didn't wait for my answer. "Fliss, I need to speak with you about what happened before I left for Avondale a few weeks ago." A wave of alarm flooded through me. "There are still things unsaid between us. I want to know—"

"Please. Stop," I begged him. I pulled my hand from his lap, stood up, and backed away. I had spent the last two weeks pushing thoughts of Alexander to the furthest corner of my mind, thinking I had more time to sort them out. The erratic beat of my heart and tightness in my chest indicated I had nothing figured out though. "I was hoping you'd forget all about it. I shouldn't have kissed you. I've made things terribly awkward. Please accept my apology."

He slowly rose to his feet. Against the bold backdrop of twilight, I was never more aware of his long, lean frame. "I'm not asking you to apologize, far from it actually. I just need you to know the truth—"

"Don't say it," I whispered. I knew then what he would say next. *I knew.* I felt it somewhere deep within my body. It was if some great truth was about to surface that I had been relentlessly trying to keep at bay for what seemed like an eternity.

"I must."

"It will change things between us."

"Would that be so bad?"

"Alexander, let me clarify: it will change *everything* between us."

"Did you not hear me earlier? Everything *is* changing. Honestly, there are some things that I want to change."

I took a step back. "Don't you dare tell me you are in love with me!" I balled my hands into tight fists at my sides. "I won't stand for it."

Alexander let out a low, rueful chuckle. It grew and bubbled over his lips, forcing his shoulders to shake wildly with amusement. "Only you would take my declaration of love right out of my mouth before I get the chance to profess my feelings. Must you always win at everything?"

"This isn't a joke!"

He glanced at the fearful expression on my face, and his features softened. "No. It's certainly not. Fliss, I have been on the brink of falling in love with you for some time. I have stayed silent because I was afraid of ruining something precious to me—our friendship."

I struggled to take deep, calming breaths. The ground spun. Alexander could not think he was in love with me! He was supposed to fall in love with Cinderella.

"There's always been *something* kindling between us, and that gave me hope."

I stomped my foot. "There has not!"

Alexander looked sorely tempted to roll his eyes at my childish outburst. "It'll do you no good to deny it. That kindling sparked into a flame, and I..." His voice broke off midsentence. He cleared his throat and tried again. "And I found that I did not have the will to douse it. So here I am, hovering between *something* and *something more*. I am, as you can clearly see, hopelessly, unfailingly in love with you."

For a moment, I—a librarian who was constantly surrounded by words—was speechless.

He continued, "Even as young boy, I admired your catching spirit of adventure, your loyalty to those you love, and your keen mind. Most of all, I loved that in a world where everyone else treated me as a prince, you treated me as your equal. I was never *Prince* Alexander to you, simply Alexander. I realized long ago there was no way to avoid falling in love with you, so I stopped trying. You astound me to no end."

Like a madwoman, I pushed him away. "Take that back! Take every word you said back!" I shouted, uncaring if Cinderella could hear me all the way from the manor.

"I will not."

Flustered and frustrated, I pulled my sword from its sheath and pointed it at him. "Take. That. Back."

"Put this up before you hurt yourself." Alexander flicked the tip of the blade away. "I anticipated your shock. I did not anticipate doing battle with you."

"Then you should have left the unsaid things between us unsaid!"

"Fliss, I'm exhausted from my journey, and, frankly, your outburst is not helping things. I have no time for games or jests. Let's act rational about this and discuss it as civilized people would."

I kept my blade level with his chest. "I'm not jesting. Also, I refuse to be rational or civilized right now, so there's that."

Instead of being outraged, he tilted his head and asked, "Then what exactly are you planning on doing?"

"Teaching you that you can't just go around declaring your love to your best friend. It just isn't done."

"*Teaching me?* Have you forgotten *I* taught *you* how to use that sword?"

"Perhaps you have a few things left to learn."

"Well, I've always been a willing student." He mockingly brandished his own sword from its sheath and bowed absurdly low to the ground. He didn't seem so tired now. If anything, his energy seemed renewed.

Before I had time to come to my senses, I lunged.

He parried, our blades meeting together with a *clang* that resonated loudly. His eyebrows shot up. "Whoa. Are we actually doing this? If so, remember that I didn't strike first."

"Because you were too rational and civilized." I raised my blade again. "Also, maybe a little scared."

His eyes narrowed. He cut over my attack, circling around me. "Watch it, Fliss."

"Why? Are you getting nervous?"

He snorted. "No. Your form is wrong. Watch it."

He struck precisely, and I barely had time to raise my defenses. With each clash of our swords we quickly found our cadence. Our blades matched each other stroke for stroke, the steel gleaming in the last golden moments of dusk. As we glided across the road, our movements felt choreographed, calculated. After several minutes, we hit our crescendo, intensity building with each determined strike.

Our swords crossed, and he leaned in close. "Are you done overreacting yet?"

"Are you done being bested by your pupil?"

Amusement lingered on his face, and Alexander's sword parried my attack, answering with one of its own. His blade swiped across the air in front of me, crossing over my blade, disengaging our swords. My weapon flew from my hand, falling to the dusty road with a *thud.*

My lips parted in shock.

He smirked. "You were saying?"

Something inside me snapped. "Enough!" I cried, throwing my hands up in the air. "We had a solid friendship going for almost eighteen years and now you have completely mutilated it."

"I see we are back to this again." Alexander remained calm, which only angered me further. "I believe that love often forms, sometimes unexpectedly, from friendship. It makes sense to me that I fell in love with my best friend."

"*Love?*" I questioned bitterly. When I said the word, it came out like an insult. When Alexander said it, it sounded like a caress. I rolled my eyes, suddenly more annoyed with him than angry. "Would you at least stop using that word? I should've never kissed you. That's what started all this."

He gave a bark of laughter. "You are a ridiculous girl. Would it help you to know that I loved you before your so-called kiss?"

"Well, you didn't act on it until now. That kiss has addled your brain."

He stopped laughing. "Stop calling that tight-lipped peck a kiss. It's insulting." He threw his sword to the ground and it dropped in a cloud of dust next to mine. "This, my dear, is a kiss."

Alexander pulled me into his arms, wrapping me into him. His lips found mine without hesitation. He held me with such desire, such longing, that I was too shocked to do anything but tremble. When my body became too light, too difficult for me to hold up on my own, Alexander's grasp tightened around my waist. Something sparked inside of me and my fingers dug into his hair, running through the dark brown strands with a fierce wanting I never knew I possessed. Alexander answered my fervor with his own, holding me close to him with one hand spanning the small of my back and the other traveling up to lightly brush the tender skin below my ear.

With ample amount of encouragement on both our parts, the kiss deepened. We pressed against each other, breathing in the other person. The world dipped in and out, bringing us back to reality only to send us crashing into another realm of existence entirely—a place that consisted of only us. I had no idea which of us ended the kiss and pulled away first, though I was almost certain it wasn't me.

Alexander smiled down at me, looking immensely satisfied with himself. The look he gave was part mischief, part boldness, and part desire—which was a lethal combination against the already discordant beat of my heart.

"I-I shouldn't have—" I spluttered over my words. I touched my fingertips to my lips, feeling the last remnants of his kiss. "You can't— We can't—"

"I think we just did, and, if I do say so myself, *that* was a proper kiss."

And just then, as the last rays of the sunset fell below the horizon and into the depths of another part of the world, a dark shadow passed behind Alexander. A sudden, eerie sensation heightened my already ringing senses. I paused and glanced over his shoulder, and my eyes widened with fear.

We were not alone on the road any longer.

Alexander, noticing my shock, squeezed my hand. "Felicity, please don't overthink what's happening between us. I beg you—"

"No," I interrupted. "Look behind you."

He curiously followed my wild gaze and his body tensed next to mine.

The monsters that had attacked Jack, Cinderella, and I in the forest weeks ago—those terrifying beasts with their shadowy cloaks and eyeless faces that had haunted my darkest nightmares—had returned.

And this time there were more.

CHAPTER 19

No, no, no," I whispered. "This can't be happening—not again."

Alexander's back straightened. He cursed under his breath. The creatures hovered over the ground as a swirling dark mist twisted up and around their bodies like black snakes. Their jagged swords clinked against the sides of their black armor to the beat of a death march.

The sun had almost disappeared, and only the faintest remains of twilight touched the sky. The dark creatures moved steadily forward, shadows rising from the underworld of a nightmare.

"You need to run. Now." Alexander's voice was urgent, demanding. He snatched his sword from the ground, prepared to fight.

I reached for my own sword. "I can't leave you here."

Hastily, I scanned our surroundings. The figures were closing in on us. The closer they crept, the more mist filled the air, causing both of us to choke as we inhaled the black substance. I mentally counted the creatures. We were definitely outnumbered.

Alexander clenched the blade in his hand until his knuckles turned white. "Go. *Now.*"

"I will not leave you here to be slaughtered."

"Now is not the time to argue," he said through gritted teeth.

"Now is not the time to be chivalrous."

He pushed me behind him. "If you aren't going to leave, then at least get out of the way. That's an order!"

Just as he finished issuing his command, one of the dark creatures lunged at him. I shuddered as their swords met with a *clang.*

Like a quick bolt of lightning, another creature rose from a swirl of mist. Its menacing, claw-like hands snatched at my skirts as I darted out of the way. I hitched up my dress and quickly started to scramble up the nearest tree. Reaching for a branch, I felt a slimy hand grasp my ankle. I shrieked as the monster hauled me back to the ground. I landed on the hard earth with a *thud* that rattled my brain.

I grabbed my sword and hoisted it over my head, delivering a swift blow to the skull of the creature that had chased me. The dark body fell to the ground with a moan. Instinctively, I ran to help Alexander.

I called out, "Behind you!"

Alexander spun around, ducked, and plunged his sword into the attacker's chest in one fluid motion. The creature let out a foul scream in agony as it collapsed and died. Several of its brethren slunk away, realizing that it wouldn't be as easy to take down the two of us as they had thought.

"What do you think you are doing?" Alexander asked. Another creature lunged at him and he leapt out of the way. An instant later he delivered a fatal swipe of his blade, slicing the monster's head off entirely. I had to stifle a gasp as it hit the ground with a *thunk* and rolled away. A putrid odor filled my nostrils.

"Helping you." I deflected a blow with my sword, thrusting it into the side of one of our foes. I couldn't help but feel satisfied as it screeched and stumbled away. My blade swiped down and across my body, slicing through the air as I met the sword of another creature that had stepped up to take its fallen comrade's place.

Our blades glinted dangerously before my eyes. I stepped back hastily as my attacker lunged forward and I counter-attacked at the last moment, plunging my sword into the creature's chest. A pair of eyeless sockets met mine with an intensity that paralyzed me for a moment—long enough to pause and shudder inwardly. When I pulled my sword out, the creature uttered a scream and fell to the ground, a heap of black mist coiling up and around its body.

The remaining creatures pulled back and seemed to be regrouping. They spoke to each other in a foreign, mysterious language neither of us could understand. We exchanged worried glances.

Alexander grimaced. "Felicity, I would prefer it if you would leave this to me."

"Spoken like a man."

Alexander opened his mouth to reply, but he was quickly cut off. The creatures let out a low rumble from deep in their chests—pure rage from being held at bay by two teenagers. They gnashed their jagged teeth as black liquid seeped through their gums. The dark mist became denser and soon turned into a suffocating fog—worse yet, we couldn't see the creatures. Their black cloaks concealed them perfectly. Panic slithered up my spine, and I blindly started swiping at the mist with my sword.

I felt a hand on my shoulder and swung my sword around, only to have it connect instantly with another blade.

Alexander's face flashed before my eyes. He batted my sword away. "It's me, Fliss. We need to get out of here. We can't fight them in this mist."

Before I could agree, one of the hooded figures emerged from the fog, tearing us apart. I whipped around to block a blow. I was too late raising my defense, and I felt the sting of metal slice across the skin on my right arm. I let out a hiss of pain as I staggered back a few steps, clutching my arm with my left hand.

Fury flashed in Alexander's eyes as he saw me stumble. He raised his blade and with two strokes, the dark creature met its maker. Three of the monstrous creatures remained. They spoke again in their language, and, as if in agreement they would lose this battle, they quickly vanished into the inky air around us—soaking up all the dark mist with them.

I swiveled my head around and noticed the rest of the creatures were lying dead on the ground. The road was quiet once more, save for our ragged breathing.

Alexander grasped me by the elbow, propelling me down the road. "We need to get out of here," he said urgently. "We don't know how many more of these things are still out there. Are you badly hurt? Can you manage?" He glanced at the hand that was still clutching my injured arm.

"This injury won't keep me from running, if that's what you mean."

He nodded. "Then let's go."

* * *

I doubled over to catch my breath when we reached the first step leading up to the palace entrance, forcing Alexander to slow down. He made a face and tried to pull me up the steps, but I remained hunched over and heaved air in and out of my lungs. My head spun from the loss of blood, my feet ached from running, and a stitch in my side felt as if it was knotting itself together with a few of my vital organs.

Alexander, meanwhile, hovered over me and no longer showed signs of fatigue, only enough relentless obstinacy to rival a mule. He tugged on my arm again. "Come on."

"Just give me a moment to catch my breath."

"No time. We need to get inside."

I ignored him and took deep, grateful gulps of air.

He pulled me to an upright position. "What were you thinking back there?"

I winced as I pressed a hand into my painful side, smearing more blood on my dress. "What do you mean?"

"Why didn't you leave when I ordered you to?"

"Excuse me?" I said. The pain in my side was nothing compared to the sting I felt from his tone. "If I hadn't stayed, you would probably be dead right now."

"I ordered you to stay away from the fighting."

Ordered. There was that word again. That was twice he had used it, and I found that I detested it.

"You couldn't expect me to watch you die, *Your Highness*," I hissed.

His eyes darkened. A moment later he gave me a nudge up the stairs. Two guards, noticing the crown prince and his companion arriving disheveled and bloody, sprinted over. Alexander issued a hasty command to secure the palace in case of another attack.

Trembling with coursing adrenaline, I slumped down on one of the steps, still not having made it all the way up them yet—and wasn't in any hurry to after Alexander scolded me like I was a child.

Alexander marched back over to me—the determined stride of his step tapping against the marble stairs grated on my ears. He stood over me, hovering like a hawk. "Get inside. We don't know if those things followed us." He tried to hoist me to my feet, but I wrenched away. I rose to my feet on my own accord, and I made a great show about doing it extra slowly.

Alexander tossed his hands up in the air. He began muttering under his breath. "Of all the—"

"Are you angry with me because I stayed to help?" I snapped.

"No, I'm angry because right now you aren't using the good sense I know you possess."

"If I were a man, it would have been expected for me to stay and help fight. I can take care of myself."

Despite my protests, Alexander pulled me into the palace, past a few curious courtiers who had arrived to see what all the commotion was about, Lady Alana and Cressida included in the mix, loitering in the spacious foyer. The group paused to glance at us, their heads tilted forward, prepared to listen to our conversation.

Once inside, Alexander surprised me by replying, "Well, the fact of the matter is, you obviously aren't a man."

"You *are* mad at me," I clarified.

Alexander continued his brisk pace. "Of course, I'm mad! You could have been killed, Felicity!" He craned his neck to look at me but didn't slow down.

"You could have too! We both could have died!" I shouted back, now thoroughly mad myself.

Cressida and another girl snickered at our biting words, while Lady Alana shot us a pitying look as our argument unfolded for everyone to hear. I knew without a hesitation that Cressida would be quick to tell the entire palace.

Alexander shot Cressida an icy glare. "Be gone," he commanded. "Have you ladies nothing better to do with your time than to eavesdrop?"

"Well, I never..." Cressida mumbled.

Alexander raised an eyebrow.

"Yes, Your Highness," she amended quickly, hoisting her skirts off the floor and turning the opposite direction. Her group followed. Even Alana, who shrugged her shoulders delicately and took off after them.

"Of course *we* both could have died," Alexander countered once the onlookers were gone. "Which was why I wanted *you*, you difficult girl, out of the way!"

We walked in stubborn silence for several more minutes. I found it easier to follow Alexander than stand around and argue with him.

When Alexander finally stopped his determined march, I nearly bumped into the back of him. We stood, tight-lipped and tense, outside the door to the infirmary. A wave of uneasiness hit me forcefully in the gut.

"Oh, my." I closed my eyes and choked back a sob. "We could have died! *You* could have died!" *We could have died.* My words echoed in my head, and I fought another wave of dizziness. The realization that death had almost claimed me—*again*—was overwhelming.

Alexander suddenly looked anxious. Apparently, he wasn't used to consoling hysterical females.

I grasped his shirt in my hands, wadding the fabric beneath my palms. "You don't understand! What would have happened to the kingdom if you had died?" My words echoed across the hallway. I thought of the unfinished fairy tale. Is this what some evil force wanted? To put an end to Prince Alexander so the fairy tale wouldn't come true?

Alexander untangled my hands. "You need to calm down," he spoke to me with concern lacing his voice, like he was trying to soothe a wild animal caught in a trap. "I didn't die, you didn't die, and we are still here." When he tugged my hands away, I noticed my bloody handprint stood out against his white shirt. For a moment, he gazed down at it with an unreadable expression on his face.

A healer poked his head out of the infirmary and started toward us. His brow furrowed with concern as he reached Alexander's side. "Your Highness? What's happened?"

Alexander jerked his head in my direction. "Her first."

I looked at him oddly. "What do you mean *her* first? What's the matter with you?"

The healer took me by the elbow and escorted me into the infirmary, a place I was becoming too familiar with, and guided me down onto a bed. I noticed a bloody gash a few inches long was swelling on Alexander's left leg. The dark blood was almost camouflaged against his black breeches.

The healer took to cutting the fabric on my sleeve and casting it aside to get a better look at the wound on my arm. A moment later, I felt the sting of strong smelling liquid being applied to clean the cut. I flinched but ground my teeth together.

I eyed the gash on his leg. "Why didn't you say you were hurt?"

"It's not a big deal." He waved away my concern. "I can barely feel anything. It's just a scratch."

"It looks like more than scratch to me," I said. On cue a few drops of blood dripped onto his boot. "See?"

The healer turned to Alexander. "Your Highness, perhaps I should attend to you?"

"No."

"Yes," I retorted.

"Her first," Alexander said firmly, once more, in a voice that indicated he wouldn't be disobeyed.

The healer nodded and resumed his ministrations on my arm. "Yes, Your Highness."

"How is it?" Alexander peered over the young healer's shoulder. He looked down at my arm. He made a face, but he quickly tried to cover up his grimace for my benefit.

"It should heal without infection if the wound is kept clean. I need to stitch it up soon and get a bandage on it. I'll be right back." The healer left to rummage through a supply closet.

I leaned back against the headboard and breathed a sigh of relief. The roaring in my ears had quieted, and I didn't feel quite so faint. I looked over to find Alexander hastily writing something on a piece of parchment he had borrowed from the healer's desk.

"I'm sending word to my father about what happened," he informed me without looking up. "I told a guard when we entered the palace, but my father needs to hear it from me that we are alive."

"Of course." I nodded in agreement.

The quill stopped scratching. Alexander glanced over at me. "I'm sorry I yelled earlier. And, for the record, I know you can take care of yourself. I have never doubted that, but, when I saw those... *things*, I was worried—no, terrified—that something might happen to you. I wouldn't have been able to live with myself if..."

"I know," I whispered. "I understand." And I *did* understand. I had felt the same terror thinking something disastrous would happen to him.

Alexander gave me a piercing look that made my lips tremble. I was certain he was going to pick up our conversation from the road. If I had been awkward around him earlier after a slight peck on the cheek, there was a good chance I would be completely mortified if he brought up the proper kiss we exchanged and his declaration of love. I felt my whole body paralyze at the very thought.

His eyes softened as they sensed my apprehension. "Rest easy. I will not demand anything else of you today." He went back to writing. There was no mistaking his choice of words. He would not demand anything else from me *today*, but I could not avoid him forever. "I need to get this note delivered to my father. Will you be all right if I leave you?"

Would I be all right if he left me?

I stared. Everything about him made me want to hold my breath and not blink for fear I would wake up from a dream and find myself in a world without him. I realized, with a pang of misery, that I *would* soon find myself in a world without him, in an entire existence without him. He would marry Cinderella—and everything from the minute details to the most influential aspects of our relationship would change. It was then, with this painful realization, I discovered what I had been trying so hard to cover up over the last few weeks, possibly the last few years.

I *loved* Alexander.

Not in the way I might love a boy who is merely a close friend or cherished like a brother. No, I loved him with all of my pathetic and confused heart. I loved his inherent courage, his incomparable charisma, and his catching goodness that made me want to be a better person. I loved him, and I was too far gone, too far into the madness, to undo my feelings for him.

I cleared my throat. "Of course. Yes, I'll be fine without you."

"Alexander!"

We both looked up and found his mother, Queen Briar, standing in the doorway of the infirmary. Her shoulders and chest were heaving as if she had run some great distance to reach us. Her eyes flashed with obvious concern from Alexander to me.

Alexander tilted his head. "Mother, what are you doing here?"

She threw her arms around him. Alexander almost stumbled backwards as she came barreling into him. After a moment, he chuckled lightly while patting her on the back.

"A guard told me about the attack," Queen Briar said. "I came as soon as I heard. I had to see for myself that you were all right."

"I'm fine," he assured her. Alexander winked at me over his mother's shoulder. "I'd have been much worse off if Felicity hadn't been there to help me."

"He's not fine!" I chimed in from my spot on the bed, ignoring his wink. "He's got a horrible gash running down the side of his leg that he's refusing to have tended."

Queen Briar covered her mouth with her hand as she gaped at the bloody mess on his leg. "Alexander, you must get that looked at right away."

"*Ladies*," Alexander said with mock exasperation. "It will be taken care of as soon as I'm able to spare the time. Right now, I need to send this note to Father and report what happened. I'll also need to make sure the guards are properly securing the palace."

"But—"

"Mother." Alexander kissed her quickly on the cheek. "I'll have it looked at later. As you can see, I'm mostly in one piece. The safety of this palace and Valencia is my first concern. I'll have my leg properly tended within the hour, but you know there's a protocol for when things like this happen, and I have to follow it."

"Must you act like a prince right now? I'd prefer it if you acted like my son instead." She frowned as Alexander backed away from her and headed toward the door.

Alexander smiled ruefully over his shoulder. "I think we both know Valencia demands that I am a prince before I am your son."

He offered us both quick goodbyes, grabbed a handful of bandages and the vial of medicine that had been applied to my wound off the healer's desk for his leg, and strode out of the infirmary before we could offer our protests.

As I watched him walk away, I couldn't help but think that Alexander was the opposite of the inadequate prince he thought he was. Even though he was injured and his life in danger moments ago, he thought of Valencia first. He didn't realize just how ready he was to rule this kingdom.

Queen Briar, who had been staring at the vacant doorway, turned around to face me. "He gets his stubbornness from Frederic," she said while shaking her head. "And how are you, Felicity?"

She sat down on a stool next to my bed. Her honey colored hair was piled high on her head, a diamond pendant glittered at her pale throat, and a dress made of dark green silk rippled to the floor. Her elegance looked out of place in the cramped, stuffy room.

"I am mostly unharmed, Your Majesty. Thank you for your concern, but I'm sure Alexander and King Frederic would want you somewhere that's safe and secure right now."

Queen Briar waved away my concern. "There's a guard posted outside this door. I'm perfectly safe. You are my best friend's daughter. I have to know that you are not seriously hurt." Her eyes traced over my person, and, unkempt though I was, she smiled softly. "It sounds selfish for me to be grateful that you were with Alexander during the attack, but I'm glad you were. Especially if it helped save my son's life."

"I can assure you, if Alexander had not been there, I, too, would have met a fateful end." My words brought a shadow across her face and her smile faded.

"Felicity," Queen Briar said, leaning forward. "I have a request."

"Yes?"

Her eyes cleared and her chin lifted with an air of regality. She was, in the span of one moment, able to transform from a devoted mother to a serious queen. She lowered her voice, though I doubted it mattered because the healer was nowhere in sight.

"I want you to destroy the fairy tale."

Of all the things I expected the queen to say, this was not one of them. I reared my head back and felt my eyes widen with uncertainty.

"Excuse me, Your Majesty?"

"Destroy the fairy tale."

"What?" My mouth fell open. "Does the king know you are asking me to do this?"

"Of course not. Frederic would be livid if he knew. He seems to think bowing to the whims of vengeful fairies is more prudent than taking action into our own hands."

"But the last time Valencia disobeyed the fairies—"

"I am well aware of what happened last time," she interrupted me. "I was, after all, cursed to sleep for all eternity because Frederic defied the fairy tale." She leaned forward, eyes flashing with passion. "But look at what is happening *this* time. You cannot tell me Alexander is anymore safe with this fairy tale than without it."

I hastened to stand. I'd get up and walk right out of the infirmary if it meant putting an end to this conversation. "I should not even be speaking to you about this—"

Queen Briar pushed me back down. "Your mother was willing to rebel though. She gave Frederic the choice to choose his destiny, which was something no other librarian ever had the courage to do. I shall always admire her for that, no matter what the final outcome actually was."

"Yes," I said. I clenched the sheet in my hands and tried, in vain, to remain calm. Queen Briar had no idea what she was asking me to do. "But that choice almost destroyed Valencia. I won't be responsible for this kingdom's demise."

"My concern is not Valencia at the moment. I fear that without being given a choice, Alexander's destiny will destroy him." Queen Briar inhaled sharply. "I am a mother before I am a queen. To see my son's future ripped so poignantly from his hands by a story book breaks my heart. I know nothing of this girl he is destined to marry."

"This girl he marries, the one from the fairy tale, she will be a good queen. I know her. We are close friends, much in the same way you and my mother were. I promise you that she will love this kingdom and its people."

"But will she love Alexander?" Queen Briar whispered. "For a marriage without love, is a fate I would wish on no one, especially not my son. Trust me, I am all too familiar with that fate."

I understood then. It was so sharply and blatantly clear. The king and queen were not in love. Their marriage, a product of a fairy tale, had not made either one of them happy. Queen Briar must have read the realization on my face.

"You must not think ill of my husband," she said. "He tried over the years to feel something stronger than mere fondness for me, but I'm afraid he always resented the fact that I was thrust upon him without his consent." She gulped and a shaky hand swiped a honey curl behind her ear. "Alexander has already lost so much control of his life because he is a prince. Even if there were no fairy tale, he would still, to a certain extent, have his life mapped out for him. I want whatever control he can take back to be his. This is why I implore you to destroy the fairy tale."

"I-I-I cannot," I spluttered. "Max and the king told me..."

"I know what they said!" Her voice rose sharply with an edge of anger. She clasped both of my hands up in hers. I fought back a wince as she unknowingly pulled at the wound on my arm. "I am asking you to spare my son from a life of misery." Her voice lowered to a soothing whisper. "I want to give him what I could not have."

"There will be nothing of Valencia if we don't submit to the fairies, though."

"There will be nothing of Valencia if we *do*," she countered. "Frederic will not listen to me. I thought perhaps you might." She dropped my hands on the bed and rose steadily to leave. "Do you know what the name Valencia means?" she asked quietly. "Valor. Courage. Bravery. What is Valencia if we do not have the courage to fight back and seize our own destiny?" The question hung in the air between us before she turned to exit the room.

"Wait, Your Majesty!"

The queen looked over her shoulder at me. "Yes?"

"In your fairy tale, *Sleeping Beauty*, it says you were awakened from the curse by true love's kiss. You say your husband does not love you, but it must be so if he was able to break Bruna's curse."

She said nothing for several moments, long enough that I was certain she wouldn't answer me at all. Finally, she broke the silence. "That is the saddest part of all, Felicity. You see, the fairy tale never specified that *I* was Frederic's true love. My husband was only able to break the curse because *he* was mine." Her smile—the sad one that so resembled Max's—resurfaced. "To live in a world where the person you love does not return your love is the worst kind of existence. It is as if a knife is thrust in your heart and remains there without you being able to release yourself from the pain." She balled her fists firmly at her side. "I can assure you, if I have any say in the matter, Alexander's future will be different than mine."

She turned from the room, her green silk gown swirling behind her as she fled. The queen had sounded so desperate, so willing to save her son that I wondered what that desperation would lead to.

CHAPTER 20

Perhaps I should just rent out a room in the infirmary for our family."

The healer had just finished stitching up my arm when we heard Max's dry, distinct voice. My uncle leaned casually against the doorway, staring at me. In fact, he looked too casual. The scary casual that meant he might explode at any moment. The healer excused himself. I sat up straighter, preparing for the lecture I was about to receive.

"How did you know I was here?"

"The prince sent me this." Max held up a small note. "It seems my own niece couldn't even take the time to tell me she was physically maimed. Thankfully, Prince Alexander showed more thoughtfulness."

"I'm not exactly maimed." I sighed and lay back down on my pillow. My previous encounter with Queen Briar was still making my head spin. I wasn't sure I could handle one of Max's lectures at the moment, too. "Go on then." I waved him into the room. "Let's hear it. Tell me how disappointed you are in me."

"On the contrary." Max whisked out a chair and sat down next to my bed. He leaned forward, intertwined his fingers, and rested his chin on the tips. "Alexander's note told me what happened. He said you handled yourself bravely."

I warmed at Alexander's praise. Then, coming back to my senses, I blinked at Max's light tone. "You aren't mad?"

"Oh no, I'm furious." Before I could explain myself, he clarified, "Not at you, Fliss. I'm actually quite proud of you."

"I don't understand." I looked over my shoulder to make sure the healer was out of earshot. "These *monsters*, for lack of a better word, they aren't magical... but they seem to be controlled by magic. Does that make sense?"

"Of course. You think there's something out there that's even more powerful than them."

"Not only that." I paused and leaned in closer to Max. "Things keep happening. Someone's trying to sabotage Cinderella and Alexander's fairy tale. I can't keep pretending everything that's happened is just a coincidence."

"I agree." Max's face fell slowly, painfully. The calm he was wearing so well drifted away. He cleared his throat. "I believe there's someone else with a broader target on their back than the prince and Cinderella."

"Who?"

"*You.*"

"Me?" I pulled back, startled. "Don't be silly. Who would want to hurt me? Alexander and Cinderella are far more valuable than I am."

"*Think.* During all these attacks—the one in the forest, the one on the road today, the unexplained sickness that tried to take my life—who was always targeted in each one? It's you, Felicity. Someone is after you. Even when my life was the one that hung in the balance, you were the one being targeted. My death would have been catastrophic for you—and someone out there knew that. Someone is making these attacks personal for a reason."

I pursed my lips. Surely it wasn't true? My life was of little consequence when compared to the important roles Alexander and Cinderella played in the fairy tale. Why was it more important to someone that I was dead rather than alive?

I looked at Max—whose face was hardened, yet his eyes pierced mine with fear—and saw that he had no more answers for the questions in my head than I did.

"What should I do?" I whispered. "If what you say is true..."

Max stretched back into his chair, crossing his ankles and scratching his chin, feigning more calmness when I knew in reality he was more likely to burst from anger. "I have half a mind to ship you to some far-off kingdom where you will be safe from whatever evil is plaguing Valencia. Avondale seems to be in about the same shape as Valencia right now, so perhaps Camelot or Aurum will do."

"But I have to stay for the fairy tale—"

"Enough about that infernal fairy tale," he snapped. "If it weren't for the fairy tale, you wouldn't be in this mess. I watched one fairy tale tear apart my twin sister's life. I'm not inclined to watch another destroy my niece's."

With the mention of my mother, I inhaled a quick breath. If there was ever a moment that I needed my mother, it was now. "I-I don't know what to do anymore. I've messed everything up, Max. And now the queen wants me to..."

Max raised an eyebrow. "What does the queen want you to do?"

"Nothing," I whispered. I didn't dare tell Max about Queen Briar's request. He'd lose his mind and go straight to King Frederic and tell him what was said, and I didn't want to get the queen in any trouble.

Max must have glimpsed my inner turmoil. "We'll figure things out," he assured me.

I slouched deeper into my covers, unsure if we could figure things out, unsure about everything. I was going to crack under all the pressure that was building up inside of me. Pressure that demanded I save Valencia, save Cinderella. More importantly, I had to do something about my feelings for Alexander or I would lose my heart to a prince I could never have, to a boy I could never truly love.

* * *

I woke the next morning with a stomach full of dread and the same agonizing sense that everything was spiraling out of my control. I had no idea what I was going to do. Max and the king told me to follow the fairy tale, while the queen pleaded with me to destroy it. Cinderella would not speak to me and had resigned herself to marrying a man who treated her like a dog. There was also that mounting tension between Alexander and myself, which consisted mostly of the words he had spoken to me that couldn't be taken back and the words that I hadn't said to him that I wouldn't dare let leave my lips. It was enough to drive any sane person mad.

I shut myself up inside my bedroom, refusing to leave or speak to anyone, and only leaving during the middle of the day while Max was working or late at night to take care of basic necessities like hunger and thirst and the chamber pot. Perhaps I thought if I pretended my problems didn't exist, they would somehow disappear. I huddled underneath my bedcovers and ignored the pounding on my door when Max asked me if I was going to ever get up out of bed.

"Felicity, get out here right now," he said. His voice was somewhat muffled by the oak door standing between us, but I could hear the irritation in his voice. "You've been in your room half the day."

"I'm not coming out!" I shouted back.

"You are being unreasonable."

"No," I countered. "Giving a teenager the responsibility of determining Valencia's fate is unreasonable."

"You are just going to hide away?"

"Yes."

"Splendid plan." I could almost hear the eye roll in his sarcasm. "That will solve everything."

Max's frustrated sigh was not as quiet as his thudding steps marching away. Several hours later there was another knock at my door. I shut the book I was reading.

"Go away, Max!" I called out.

"Fliss, it's me," Alexander's gentle voice answered. "Open up. We need to talk."

I looked up at the door. Panic struck me. I glanced out my window and considered scaling the side of the palace walls just to avoid having a conversation with him.

"Felicity?"

"I-I-I can't talk right now," I spluttered.

"Why not?"

I fumbled for an excuse, any excuse. "I'm not feeling well." I coughed loudly. "I might be contagious."

"I'll take my chances." He jiggled the doorknob.

I leapt forward, prepared to thrust my weight against the door to keep him out. "Well, I look hideous! Like death warmed over. You don't want to see this."

"I don't care what you look like."

When I didn't respond, Alexander sighed. "Very well. I'll try again tomorrow."

Alexander came back the next day, rapped assuredly on the door, and kindly asked me to let him in. I told him I was still sick—worse than yesterday, in fact. I even threw in some more coughing and gagging noises to make it believable.

He rattled the doorknob. "Open this door. Max and I are worried about you."

I ran to the door again, making sure that the lock was still securely in place. "I can't talk... not today."

"Then when?"

I didn't respond.

"Very well. I'll try again tomorrow."

Alexander came back, day after day. By the fourth day he had stopped asking nicely. He demanded to see me, threatened to lock me up in the dungeons or throw me into the stocks if I didn't obey his command. I knew they were mostly empty threats, but his voice held an edge to it that I had never heard before. He ranted and raved outside my door, pounding on it when I wouldn't open.

On the fifth day, his anger had vanished into despair, and he begged me to open the door. Alexander, who was the prince of the realm and who asked for nothing twice, sounded desperate and miserable. It almost weakened all of my resolve, but not enough to coerce me to open the door.

"Why, Felicity?" he whispered. "Why won't you let me in?"

Alexander pleaded with me to spare a moment of my time to speak with him. I turned away from the door and ignored his pleas. If I did open the door, he'd tell me he loved me once more, and I'd finally confess my feelings for him. I'd forget about curses and fairy tales and magic—I'd forget about my task.

On the sixth day, the day before the ball, I heard his weary steps trudge up the stairs to my bedroom. I had steeled myself for this moment all day. Instead of Alexander's usual command to open the door, there was a *swooshing* sound as his back pressed against the door and he slid down it.

"I'm here."

That was all he said. It was so simple, so hollow that it didn't even sound like him. There was nothing vibrant in his voice, no passion in his words. I almost preferred the ranting and raving Alexander to this dejected one. I found myself sliding down against my side of the door, too. I could almost feel his warmth seep into me from the other side. I pulled my knees up to my chest and cried into the palms of my hands. My shoulders shook as I took quick gasps of air between tears.

He must have heard my cries through his side of the door.

"Don't cry."

"But I'm scared," I whispered.

"You are not the only one."

I longed to reach through the door and touch him, to see him. I imagined him lonely and solemn on the other side, his blue eyes dull without their usual vitality.

"I'm afraid, too," Alexander said. "I'm not so frightened when you are near, though. You make me braver—a better person, a better prince." I heard him stand. "Whether you return it or not, I do not regret confessing my love for you. I might regret the toll it took on our friendship, but I do not regret the freedom my heart feels knowing that I finally told you the truth."

I said nothing.

"Open the door. Talk to me. Let me in."

I covered my mouth, muffling a sob. "I cannot."

"*Please.*"

I shuddered at the thought of what was inevitably coming. Silently, we both took in that last binding moment. I felt a force start to wedge between us, something trying to shatter the bond we had created together over the years. It was almost stronger than any magic a fairy tale could create—almost. My hand grasped the doorknob, tempted to open the door.

"I cannot," I repeated.

I heard him walk away. In that moment, I felt us both carrying the weight of a kingdom's future on our shoulders.

CHAPTER 21

A few hours later, I heard the lock to my room spring open. Turning sharply, I stared in surprise as the door swung open. I half expected it to be Alexander, but Max was standing in the doorway, holding a key and a long box tucked under one arm.

I crossed my arms over my chest. "I had that locked for a reason."

"There are keys for a reason, too." Max placed the box on the bed, shuffling aside the many dishes I had accumulated over the past several days. "I have something for you."

I lifted the lid off the package. A gasp caught in my throat. Inside was a beautiful white dress that shimmered with tiny crystals and ornate beading. I caressed the tulle skirt with care. "Where did you get this dress? It's stunning."

"It was your mother's wedding dress."

I looked at Max with wide eyes. "From when she married my father?"

"Yes."

My heart did a little leap. It was only a dress, but it was also a clue. It was my one link to my father. More than that, it was a link to my mother, who I missed so much it almost made me physically ache.

I picked up the dress, hugging it to my body gently. It even smelled like her still; there was a faint whiff of lilacs. If I tried hard enough, I could almost imagine I was hugging my mother again. I wanted her here with me. I missed her like a person misses a piece of their heart that they've given away. I missed her laugh, her teasing spirit, her love for books and knowledge. I missed the way her personality could fill up a room when she entered and leave everyone in wonder long after she left. But most of all, I missed her love.

"She meant to give it to you herself someday." Max watched me with uncharacteristically misty eyes. He cleared his throat. "She thought you'd want it."

"I do." I ran my hand over the intricate beading on the bodice. "I wish she were here. More than anything, I wish she were still here. I would give anything to know what took her from us."

I almost laughed at my own poor choice of words. *Took her from us.* As if there were a chance of getting her back.

I couldn't bring myself to look at Max. "The sickness that killed her, the same one you had, if only I had known about Katrina at the time Mother was ill... perhaps Katrina could have saved her, too." I laid the dress down on the bed. "I've come to realize there's magic in this world, but I wonder what good is magic if it can't protect the people we love?"

Max peered at me over the top of his spectacles. "I'll start by saying that Katrina should not have interfered with my death. There could still be a price to pay for her meddling. Furthermore, you do not get to decide who lives and dies. I hope you know that you can't live with that kind of impossible responsibility. We are in control of very few things that happen in this world—life and death are certainly not among them."

I began to pace across the small space from my bedroom to my window. "I wonder so many things, Max. Did I tell Mother how much I loved her, how much I admired her? Did I leave too many things unsaid?"

"Rosalind knew you loved her. You were her greatest treasure on this earth. She would not have parted with you for anything. She was a lot of things, but she was your mother first and foremost."

"I just wish my mother were here. I would tell her to fix this giant, gaping hole she left in my heart." I covered my chest with my hand. "I would tell her to make me feel whole once more."

"That giant, gaping hole is just proof that you loved someone more than you love yourself. It's called grief, and it's the price of love."

My insides twisted, writhing with sparks of anger as I turned sharply away. "The cost does not seem worth it," I grounded out through clenched teeth.

"It costs us more to never love at all, though."

"What good did love do my mother? Her husband died and she was more than likely murdered. What good did love do Cinderella? She is an orphan and she is treated like a slave. What good did love do Alexander? He is controlled by some unseen fairy tale." I let my words fly rapidly like arrows being released from a tightly strung bow. "Tell me, Max, what good did love do you? You lost Katrina. Twice."

He brought my chin up to look at him. "Felicity, we give love a power over us that death will never have, because we *choose* love. We choose it, knowing it is capable of inflicting grief upon us someday, but that choice is what ultimately saves us. It is the peace we find in chaos; it is the sanity we find in madness; it is the hope that reveals itself when darkness covers us. Love is more than an emotion. Love is an endeavor we pursue all our lives."

Neither of us said anything for a moment, only the soft in and out of our breathing filled the room.

Finally, Max broke the silence. "I'm really bad at these sorts of things, Felicity."

"What things?"

"Feelings."

I almost laughed. "Actually, I think the opposite is true."

He cleared his throat once more and smiled down at me. "You should know if I ever had a daughter, I would want her to be just like you."

"You've been a father to me in more ways than you will ever know."

Max nodded before he left my room. The door closed behind him with a soft click.

I turned my attention back to the wedding dress.

I held the dress up and let the sunlight streaming in from the window shine down on it. It really was extraordinary. I couldn't pry my eyes away from the way the fabric shimmered in the light, giving the dress a silvery sort of gleam, as if it was made of glass and icicles and crystal.

I wondered what Alexander would have said if he saw me in it. Perhaps he'd ask me to dance. I'd tell him I was a terrible dancer, but he'd pull me into a dance anyway. He'd set his hand on my waist and I'd put mine on his shoulder, both gestures would make my heart do somersaults. He'd tease me and tell me I was blushing. I'd retort that it was merely too warm in the room and my cheeks weren't red thanks to any effect he had on me—which we would both know was a lie.

I uttered a gasp when a gleam of silver tied on the end of the dress' sash caught my eye and brought me out of my daydreams and into the present. I reached for the shining piece of silver. It was a wedding band. I tugged it loose, letting it fall into the palm of my hand.

A sense of joy swept over me. Even though Mother never spoke about my father when she was alive, he must have meant something to her. This was proof. Why else would she keep the ring?

I secured the ring around a chain on my neck. The ring had small, intricate roses etched around the circumference that must have taken hours of painstaking care to engrave. It was another clue. If I could figure out which silversmith made the ring, I might be able to discover where my father was from and perhaps if he had any family still living. I reached into the box to pick up a silk shawl that matched the dress. My hands stilled as I discovered something else, something greater even than the ring.

Gingerly, I pulled out a pair of sparkling glass slippers. The glass was cool against my fingertips and magically lightweight in my hands, feeling hardly heavier than a feather. I smiled wistfully, somewhat saddened by this turn of events, as I laid the dress and the shoes down on my bed. My mother had given me the one gift I still needed to complete the fairy tale. Though this gift was not really for me. It was for Cinderella.

My mind turned to thoughts of my dear friend. She was what Alexander needed. One second spent with her and he would see her goodness, her beauty that ran much deeper than appearances. It dawned on me then that *they* deserved each other. If I had to choose a heart other than my own for Alexander to claim, I would choose Cinderella's. If I had to leave him, I wanted to leave him with her.

With a sudden spark of determination, I decided, no matter what it took, Cinderella would go to the ball tomorrow night.

* * *

"Tell me again why I can't borrow this carriage?" I asked Thomas the next morning, flitting my hand in the direction of the large, looming black carriage next to us.

We were standing in the marketplace, surrounded by busy villagers who bustled about finishing last minute preparations for the ball. A nearby baker was stacking piles of pastries on pans to take to the palace kitchens, the sweet scent of freshly baked spice cake and rich vanilla glaze hung in the air. Two seamstresses were rushing in and out of their shop to deliver last minute alterations, the shop bell continuously jingling behind them. The livery was packed with carriages and horses that waited to pull hundreds of ladies up the winding road from the village and to the palace entrance later this evening.

Thomas, who I had discovered outside the livery waiting for the blacksmith to repair a horseshoe, leaned on the rump of a horse, chewing on a piece of straw with care. "Because Lord Reginald would have my head on a fancy platter if he knew I let some girl borrow one of his nicest carriages."

"Let me borrow one of the lousy ones then."

"Why?"

"I need it for the ball tonight."

Thomas scratched his chin. "I thought you lived at the palace already. Why would you need a carriage to get you someplace you already live?"

I huffed impatiently. I had one day to throw every single piece of this fairy tale together, and, since I hadn't seen Katrina after her reunion with Max, nor was I certain she would be at my disposal to turn a pumpkin into a carriage, I had to resort to asking Thomas and Harold for a ride to the ball.

"I don't need it for me," I explained. "I need it for a friend."

Thomas' eyebrow traveled halfway up his forehead, almost reaching the sandy tendrils that fell in front of his face. "A certain friend that may or may not be marrying my master?"

"Possibly. And your point is?"

"I'd lose my job and more if Lord Reginald found out I was helping his intended bride get to a ball to secure the attentions of a young prince."

I walked around the horse and took the collar of Thomas' shirt in my hands, pulling him forcefully down to my eyelevel. "Listen here, Thomas, I am going to get Cinderella to that ball tonight whether or not I have your cooperation. Though I'd prefer it, especially since I figured you for a gentleman. Cinderella needs a carriage because she can't walk all the way to the palace in glass slippers."

"Glass slippers?"

"Never mind," I scolded, shaking him a little. "Are you going to help me or not?"

"Easy there, lass," he soothed, like I was one of his temperamental horses. Thomas pried my hands off his shirt. "I'll help you. Mostly because I don't want to see some nice girl forced to marry Lord Reginald, but I'll lose my job if he finds out I'm helping you. I need this job." Thomas tugged on this collar, only this time out of a different type of nervousness, not because he thought I might strangle him if he didn't comply. "You see, I'm going to ask Mary to marry me soon..."

My eyes widened.

"Well," he explained, turning out his palms and shrugging, "I can't ask her to marry me if I don't have means to support us. Mary hasn't found work yet herself, and, if I lose my job, then I can't support us..."

I understood his concerns, and my mind raced with ways to help the couple until it firmly latched onto one. "What if I told you I found Mary a job? It's a job that pays well and the employer is decent and one of the most caring men I've ever met, though he's somewhat eccentric at times."

Thomas straightened. "Really? Who? Where?"

"My Uncle Max and in the palace library." I hastened to explain my uncle was looking for someone to help cook and clean our home above the library. I promised Thomas that I'd give Mary a glowing recommendation. I was certain my uncle would go for the idea.

"Can Mary cook?" I asked him.

"Can she cook?" He raised his eyes to the heavens. "She can turn even the most meager of rations into a banquet fit for a king."

"Then she's got a job," I assured him. "Max has suffered through my poor attempts at cooking for us the past four years, and he's complained more than once about how malnourished he is." I almost laughed at the excited look spreading across Thomas' face. "Just be at Lady Maura's manor at half-past eight to pick Cinderella up with a carriage." I paused and looked up at him thoughtfully. "You don't happen to have one that looks like a pumpkin, do you?"

"*A pumpkin?*"

"Yes, well, I thought not."

Thomas opened his mouth to reply, but before he could utter another word I dashed across the street as a flash of familiar golden hair on the head of an even more familiar person traveling from the seamstress' shop caught my attention.

"Cinderella!" I shouted. I dodged a wayward child being chased by his mother and then a wandering shopkeeper with a cart full of vegetables. I stumbled across the street, kicking up a cloud of dust that gave me a coughing fit. I came to a crashing halt, almost spilling the stack of packages piled in her arms.

"Felicity!" Her eyes widened with surprise. "What are you doing out in the village today? I haven't seen you since..."

"The unfortunate incident with Lord Reginald?"

"Yes. That." Cinderella shifted her weight from foot to foot.

"I'm in the village to speak with someone about securing a carriage for the ball tonight, but I was also on my way to see you. I felt bad about how I left things between us. I wanted to say that I was sorry, and you were right."

Startled, she blinked. Apparently, Cinderella was not used to being offered apologies. "I was right about what?"

"I shouldn't have tried to tell you what to do. I should have..." My words trailed off as pools of moisture filled Cinderella's eyes. The packages in her hands shook as she fought back tears. "Hey, what's wrong? Come sit down."

I led her to a bench outside the seamstress' shop and took a few of the packages from her hands as we sat down next to each other.

"Oh, Felicity," she whispered. "Things have been terrible at the manor since you've been gone. I didn't realize how much I had come to count on your presence.

My stepmother heard about Lord Reginald's injury, but she can't trace it back to me. Lord Reginald doesn't remember the incident but has his suspicions. I've refused to speak about the matter, so Lady Maura has made my life more miserable, and my stepsisters have never been more willing to help her. I think they are jealous I received an offer of marriage before they did, especially Cressida. If only they knew how vile Lord Reginald was and that I'd gladly hand him over to either of them." She slouched back against the bench. "Not to mention I've felt awful about the way I treated you last week. You were only trying to help."

"It's forgotten," I assured her. "Now tell me the truth. Your stepfamily has always treated you poorly, what else is really bothering you? There used to be a sparkle in your eyes, even during the most trying of times, and your stepmother has robbed you of that."

"That's not all she's robbed me of," Cinderella whispered. She swiped at a falling tear. "She sold my mother's harp to pay for three ball gowns for her and my stepsisters to wear to the ball tonight." She gestured to the packages on my lap and her own. "Since I refused to speak about Lord Reginald's injury and how he acquired it, she found some other way to get back at me. I woke up one morning this week and the harp was being peddled off to some merchant... I'll never be able to get it back."

I was sorely tempted to throw the package in my hands into the busy street to be trampled on by vegetable carts and children. I was more than willing to let one of those horrible stepsisters go to the ball in a rumpled, ruined gown.

"I know you told me not to interfere," I said after a few moments of silence between us. People bustled in and out of the seamstress' store and the jingle of the shop bell kept cutting into my thoughts. "I know it's not my place to, either."

Cinderella craned her neck to look at me. "Yes?"

"However, I think... I think you should go to the ball tonight."

"The ball?" She laughed. "*Me?* Go to the ball?" She smiled to herself as though I had made the most amusing joke in the world. "I could never go to the ball."

I frowned. "Why not? The entire kingdom is invited."

"First, my stepmother wouldn't let me leave the manor."

"I'd sneak you out."

"Second, I've nothing suitable to wear. I doubt the dress code includes soot and grime."

"I've the perfect dress for you to borrow."

"Third, even if I did sneak out and borrow a dress, there's always the chance I'd run into my stepfamily at the ball and they'd discover I was there."

"But—"

"I can't." She rose from the bench and reached for the packages in my lap. "I just can't go, Felicity."

I stood up, too. "What's really stopping you from going? There's something else... something that runs deeper than your stepmother's disapproval or your lack of a proper dress."

She was silent for a moment before meeting my gaze halfheartedly. "I can't go to the palace and pretended to be someone I'm not." She glanced down at her soiled apron and dress. "Look at me, Felicity. I'd take one step into the ballroom and everyone would see me for who I truly am."

"I sure hope they would."

Ruefully, Cinderella shook her head and started off down the street, while I trailed after her. We zigzagged in and out of the crowd of people, and Cinderella took care to make sure the packages in her hands didn't tumble to the dusty ground.

"Cinderella! Wait!"

She called over her shoulder, "I'm a coward. I'm a coward who would rather continue to live an existence that makes me miserable than have the courage to find a new one out of fear it would be ripped from my grasp. I told you once I was tired of living with false hope. That's just what going to the prince's ball would be—false hope, a tempting morsel of the life that I could never have."

I finally reached her side. "You could meet the prince. Perhaps you'd even have a chance of winning his heart."

"I'm not interested in winning Prince Alexander's heart." She looked over at me as if I were mad, as if I didn't know her at all. "I want something else entirely."

I took a deep breath and threw out the only words I knew would make her think twice. "Jack will be there."

"What?" She paused before turning slowly to face me.

"Jack will be there," I repeated. As far as I knew, this was a lie and Jack was still in Avondale on unfinished business. "He'll be at the ball. If you don't want to win the heart of a prince, perhaps you could come to see the knight whose heart you've already captured."

"Do you think it's possible that Jack likes me?"

"No." My abrupt answer made her flinch. Cinderella frowned and continued on her way with a slight shake of her head. I called after her, "I think it's more likely that he's already halfway in love with you."

My words stopped her retreating steps. Cinderella cast a hopeful glance over her shoulder. "Do you really believe that?"

I confessed that I did.

It was easy to see that Cinderella was in love with Jack, and I was going to use that to my advantage—rather

Valencia's advantage. I could only hope Cinderella would come to the ball for Jack's heart, but that she would leave with Alexander's. I also desperately hoped that someday, if it came down to it, she'd forgive me for meddling in her life once more.

CHAPTER 22

I hid outside the manor and waited, not-so-patiently, for Cinderella's stepfamily to leave for the ball. My legs were quaking as I crouched behind a bush with the box containing my mother's dress pressed tightly against my chest. At a quarter till eight, the three of them piled into a carriage in their frilly hoop skirts and obnoxiously bejeweled masquerade masks—a sight that made me seethe with anger at the thought of Cinderella's mother's harp being sold simply to satisfy their vanity.

My legs rejoiced when the carriage finally rounded the bend in the road. I was free to spring up and head to the manor.

"Are you sure they are gone?" Cinderella whispered after I knocked on the door.

I stepped inside. "Of course. I watched them pack into that carriage, cackling as if they were a hoard of buzzards. Also, your stepsister's rouge was dark enough for me to see from my hiding spot."

"I told her not to use so much. Agatha was convinced the prince preferred rosy-cheeked women, though."

"Rosy-cheeked, yes. Enough to rival a bad sunburn, no." I set the box with the glass slippers and my mother's wedding dress down on a chair. I smacked my hands together. "Well, are you ready to get dressed?"

"I'm afraid I haven't been able to do much to get myself ready." She pointed dismally to her limp hair and raggedy dress. "I had to help my stepsisters with their wardrobes."

"Don't worry," I said, giving her a mock curtsy. "Tonight I'd be honored to be your lady's maid." I gestured toward the box. "I brought you something to wear this evening."

Cinderella hesitantly opened the box. Her eyes lit up in surprise and a smile played at her lips. She cast me a look of wonder. "Where did you ever find such a magnificent dress?"

"It was my mother's wedding dress," I replied simply. I pulled it out of the box and shook out the train. The yards of white fabric spilled over my arms and swept the floor in ripples of snowy silk and tulle. "Also, there are some slippers for you to wear."

Cinderella gasped, stepping away from the dress. Though I noticed her eyes hadn't left it yet, they continued to stare at it with amazement. "I can't wear your mother's wedding dress."

"Sure, you can. In fact, I insist that you do."

"You should be wearing this dress tonight, not me. Your mother would want you to wear it."

I faked a laugh, pretending I didn't care. "Honestly, my mother wouldn't mind. I'm sure she would just want it put to good use." I reached down to pick up the glass slippers. They caught the light from a candle's flame and sparkled brilliantly as if they were made of diamonds and not simple glass. "Try the slippers on."

Cinderella unexpectedly pushed the shoes back into my arms, and I almost clumsily dropped them to the floor. "Nonsense. I insist that you wear your mother's dress and slippers."

"Watch it with the shoes. They are made of glass, you know." I placed the shoes on the floor next to her feet. "Go ahead, try them on."

"Felicity..."

"Just try the stupid slippers on."

Cinderella nodded reluctantly. "All right, if you insist." She sat down and placed her foot inside the glass slipper, working her heel into the shoe. Once it was on, Cinderella raised her leg to examine the shoe more closely, admiring the bewitching way it glittered in the candlelight.

"They are a little tight. Even if the shoes were two sizes too small, I'd still manage just to get to wear something this lovely," she whispered with awe.

"Good." I held up the dress in front of her. "Are you ready to try this on?"

Cinderella clapped her hands together. Her excitement was hard to contain, and I found myself smiling as she cried, "Yes!" with no small amount of enthusiasm.

I tugged the dress over her shoulders and buttoned up the long row of buttons tracing down the back. I fluffed the skirt out and smoothed down a few wrinkles in the tulle with my hands. I patted the sleeves of the dress down. "There," I smiled at her in the mirror, "I think it's a perfect fit."

The dress molded around her delicate figure perfectly and the skirt belled out around her waist like a fountain. Her eyes filled up with tears. "It's the most beautiful dress I've ever worn, Felicity." She spun around in a circle, and the dress glided around her like a cloud. "How can I ever repay you for the kindness you have shown me?"

I looked away, embarrassed. "We're friends. I don't need you to repay me."

"What will you wear to the ball if I am wearing your mother's dress?"

"I'll find something."

She tilted her head slightly. "Is there something wrong? You don't seem like yourself tonight. You seem so... distant."

"If you must know, I just don't feel like going to the ball and celebrating tonight. Here I brought you a necklace to wear." I reached inside the box and extended the strand of pearls that had been passed down to me from my mother. I gently shook the necklace in front of her face. "It'll look good with the dress."

Cinderella ignored the necklace. "Why don't you want to go to the ball?"

"I'm a terrible dancer," I said, looping the pearls over her head.

"I'm sure you aren't all that bad."

"Two left feet."

She looked thoughtful for a moment until her face softened with realization. "Oh. Wait. I see. This wouldn't have to do with a certain prince? Are you avoiding him for some reason?"

Her statement caught me off guard.

"Of course not," I stated. I frowned and shook my head. "I, um... *no*. What makes you say that?"

"Jack told me how close you two are, and that you've been inseparable friends for years. It's Prince Alexander's birthday, and I know you wouldn't miss tonight unless something had happened between you two. Why else would you be so reluctant to go to the ball if you weren't avoiding him?"

"I'm not avoiding him!" I answered, much louder and snappier than necessary.

She ignored my rise in volume. "I hear the way you speak about the prince, the way you unintentionally bring him up in conversations. It's as if—"

"It's as if what?" I whispered. I was suddenly afraid that she'd voice my deepest secret—that I was in love with Alexander.

"As if..." she trailed off. "Never mind." Cinderella looked like she wanted to say more, but to her credit she dropped the subject. "Will you help me with my hair?"

So that's what we did for the next half hour. We primped, trimmed, plucked, and styled Cinderella into a complete picture of a princess. I curled her hair and pinned it up to the top of her head in the latest court fashion. She painted her lips and cheeks pink with some of her stepsister's cosmetics, though, to my immense relief, she had a lighter touch with the rouge.

After the last curl was pinned, I sat back, satisfied. She looked like royalty. She looked like just the right kind of girl to win Alexander's heart. However, she did look nervous, if the crease between her eyebrows was any indication. Truthfully, I felt a little anxious myself. I could only imagine what she was feeling as she attempted to waltz into a court function as a commoner. Not just any court function, but the event of the year. She twisted her hands nervously in her lap.

"Every man at the ball will be captivated by you tonight," I said as I leaned over her shoulder. "You won't be able to keep them at bay."

"I don't want them all." She sighed wistfully before the mirror as she peered at her reflection. "Just the one."

"Still, you'll have the entire court enraptured with you by night's end. I have no doubt."

"What if someone asks me to dance and I don't know the steps?" A horrified look crossed her face, as if the greatest blunder in the world was to misstep during a waltz. "Or what if the prince speaks to me, but I can't find the right words to say? I'll look like a fool."

"Stop worrying. Enjoy the experience, Cinderella. Don't try to control it." That was my job.

"What if my stepfamily sees me? What will I do?"

"It's a masquerade, and you'll be wearing this." I pulled out a small white mask with beads lining the edges. I was thankful I had remembered to purchase a mask from a shop in the village. "They won't be able to tell who you are."

A noise from outside caught my attention. "I think the carriage is here. You finish getting ready, and I'll tell the coachman where to park it."

Nodding, she turned back to the mirror and started securing the mask.

I let myself out the front door and surveyed the yard from the porch. I didn't see anyone. The wind picked up and rustled the leaves in the trees. I covered myself with a shawl to keep the cool air off my arms and stepped off the porch to check the side entrance to the manor.

"Thomas?" I called loudly. "Are you here?"

Swish. Swish. A giant gust of wind answered my call.

"Thomas?"

"There's no Thomas here," a soft voice answered.

Surprised, I spun around to find a certain small, dainty minx of a fairy smiling at me. I took in her tiny figure and outrageous orange hair with wide eyes. "Katrina?" I breathed with excitement. "I wasn't certain you would show up."

"I believe the fairy tale said I would."

"I wasn't certain after what happened with Max."

Katrina gave a formal bow. "As promised in the fairy tale, I came to help you."

"Don't you mean you came to help Cinderella?"

"No, I'm here to help you—my goddaughter," she replied, sauntering over to me with such ease it was more like she was walking on clouds than a gravel pathway to the porch.

"What do you mean?"

She came to stand before me and, with a grin, took my hands in hers. "I was never Cinderella's fairy godmother. I was yours, Felicity."

"What?"

"Why do you think I've made it a habit of keeping such a close eye on you? It's not been for my own entertainment. Mind you, it has been entertaining in its own way."

"Did my mother know? Does Max know?"

"Rosalind was the one that asked me to look after you. As for Maxwell, I'm sure he had his suspicions. Here I am, fulfilling my promise. I figured you couldn't get your hands on a pumpkin carriage without a little help from a fairy godmother." She bowed again. "Unless you have some way of conjuring up a pumpkin carriage on your own that I don't know about?"

I shook my head, tendrils of hair falling out of my kerchief as I did.

"I didn't think so."

Katrina waved her hand in the direction of the garden, and moments later a great, hulking pumpkin came bouncing over the weeds in the front lawn and landed squarely in the driveway. I eyed the pumpkin and tried to keep back the frown forming on my lips.

"Isn't it supposed to, um, turn into a carriage or something?" I questioned.

"Patience, my dear girl." Katrina flicked her hand once more, a beam of light springing out of her fingertips. "I'm not done with it yet."

The pumpkin swelled to the side of a small house, rounding and contorting itself into such a large structure I feared it would loudly burst and bring Cinderella flying from the manor, demanding to know what the commotion was. I wasn't certain I could explain Katrina's presence to her in any way that seemed remotely believable. Still, the pumpkin continued to grow. The vines growing from the pumpkin wrapped around into impressive carriage wheels. The bright orange coloring turned into a brilliant, luminous silver. Exquisite mother-of-pearl handles and stepladders formed on either side.

I reached out in breathless awe to stroke the silver carriage, the surface flawless beneath my touch. I was afraid I would wake up and find myself in a dream. I knew if I touched the carriage it would make it all real, tangible—a true moment I could keep locked in my memory forever. Katrina joined me next to the carriage.

"I forget how easily impressed humans are by even the simplest of magic," she said.

"It's beautiful, extraordinary," I breathed. "It looks like something out of a..."

"Fairy tale?"

I half-heartedly laughed at her joke.

"Beautiful it may be, lasting it is not. Don't forget it turns back into a pumpkin at midnight. You must remember to tell Cinderella to leave before the stroke of twelve. Every part of the fairy tale must be followed."

I turned to Katrina, still enraptured. "You have saved me from monsters, spared Max's life, and now you create a carriage out of something as ordinary as a pumpkin. What else can you do?" I asked her.

She chuckled, throwing her head back to laugh. Her curls danced in the wind. The moonlight splashed across her face, enhancing her eternal youth and beauty. In that moment she was all fairy—wild and whimsical, magical and mysterious.

"More than I can explain, my friend." Her smile faltered, fading almost completely as her eyes caught the night sky. I wasn't sure what made her frown. I glanced up at the stars above us, wondering if she was reading some foreboding message in them that mere mortals were not privy to see.

I cleared my throat. "Katrina?"

"Yes?"

"You said you were my fairy godmother. But why would you agree to be my fairy godmother? I can't imagine it makes you popular with the other fairies in your realm, especially since most seem to despise humans." I continued to gaze at the magnificent carriage before me, a carriage fit for a future queen. "I don't want you to get into more trouble."

"Oh, they know I'm a fairy godmother." She leaned up against the silver door and folded her arms over her chest. "It was one of my conditions."

"Conditions?"

"For agreeing to write this fairy tale."

I suddenly lost all interest in the carriage. "*What?*"

"Why are you so surprised? Didn't Maxwell tell you a fairy wrote each fairy tale?"

"Yes. I didn't think *you* wrote this one, though. Especially not after I got to know you." I took an uncertain step back. "I thought the fairies that wrote the fairy tales would be... I don't know..."

"Evil?"

"Well... yes."

"Some of them are. It's the same with humans; you have your good and your evil and all those in between. Some fairies write horrible fairy tales with nary a happy ending in sight. Trust me, there are worse fates for

Cinderella than having to be home from a ball by midnight."

"Felicity!" Cinderella called from inside the house, breaking into our conversation. I spun around to find her standing in the doorway, looking like a hauntingly beautiful vision in white as the dark shadows of the night and the moonlight spilled over her dress like contrasting claw marks.

Numbly, Cinderella stepped off the porch as she stared at the spectacle behind me.

"Cinderella, I can explain—"

Her hand rose to cover her mouth. "Where did you get that carriage?" she whispered.

I blinked. *The carriage?* She was more curious about the carriage than the bizarre fairy standing behind me that conjured magic with a flick of her wrist? I glanced over my shoulder and was surprised to find that Katrina had vanished without so much as a goodbye or an explanation—again.

"Oh, this..." I tapped the carriage, ruffled by Katrina's disappearance. Why did that fairy always seem to disappear right when I started asking questions? "Yes, well, I'm borrowing it from a friend."

"Which one of your friends is wealthy enough to own a silver carriage?" she asked. Her eyebrows rose up an inch or so. "Perhaps a certain prince of Valencia?"

Before I could reply, the rumble of wheels churning around the bend cut me off, and, for a moment, Cinderella and I froze, thinking her stepfamily had returned to the manor for some unexplained reason. I let out a sigh of relief when I noticed it was only Thomas and Harold with their own carriage.

Cinderella's hands shook. "What are Lord Reginald's servants doing here?"

"They won't say anything to him," I promised. "They have come to escort you to the ball as a favor to me."

Harold pulled one of Lord Reginald's finest carriages to a stop, which looked entirely dowdy and plain in comparison to the brightly glittering silver one next to it. Thomas jumped off the footman's perch with youthful ease. He took a moment to stare at the pumpkin carriage, then at me, and then finally back at the carriage.

He whistled low, appreciatively. "Gracious, Felicity. What did you need our carriage for when you've got this gorgeous ride?"

Instead of explaining, I barked out hasty instructions for them to hook the team of horses up to the new carriage. Thomas and Harold, more than willing to drive the new carriage, seemed eager to follow my directions without any further questions.

I turned to Cinderella. "Are you ready?"

Cinderella looked up, worried. "Did you know each girl has to be introduced to the prince in the receiving line?" She bit her lip. "What will I say?"

I ushered her toward the door of the carriage. I noticed her feet dragging behind her, like I was sentencing her to exile in a foreign land and not to a ball in the palace. I supposed they were the same thing to her. "In the case of introductions, I find that it's always a good idea to start with your name."

Thomas came forward, opened the door, and offered Cinderella a hand up. "My Lady," he murmured with a practiced bow.

Cinderella stared at Thomas' proffered hand but refused to step forward. Her hand went to her stomach. "I can't seem to breathe properly."

"It's probably just your corset," I replied.

"It's more likely the nerves in my stomach that have all jumbled together and are slowly making their way up my throat. I feel like I'm going to be sick all over my slippers."

"Don't you dare! Those were my mother's."

Cinderella backed away from the carriage, as if she planned on bolting. "I don't even know what to do, or say, or even think, actually. This is all happening too fast. I-I-I can't do this—"

"Hey." I caught her hand before she could dart away. I was grateful the night was already dark enough to conceal my watery eyes. I was handing her over to marry my best friend. If only I could tell her the truth, tell her that there was a destiny ahead of her that would change the course of history. She needn't be afraid, especially not when Alexander was waiting on the other end of that destiny.

"I'm scared. I've never done anything like this before," Cinderella said.

"Once in a while, you need to give yourself permission to do something daring."

"For one night I want to live the life I deserve. I just wish I had more courage."

"Courage has a way of making an appearance when we least expect it and when we most need it."

"Yes. Courage," Cinderella whispered. She straightened her shoulders and nodded before reaching out to squeeze my arm affectionately. "Thank you, for all of this. How fortunate am I to have found a friend in you?"

"Go on," I urged her, ignoring the tension in my chest. "Go charm the entire court tonight."

Charm the prince, too.

Cinderella picked up her skirts and let Thomas hoist her into the carriage. Once inside, she leaned out the window, a smile, more confident than any I had ever seen on her, graced her lips. "Don't you want a ride back to the palace?"

I shook my head. The fairy tale indicated she needed to make her grand entrance and meet Alexander alone. "I need to walk back tonight. Clear my head. I'll find you at the ball later."

"But—"

"I'll see you there. I promise."

I heard Harold flick the reins, and the carriage jolted forward, rocking Cinderella to and fro in the window frame. She waved to me as the carriage took off, and I started after it as I remembered the warning Katrina had issued.

"You'll need to leave the ball before midnight!" I called after her.

Her smile disappeared. "Why?"

"Trust me," I answered. "Nothing good happens after midnight."

Especially not in fairy tales.

She laughed and waved to me as the carriage disappeared into the dark night.

CHAPTER 23

The walk back to the palace was long and tiring. The sleepless nights, the exhausting days, had finally caught up with me, and I had to force myself to put one foot in front of the other. When the glittering lights of the palace finally came into view, I felt relief coupled with a mix of despair. After tonight, everything would change.

I took a different entrance into the palace, avoiding the hustle of the ball and the hundreds of carriages and guests milling around outside the main entrance. Flashes of blue and green and pink silk dresses caught my eye. Tinkling laughter and the deep, resonating sounds of a grand orchestra filled my ears, and I knew I wouldn't be able to stand the embarrassment of walking past the guests at the ball in my wrinkled homespun dress, dirty boots, and wind-blown hair. I'd have to hurry back to the library if I wanted to have enough time to change into my own dress.

When I reached the library, I found a note pinned to the door.

Fliss,
I joined the festivities in the ballroom. If you don't join me soon, I shall be forced to make conversation with strangers and neither party will want that.
Also, be careful where you step. The feline's instincts finally kicked in and I found remnants of a mouse in the sitting room.
Max

I shook my head as I read Max's note with a smile on my face. Even Max, the social recluse that he was, wasn't going to miss the ball tonight. It felt as if the entire world had shown up to watch how this fairy tale played out.

A throat cleared behind me.

Startled, I looked up. I dropped my hand and the note to my side. "Your Majesty?"

Queen Briar stepped forward out of the shadows in the corridor. I took in her lovely midnight blue dress with silver piping on the sleeves and train. Her honey hair was swept back into a bun at the nape of her neck and a small silver chain intertwined within her curls. She had a dainty tiara bejeweled with sapphires and diamonds sitting atop her head. She looked like something out of a fairy tale herself. I suddenly felt very plain in comparison.

I bobbed a curtsy.

"Hello, Felicity," Queen Briar said. "I've been looking for you at the ball. Maxwell said that you might be up here." She looked at my plain gray dress, smudged apron, and frizzy, unruly hair. "I take it you aren't ready yet?"

"Is it that obvious?"

"Well, hurry up, my dear. You don't want to waste the night standing around in an empty corridor when you could be dancing at the ball."

"I'm only going to the ball to make sure the fairy tale is fulfilled. I'll probably just stand discreetly in some corner." I turned back to the door, grasping the knob in my hands. "I don't want to keep you, Your Majesty. I'm sure you need to get back to the celebration."

"Stand in the corner on a night like this? That won't do. You are living in a story book right now." The queen tugged my hand away from the door. "Hmm," she murmured. "I think I might have something you can wear."

"Oh no," I said, taken aback. "I don't need anything special to wear, Your Majesty. I just—tonight is hard for me. I think I'd rather wait in the shadows until the evening is over."

"Is there something wrong with my ball, Felicity?" The queen raised an eyebrow in question. "You were the one who asked me to throw a ball in Alexander's honor."

"It's that... I can't..."

The queen's eyes snapped to mine. "You are in love with my son. You are afraid that if he sees you at the ball tonight it will only complicate things. I know you've been avoiding him. He's been sulking all week."

I gulped.

"Am I correct or not?"

"Well, yes." It felt odd confessing my love for Alexander to his mother when I had never confessed it to him. "You can see my predicament. I need to go to the ball for the fairy tale's sake, but I also need stay hidden."

The queen, undaunted by my response, looped her arm through mine. "Come on, we'll find you something suitable to wear. I'm sure Alexander would love to see you this evening. You wouldn't want to disappoint him. It's his birthday, after all."

I looked longingly at the library's door, wanting to escape this evening all together. I started to protest. "Your Majesty, I can't..."

"As your queen, I insist that you come with me." She pulled me down the hallway. "And as Alexander's mother, I insist even more." She stopped to look at me solemnly, and I was forced to come to a halt as well. "Make a mother's wish come true, I would like to see my son dance with the woman he cares for tonight. There will be a line of young ladies trying to win his crown this evening, not his heart. I want him to dance with at least one girl who admires him more as a person than as a prince."

I didn't quite know how to respond to that statement, but what could I do? If the queen wanted me to go with her, it's not like I had much of a choice. She was the queen. "Of course, Your Majesty." I let her continue to pull me down the hallway. "But I don't know if I can stay long."

Queen Briar winked at me. "You'll stay at least until midnight, Felicity. If I know fairy tales, and I believe I do, nothing good happens until midnight."

* * *

The ball was in full swing by the time we made it down to the ballroom. I paused with Queen Briar outside the ballroom doors, and a swift feeling of panic welled up within me, sending jittery tingles up my arms and spine. I tried to shake them off.

You should not be here, my head warned.

But my heart was telling me something else entirely—it beckoned me to stay. I twisted my gloved hands together. Queen Briar reached out to still them.

"I'm nervous," I admitted.

"I know." She squeezed my hand. "But you deserve this night, Felicity."

Self-consciously, I ran my hands over the folds of my gown. The queen had found me a dark crimson colored dress that was made of a luxurious satin material. Tiny satin rosebuds gathered at the bosom, and the sleeves were trimmed with delicate crimson lace. The shimmery material fanned out at my hips and fell into a graceful train with lace rose patterns giving the back of the dress tiny sparks of detail. My cotton stockings were replaced with silk ones, and my riding boots were replaced with satin slippers that matched the dress.

I touched the lace dangling from my sleeve. "Your Majesty, do you think this color is too bold?"

She dismissed my concern with a wave. "In a sea of cautious pastels and prudently thought out patterns, this dress will stand out."

"That was my fear."

The queen patted down a wayward curl falling over my ear and stood back to survey her work. It was a beautiful dress, not as lovely as my mother's wedding dress, but still breathtaking nonetheless. It felt completely out of place on my body. Queen Briar was right—the dress was a standout color. The hue made my unruly curls mirror the night sky, my skin shone in the candlelight, and my eyes were a dark, vibrant green against the deep red silk.

I fiddled with the black masquerade mask on my face as we descended the staircase, feeling more than a tinge of the nerves Cinderella had felt earlier. The air hummed with something more profound than excitement—it hummed with sheer anticipation. Everything would change after tonight, maybe the people in this room didn't know they were standing on the brink of destiny, but they could certainly feel something magical in the air. I even felt myself falling toward the magic that surrounded me.

The ballroom, which was always beautiful, seemed infinitely more splendid this evening. As if it knew that somehow it had to muster up more grandeur tonight than ever before. The glittering chandeliers towered over the guests, and the flicker of the candles' flames caused prisms of light to drip off the hundreds of crystals dangling from the ceiling. The marble floor was polished so perfectly that you could see your reflection. An orchestra was playing off to the side of the room, and couples filled the dance floor, making the room come to life with a sea of colors as the skirts of all the eligible maidens whisked by me.

My eyes traveled the room, searching for Cinderella or Alexander.

I saw the prince first, bowing ever so politely to the next young lady in the longest receiving line I'd ever beheld. Moments later, I caught an unmistakable glimpse of my mother's silvery white wedding dress in the far corner. The dressed glinted magically beneath the rainbow prisms falling from the ceiling. Cinderella leaned in to whisper something amusing to a young gentleman next to her. Unfortunately, that gentleman was not Alexander—it was Jack. For all I knew, Cinderella had yet to meet Alexander.

I huffed a little in frustration. I had counted on a lot of obstacles tonight, but Jack had not been one of them. He was supposed to still be in Avondale.

Midnight would come a lot sooner than I wanted it to, and Alexander and Cinderella needed to meet and have a connection as soon as possible. I started to make my way to their side of the ballroom with every intention of separating Jack and Cinderella once and for all, when Queen Briar stopped me.

"Not that way, Felicity. There's something I want to show you."

"But—"

Queen Briar had once again commandeered my hand and was whisking me to a large balcony off the side of the ballroom before I could finish my protest. She all but pushed me out onto the balcony, and my bare arms prickled with chill bumps as the cool night air washed over me.

To my relief, I found my uncle outside. He was probably avoiding the crowd as I had intended to do.

"Max!" I cried. Max turned at the sound of my voice, his eyes lighting up. I rushed forward, relieved to see another familiar face.

"*Felicity?*" Max whispered. His voice came out sounding strangled, as if something were caught in his throat. "You look..."

I tugged at the sleeves of the dress. "Ridiculous?"

"Like your mother." He gave me a wistful, sad look as he urged me to spin around. I complied, twirling around in a circle to let my dress billow out around me. He reached out to steady me as I wobbled, the earth still spinning even after I stopped. "For a moment, I thought you were her."

The compliment warmed my heart. I often had to remind myself that it wasn't just I who had lost a mother. Max had also lost a sister. Not just any sister, either—his twin. The person who knew him better than anyone else.

"Though I don't think I've ever seen you wear that particular dress before. I would have remembered the low neckline and told you to wear a scarf."

"That's because it belongs to Queen Briar." I felt my cheeks flush. I looked over to see how the queen had reacted to my uncle's comment, but I found she had left us alone. Trying to shake off my embarrassment, I reasoned with him. "It's not that low, Max. If I wore a dress with a collar up to my earlobes, you would think that's low too." In an effort to change the subject, I said, "You look very handsome. I must admit though that I'm surprised you came tonight. I don't remember the last time you left the library to attend a social event."

Max was dressed in a dark green dress coat and cream-colored pants. His spectacles sat perched atop his nose, and it looked as though he'd actually taken the time to run a comb through his usually mussed up chestnut hair. He looked distinguished and scholarly, but his eyes were all kindness. I felt a surge of pride to be his niece.

"Probably at least a few decades, but I wanted to be here to offer you my support tonight. I hope you are not too disappointed about how this evening will play out."

"If Cinderella and Alexander fall in love, then everything's played out as it should."

Coincidentally, at the mention of Alexander, I heard his voice, agitated and brisk, come crashing through the stillness of the night air and shattering my nerves.

"Mother!" Alexander groaned. "You can't just drag me away from the ball without giving me a reason. It looks rude. And, might I remind you, it was *you* who insisted we have this ball in the first place."

I watched—half-horrified and half-entranced—as Queen Briar came clambering onto the balcony, clutching her son by his elbow and dragging him after her much in the same way she had done with me.

"Hush, son," she commanded in a voice that was more mother than queen. "You'll thank me when you see what I have to show you."

"What's going on?" I mumbled to Max. I was tempted to hide behind him.

Max's worried glance gave me the impression that he was just as surprised as I was. "I have no idea. Though it seems the queen has her own idea about how the evening should play out."

Alexander pulled out of his mother's grasp and turned to go back inside. He paused mid-stride when his eyes scanned across the dark balcony and found me standing— completely still—in a wash of moonlight.

Alexander shook his head in disbelief. "*Felicity?*"

I gulped, taking a few uneasy steps back.

Alexander approached me with what I recognized was, unfortunately for me, his look of sheer determination. The moonlight hit him at a certain angle, and I feared I might not recover my breath for he almost stole it completely. He was achingly handsome in his navy jacket and polished boots. His dark hair fell forward, eyes flashed brightly, and he offered me a boyish grin that reminded me of one he wore when we were children fishing by the creek or playing hide-and-seek in the palace gardens.

If this was to be our moment of reckoning, Alexander was much more prepared to steal my heart completely than I was to surrender his over to Cinderella. I suddenly wished we were on opposite sides of a locked door again.

The queen all but danced around her son in giddy delight as she took in the look on his face.

"Mother," Alexander said before Queen Briar turned to leave.

"Yes, dear?"

"Thank you."

The queen cast a mischievous glance over her shoulder at us before making her way back inside the ballroom. "Maxwell, come along," she beckoned him. "I have a few questions about the library that I've been meaning to ask you. Let's discuss them over a glass of cider, shall we?"

"Of course, Your Majesty. But I thought for the moment I might stay with—"

"Splendid!" The queen waved to us. "We'll be just inside the ballroom, dears."

Max was whisked away by the queen before I could convince him to stay. Once they had left and closed the doors to the balcony firmly behind them, my heart leapt up from my chest and into my throat. I felt the urge to run. Dismayed, I noticed Alexander stood between the door and myself, effectively blocking any escape I might try to make.

I glanced over my shoulder at the edge of the balcony, trying to determine how far of a jump...

"Don't even think about it, Fliss," Alexander cut into my thoughts.

"I wasn't going to actually jump," I insisted. I didn't tell him that shimmying down the trellis was still an option, though.

He cracked a small smile, but his eyes never left mine. "I thought you were going to avoid me forever. Why are you here?"

"To tell you happy birthday?"

Alexander chuckled as he circled around me with keen interest and something that closely resembled appreciation.

"Didn't anyone ever tell you it was rude to stare, Your Highness?"

"It's your dress." He moved in closer. "Rather it's the girl wearing the dress. If you were seeking to come to the ball and capture my attention, it is now undividedly yours, m'lady."

"I was not seeking to capture anyone's attention; least of all, yours."

"It's a little late for that."

A burst of cool wind picked up, reminding me that though it was April, the nights could still get impossibly cold. I crossed my arms to cover myself from the chill. "It's cold out here. I'm going inside." When Alexander didn't move out of my way, I huffed in frustration. "Are you going to stand there all night staring at me?"

He ignored my question and asked one of his own, "Why did you come tonight, Felicity?" His voice was firm, but his eyes were kind. "I was certain I had scared you off for good."

I turned away to look out over the balcony. More importantly, I turned away to evade his gaze and eye the rather sturdy looking trellis next to the balcony. Yes, it could probably hold my weight.

"If you must know, I came for the food, particularly the cake. It's chocolate again this year, right?"

Alexander sighed impatiently. "Must you make everything so complicated? Just tell me the truth. You've avoided me all week. If you had just been honest with me from the beginning as to why you don't think we should be together..."

"It's not that easy!" I banged a clenched fist onto the hard railing, frustration snapping within me. "You can't just demand answers from me because you are a prince!" I turned to go, storming past him in a fit of silk skirts.

"Wait a moment!" he called after me. He took three quick strides and caught up with me. "Fliss, that's hardly fair." His hand found mine and gently tugged me back. "It has nothing to do with being a prince. I am your oldest and closest friend. I deserve to hear the truth. Why are you avoiding me?" His nearness, his touch, was making my stomach flip-flop in an unwelcome manner.

"Please... just let me go," I whispered, unable to look him in the eye. I stared at the collar of his jacket. "If you care about me at all, you'll let me go."

His finger tipped my chin up and he peered down at me with furrowed eyebrows. It was a look of deep, genuine concern. "Felicity," his tone was serious and tight. "What has happened? Something is wrong. I can feel it."

"Please, j-just let me go." My voice trembled and broke. "*Just let me go.*"

"Don't you think I've tried? I resolve every day, every hour, every minute of my miserable existence to let you go, only to find myself in the next breath petrified at what it would cost me if I did—so I cling even more fiercely." He reached out to pull back a curl that had flown in front of my face. "I spend every night dreaming of being in your company, and every day trying to seek it out."

"What do you expect me to say to that?"

"You know exactly what I want you to say."

Alexander leaned forward, and his lips hovered slightly over mine. His warm breath on my face seemed to fan the fire that was burning in my belly. He pulled me even closer to him. His arm wrapped around my waist and his other hand grasped mine. I knew I should have pulled away, but my traitorous heart had other ideas.

"I don't love you," I whispered. Whether I was trying to convince him or myself I wasn't certain.

"You little liar."

Alexander somehow managed to make *liar* sound like a term of endearment. He reached up and tugged at the silk ribbon holding my mask onto my face; it slipped off and fell to the ground. He lowered his head, and I eagerly rose up on the tips of my toes to meet his kiss. I closed my eyes, tilting my head back, expecting and wanting what I knew would come next.

Except his lips never met mine.

Instead, his breath tickled my ear as he whispered, "Dance with me."

CHAPTER 24

I s that a request from a friend or a command from a prince?" I asked.

"A request," he said softly. He tilted his head, waiting for my answer. "Even though I'm a prince, I've learned that it's hard to command you to do anything."

Our eyes met—his teasing, mine entirely confused. I was certain my face had turned as crimson as my dress when I realized how I must have looked anticipating his kiss. Biting my lower lip, I nodded. For better or worse, I wanted this dance. Alexander swept me up into the waltz the orchestra played, and my skirts swirled around us.

"We've never shared a dance with each other before," he said.

I accidentally stepped on his foot after missing a step.

"Ah." He pulled me tighter into him with a chuckle. "Now I can see why."

"Sorry. I-I'm just a little..."

"Yes?"

"Disoriented."

"Because you thought I was going to kiss you just now?"

"No. Yes." I missed another step. "No. I mean—"

"I was afraid I might scare you off again if I did, so I settled for a dance. No harm in a dance, right?"

No harm in a dance? His hand on my waist was sending sparks of something dangerous up my spine. At least if he had tried to kiss me I might have been able to run away afterwards. Instead, I was locked into his embrace and pressed close to him like a lifeline. No harm, indeed.

"Speaking of," I said as he spun me out and back into his arms. "You should not have kissed me on the road last week."

His eyebrows rose. "I heard no complaints from you at the time."

I clenched my teeth, steeling myself against his charm. "Well, you are hearing them now."

Alexander came to an abrupt stop, and I had to stop myself from crashing into him. He released me as if my skin scorched his hands like white hot metal, baffled at my reaction. "I've never met a girl who denies such an obvious attraction like you do."

The orchestra's music gently wafted over the night, a distinct contrast against my racing heart as I tried to sort out my feelings for the young man that stood across from me. I felt as if I was suffocating on nothing and everything all at once. I couldn't catch my breath, and I couldn't stop a sudden dizziness from circling around me like a cyclone. I tried to cling to something sturdy to help me remain standing, but there was nothing around me—save Alexander—and clinging to him induced an entirely different wave of dizziness and heavy breathing.

"Are you feeling okay?" he asked.

"Just stay back." I ran a shaky hand across my face. "I need to think about all of this."

"Perfect," he muttered. "Now I've definitely scared you."

I ignored him as he hovered, close enough to catch me if I did indeed plummet to the ground as we both half-expected me to do, but not close enough to where I'd snap at him for touching me.

"You are making too much of this," he said.

Too much? If my actions were any indication, I was being too cavalier with the situation.

My mind buzzed with questions. *How are you going to fix this? He should have been dancing with Cinderella—not you. She should be the one in his arms, the one he declares his love to tonight.*

"Fliss, are you listening to me?"

Fix this, Felicity. For goodness' sake! Use the brain you profess to have.

I looked at Alexander, which made my resolve weaken. He was not making this easy. He obviously didn't believe me when I told him I didn't love him. That left me with *showing* him I didn't love him.

Fix the mess you've made.

"I do not love you," I whispered.

"So you've said."

Think, Felicity. Fix this, save Valencia.

"The truth is... I love another."

He started toward me but paused mid-step, tilting his head ever so slightly to the side. "I do not believe you," he said.

"It's true."

"No. It's not."

"Yes." I didn't even blink as I replied, "It's true. I'm in love with... Jack."

He let out a bark of laughter. "*Jack?* Be serious."

I said nothing.

Alexander stopped smiling when he noticed my solemn face. "As in my friend *and* cousin Jack?"

"Yes."

He looked off over the balcony, staring into the darkness of the night. It took him a few moments before he finally said, "This is maddening. Why on earth are you saying this?"

"I just felt you deserved to know the truth—"

Alexander's eyes snapped forward, flashing as they found mine. "The truth? Yes, that's a splendid idea. Why don't you *finally* tell me the truth? Your lies grow tiresome, Felicity."

I fought the tears that were forming in my eyes. I could see the hatred start to form on his face. Pure hatred. I never thought he'd look at me that way. "I never meant to lead you on. That was never my intention."

He shook his head so hard I was afraid it might roll off his neck. He let out a frustrating hiss of air. "I don't understand you. Don't you realize I would have given you my crown? I would have asked you to be my queen, my wife. This palace could have been yours and every single thing within its walls." He gestured wildly around him and towards the ballroom. Suddenly, he grew still. "Even my heart. I would have given it to you a thousand times over until the day I died, until there was nothing more to give."

I bit back a sob and forced my face to remain impassive. "Why would you think that's what I wanted? In all our years as friends, I never asked for those things."

The orchestra transitioned to a fast-paced song, which I took as a cue to flee to the ballroom and escape Alexander's stare. I darted around him. If I was going to do what I had to do, I needed to act fast. I ran through the double doors leading to the crowd, looking for Cinderella.

I heard Alexander call my name and his boots *smacked* across the tile with authority as he followed me. I peeked over my shoulder. As soon as he reentered the ballroom, he was swarmed by a flock of maidens waiting for a dance.

"Felicity!" Alexander shouted. "Wait!"

I pressed on.

Across the crowded room, I sought out the glimmer of my mother's wedding dress and the girl wearing it. I ran past the orchestra, dodged the swirling ruffles of petticoats from a cluster of village girls giggling, and avoided making contact with a knight's elbow as he turned to ask a lady to dance. When I finally reached Jack and Cinderella, I practically slid across the polished floor and tumbled into them.

"Fliss, are you all right?" Jack asked. His rusty hair swept over his forehead. I noticed he looked different than I had remembered him—older, darker. He and Alexander had both come back from Avondale with a different air about them. His hazel eyes flashed with concern as he took in my anxious state. "Fliss?" he asked again when I didn't respond.

"Felicity?" Cinderella's eyes widened. "There you are! You look as if you're being chased by an angry mob..." Her voice chattered on, but I ignored her. I knew if I looked at her I wouldn't have the courage to do what I must.

Instead, I glanced up at Jack apologetically. It was now or never.

I'm sorry, I mouthed silently.

He raised an eyebrow.

I stood up on my tiptoes and pulled him down to my level by the collar of his jacket. I placed my lips on his and kissed him, harder than I anticipated. His lips were soft, hesitant, and, surprisingly, warm. I could feel the uncertainty radiating off him.

I pulled him closer, clutching him tightly. I made the kiss count. If not to convince Alexander and Cinderella, then to convince Jack so he wouldn't pull away.

Jack, too shocked to move from my unexpected kiss, stood there stunned. After a few seconds, I pulled away, but my hands continued to clutch his collar. I looked over my shoulder and saw Alexander staring at us from a few feet away where he had come to a halt. His features were schooled in such a way that if he hadn't been forming his fists into tight white balls of fury at his sides, I might not have detected his anger.

The damage was done.

Jack tried to squirm out of my grip, but I held fast. "I love you, Jack," I said loud enough for Cinderella and Alexander to hear, and several other guests surrounding us.

Jack stopped squirming and blinked several times. If the kiss didn't catch him off guard, my declaration did.

"Did you hear me?" I asked, shaking him a little.

He narrowed his eyes. "Oh, I heard you all right. I gather half of the court did, too."

From behind me, Cinderella gasped. She reached out and wrenched her mask off her face to take a better look at the scene before her, and I could see tears forming in her eyes.

Jack reached out for her, but I held on tight and pressed against him.

"Stop it, Felicity," he said, trying to shake me off. "Cinderella, you don't understand—"

"*Enough*," Cinderella commanded in a furious whisper. "I am tired of being used."

"No. Wait. It's not what it seems."

"Enough!" Her cry echoed across the ballroom, sending curious eyes and swiveling heads in our direction. She stomped her foot on the floor, and I feared the thin glass slipper would shatter underneath the sudden force, but it held strong. "I am tired of being used," she repeated.

She stood there silently for a moment, looking between Jack and me. The hurt was visibly etched across her face. It wasn't the anger I had seen from Alexander; it was something much worse and more akin to betrayal.

"Cinderella," Jack said, attempting to reach for her again.

"No," she whispered. "Stay away from me." When she could no longer stomach the humiliation, she turned on her glass heel and ran away. Her slippers hit the floor and made a quiet *click clack* as she ran from Jack's side. She bumped into Alexander on her way out of the ballroom.

"I'm sorry," she whispered.

Sensing her unease, Alexander steadied her.

Their eyes locked.

I held my breath, pleading with Fate to make them see each other in the same light that I saw them in separately. It was as if the ballroom melted away and the only two people in it were Alexander and Cinderella, while I, a spectator looking through a window, watched as their world and mine came together and fell apart in one pivotal, magical moment.

Alexander tilted his head and stared at her, taking in her beautiful features and sparkling white dress. "*Who are you?*" he whispered reverently.

Cinderella straightened. "No one. No one at all."

She tore away from his grasp and fled the ballroom, a sob of pain following her. Alexander's gaze trailed after her as she left the room. He had *finally* noticed her. Something immediately changed about him when he looked at Cinderella. I saw it in his eyes. More importantly, I felt it in my heart.

Now came the crucial part of the story—the part that perhaps would go down in history as the turning point of the fairy tale. I silently willed Alexander to follow her. I willed him to go after her and forget about me. Alexander watched Cinderella's figure disappear into the night. He looked back at me, questioningly. Then he looked to where she had vanished, as if he was trying to decide between the two of us whom he wanted to pursue.

After a moment's hesitation, Alexander ran after Cinderella. He did the one thing I knew a prince in a fairy tale wouldn't be able to resist. He chased after the damsel in distress.

CHAPTER 25

J ack spun around to face me, his eyes filled with thunder. "What exactly do you think you are doing?"

I took him by the hand and pulled him through the milling crowd and their unforgiving stares. He followed me, reluctantly, out onto the balcony where Alexander had professed his love only minutes before. Had it only been minutes? It seemed like a lifetime ago.

"What is going on?" he asked. He pulled away from my grip. "I need to go after Cinderella—"

"Don't go after her," I pleaded. "Let her go."

"Not likely." He paused and peered down at me. "I'm not sure what all of that was about, but I know you don't love me. It was all a show."

I lifted my chin a little defensively. "Well, I *might* love you."

"Liar." Jack rolled his eyes. "You gave a stunning performance. However, I know Alexander's the one you have feelings for. Are you going to explain what's going on?"

I huffed loudly and leaned against the railing. It was no use denying my feelings for Alexander. "I can't explain everything to you, but you should know there was a reason for my madness."

"Reason? There had better be a spectacular reason, because Alexander will probably never speak to me again,"

Jack pointed out. "The girl he loves did kiss me and declare her love for me in front of an entire ballroom of people... on his birthday, no less. That's not something he's likely to forgive."

I gazed out over the balcony, and, after finding what I suspected we'd be able to see if we came out here, I pointed and said, "Look!"

Alexander and Cinderella were sitting together on the steps of the palace, and we both instinctively leaned over the railing to watch. Moonlight washed over them, bathing them in a celestial light that seemed to pour through the starry sky. Night-blooming jasmine grew on the nearby trellis and its simple scent floated over the balcony. The white flowers reminded me of Cinderella. They were a rarity, capable of blooming despite the darkness that surrounded them.

"What do you think they are talking about?" Jack asked.

"How much they hate me?"

"Alexander could never hate you."

"Did you see the look he gave me before he left the ballroom? He hates me."

"Of course I saw the look, as it was also directed at me."

We watched them silently as several more minutes ticked by, and I truly did wonder what they were discussing. Was Alexander asking her where she lived or about her family? Was Cinderella asking him about his birthday or what it was like to be a prince? Were they truly talking about me?

"I can't be with her, can I?" Jack asked, more to himself probably, after watching Alexander lean forward and whisper something in Cinderella's ear that made her laugh. "I suppose Alexander will get her. He is the prince, after all." Jack tore his eyes away from the couple below us, refusing to look at the scene anymore. "I must ask *why* though. Why did you think it was so important for them to be together that you were willing to ruin two of your closest friendships?"

"Because all of this," I swept my hand out over the dark horizon of Valencia and then gestured across my body to the palace, "hangs in the balance if Alexander doesn't marry Cinderella. I know it seems unlikely, and I am truly sorry I can't give you a better explanation, but it has to be this way."

"I want the truth."

Jack's demand sounded so much like Alexander's earlier one that I jumped a little. Didn't they know the truth was complicated and almost impossible to explain?

"You would never believe me if I told you the truth, Jack. Things have been happening lately that can't be explained with mere words, and, trust me, I'm pretty good with words. After all, I am a librarian."

Jack took a step towards me, taking one of my trembling hands in his. "Fliss, I've seen something, too... something unfathomable. I found..."

"Yes?" I leaned forward curiously. "You found what?"

Jack dropped my hand. "Let's just say I found something I can't explain with mere words myself. It was something, for lack of a better word, *magical*."

"Magical?" I echoed. Something crept up my spine, something that sent several warning signals to my brain to tread cautiously. "What did you find?"

"What would you say if I found a realm of giants on the other end of a beanstalk?" Jack shot me a sideways glance. "Would you laugh in my face and call me crazy?"

I froze. How did Jack know about the giant realm, about any other realm besides the one the humans lived in? I forced my voice to remain calm as I asked, "How did you find this realm?"

"You don't think I'm crazy?"

"How did you find this realm?" I asked again, louder this time.

"I was in the right place at the right time."

"How fortuitous."

I leaned against the railing once more, trying to sort things out. Jack always seemed to be in the right place, at the right time. My mind started racing, linking together pieces that had been missing from a puzzle. Jack had been with Cinderella and I during the attack in the forest. He had escaped without so much as a scratch, even though I had almost been killed and Cinderella nearly abducted. Jack had been the first to alert me about Max slipping into unconsciousness during the queen's dinner party. Had that been a coincidence or had he played some role in plotting Max's demise? Jack had been mysteriously missing for days, choosing to stay behind in Avondale, a kingdom riddled with secrets, even after Alexander had left. Yet he had somehow managed to show up at the ball and woo Cinderella the very night the kingdom's destiny was set to change, a destiny he could alter if he succeeded in having Cinderella fall in love with him and not Alexander.

Surely not...

I tipped my head back to look at him. "Tell me it's not true," I whispered.

"What's not true? The giant realm? No, it's quite true."

I shook my head fiercely. "Tell me you aren't behind all the attacks."

His brows furrowed. "What attacks?"

"The one in the forest a few weeks ago. Max's unexplained illness. What about the one on the road last week that could've killed Alexander?" I stepped away from him. "Was that your doing too? Is that why you *pretended* to stay in Avondale, so you wouldn't be accused of being the mastermind behind another attack?"

A shadow crossed his face. "What are you talking about? You think *I* orchestrated those horrible things? For crying out loud, I'm a knight, sworn to protect this kingdom, not destroy it."

"It's no secret you are jealous of Alexander," I countered. "It's also no secret that you are next in line for the throne if something were to happen to him."

There was a deafening silence. It filled a chasm between us. I hadn't stopped to consider the weight of my words and the accusation they held. Only the whispering wind and the rustling noise from the ballroom echoed in the background.

"Are you serious?" His whisper was like a fierce blade, slicing through the silence. "You actually think I would put you, Alex, and Cinderella in harm's way? The three people I care about most in this world?"

"I-I don't know. There are too many coincidences, and you *are* next in line for the throne."

"Yes, but I wouldn't try to *kill* Alex! He's family," Jack practically growled. "Listen to yourself. Have you gone mad? Do you know me at all?"

"I know you were trying to sabotage his fairy tale!"

"What are you talking about?"

My breath caught in my throat. I couldn't breathe. It felt as if someone had punched me in the gut. My next question came out in a choppy whisper. "Was it you all along?"

Jack said nothing, but he continued to look at me as if I'd lost every ounce of sense I'd ever possessed.

I had to find Cinderella and Alexander to warn them. I turned to flee, but Jack pulled me back before I could escape. His hand gripped my wrist.

"You've got it all wrong, Fliss."

"Let me go."

"You don't know what you are saying."

"Let me go!"

He released me, and his hand fell numbly to his side. This time I did make my escape. I could feel his eyes on me as I sprinted to the double doors that led back to the ballroom. I had to find Cinderella and Alexander, to warn them.

I flew past the guests who stood on the side of the ballroom waiting for a turn to dance. My satin skirt and petticoats kept getting caught under my slippers, so my exit was not as graceful as Cinderella's had been, but it was no less dramatic. I caught the queen's questioning stare from across the room, but I didn't stop to explain what was going on. I didn't stop to explain that her nephew was possibly a traitor to the crown and his family.

I raced outside to the palace steps. When I arrived on the landing, in a tangle of satin, I noticed Cinderella and Alexander were gone. Instead, a lady sat on the steps where they had been earlier. She seemed small and her back was hunched over.

"Excuse me," I called out. "Have you seen the prince? He was just here a few minutes ago. You see, I'm looking for him."

The lady looked up at me. I blinked, shocked to find that it was Cressida. Her tears streaked through the charcoal lining her eyes and the rouge applied to her cheeks. Her brown curls fell limp over her shoulder, as if she had been running her hands through them all night. She sniffed loudly as she replied, "I know who you were looking for."

How close was it to midnight? What if I hadn't arrived in time? "Yes. Well. Have you seen him? It's important that I find him—"

"Seen him? *Seen him?*" Her voice was high and shrill. She stood up, swiping at her tears angrily. "Yes. I saw him with *her*."

Icy dread chilled my bones. I silently prayed she hadn't seen Cinderella too. "Who?"

"*Cinderella*," she spat. "All along I thought *you* were my biggest competition for his affections, but it turns out it was my stepsister—the scullery maid! Oh, how the court will relish my embarrassment. Thankfully, my mother has already gone home. If she were still here and had seen that brat cozying up to the prince..." Cressida shuddered. "Well, there's no telling what she'd do. I'm going to find my sister and we are leaving."

I stifled a groan. *If Lady Maura is already at the manor, she'll know Cinderella's missing.*

Cressida stalked up the stairs.

I chased after her. "Wait. If you saw them, where did they go? It's important that I find the prince."

"To believe that I thought she wasn't a threat," Cressida muttered to herself, ignoring me. "She is nothing but a maid."

I took the stairs two at a time to keep up with her swift pace. "Listen to me—"

She turned sharply to face me, nearly knocking me down the steps. "Listen to you? I shall listen to no one else from this moment on. That's what got me into this mess. To think that I *listened* to Lady Alana." She huffed in frustration. "She convinced me to persuade Lord Reginald to marry Cinderella."

A new piece of information in her enraged prattle caught my attention. "Hold on a moment."

"She told me I had a chance of marrying the prince. If I hadn't listened to her, then I might at least be somebody's wife right now!"

I paused as the weight of her words sunk in. In another instant, I was chasing her up the stairs again. "Wait. What did you say about Lady Alana? Why would she care if Cinderella married Lord Reginald?"

"How do you know my stepsister? Never mind. I don't want to know."

"Why would Alana care if Cinderella married Lord Reginald?" I asked again.

Cressida batted away my question with the flick of her hand. "Does it matter?"

I grabbed her wrist to hold her back. "Yes! It does!"

She shook me off with a grimace. "I had an offer of marriage from Lord Reginald. I detested him at first, but he was wealthy enough to tempt me even if he was only nobility and not royalty. Lady Alana convinced me to turn his interests toward my stepsister and set my sights on the prince instead. That's all. I've been played a fool. Now I've lost the prince *and* a wealthy suitor to that wench."

Thinking I had heard her wrong, I started to ask her to explain again, but a soft black mist appeared and enveloped the air around us, pouring over the stairs like the fog from a cauldron.

The mist was so dense it caught Cressida's attention too and she reached out to touch it. "What is this?" The mist swirled around her fingertips.

"*No,*" I said under my breath. Horror crashed into me, and I suddenly knew what *creatures* this mist belonged to. "This can't be happening again. Not here. Not tonight."

I heard a low laugh echo from somewhere behind us. The sound rumbled over the night, and I turned quickly to see where it was coming from.

Cressida frowned. "Did you hear that?"

We heard the laugh again, louder this time. The guests milled around inside the ballroom, but they sounded as if they were miles away.

All I could see was the black mist. It swept up over my face and swirled around my body like slick steam rising off a murky swamp. Cressida coughed after she inhaled some of the foreign substance.

"Not again," I whispered, turning to run up the stairs. I pulled Cressida along with me, but our steps were uncertain and wobbly as the mist churned into smoke that clouded the air around us.

Several of the monstrous figures that had attacked me in the forest appeared from almost thin air, slithering up the steps with purpose. A thick, tangible fear swept over me. I felt my pulse quicken and the overwhelming urge to scream bottled up inside my throat. I took an uneasy step back as the cloaked creatures surged forward.

One lunged at me, wrapping its claw like hands around my arm.

Cressida fell as one tackled her.

My sudden scream echoed across the night much in the same way the mysterious laughter had moments before. I tried to run, but the creature threw me to the stairs, replying to my scream with a deafening screech of its own. It pinned my arms above my head, gnashing at my face with jagged teeth as black liquid seeped between its gums and fell onto my cheeks. I screamed again, louder this time, while I kicked and squirmed underneath the dark cloak of the monster. My foot knocked its sword from its grasp.

"Help us!" I screamed. "Someone help us!" I kneed the creature above me in the middle, and it shrank back in anger. I rose to my feet as more black mist twisted up and around my body, wrapping around me like wayward vines on a decaying tree. I reached for the creature's fallen sword, only to be thrown back to the ground. My body bounced as it hit the hard steps and my head felt as if it would roll off my shoulders.

I blinked, dazed by the fall.

A smaller, thinner hooded figure arose from the haze and walked forward, gliding seamlessly up the marbled stairs. The mysterious laughter, strong and clear, snapped across the night like cracks of lightning.

I knew then who was behind all of this, and it was not Jack.

"Oh, Felicity. Isn't this a predicament?" a female voice rang out. The figure laughed again, taunting us. She reached up and pulled down her hood. Lady Alana showed her face beneath the shroud.

"*You* are behind all of this!" I shouted, scooting backward up the steps, painfully.

Alana inclined her head regally.

"How could you betray the royal family after they welcomed you into this court?"

Alana had sent the monsters to attack Jack, Cinderella, and myself in the forest after seeing me the day before with the fairy tale in the garden. She was the one who had brought a deathly sickness upon Max to weaken my defenses, to weaken my spirit so I might abandon the fairy tale. She was the one who had tried to have me killed again on the road last week. She had been behind the ploy to get Lord Reginald to marry Cinderella, yet another way to sabotage the fairy tale.

I shook my head angrily and lunged for the sword again, but she pinned my hand to ground by smashing the heel of her boot into my knuckles. I cried out in agony as tears threatened to fall.

Alana kicked the sword away with her other boot, amusement lingering on her exquisite features. "Always ready for battle, aren't you, little librarian?"

The heel of her boot dug harder into the back of my hand, and I bit my lip until it bled to hold back another cry.

"What is going on?" Cressida cried. She rose shakily to her knees. "Alana, what are you doing? Let us go. The guards or other guests will come soon."

Alana laughed so shrilly this time that the cackle skewered through the night. "Simple, foolish, Cressida. Do you think this is not part of my plan?" She gestured wildly toward the double doors leading into the ballroom. "Listen to them in there. This court sees and hears nothing but what is before them. They are blinded by the gilded and opulent world they live in, content to be oblivious to all else, and you are one of them. You will have no saviors from the ball come to rescue you. Those people in there could not even rescue themselves if they desired it. As I'm sure you are now aware, since you were the perfect pawn."

I faintly realized the music and the laughter from the ball had not stopped, despite my earlier cries for help. Alana could kill us right now and no one would notice until it was too late.

I tugged my hand out from under her boot with another cry of pain, clutching it to my chest as I slunk away from her.

I ground my teeth together to fight against the throbbing in my fingers. "You realize your folly, correct? You've attacked a lady of the court and personal friend of the royal family. You won't make it out of the palace alive if you harm us."

"Your threats are amusing, but I gather not many people will make it out of the palace alive tonight."

"What do you want?" I croaked. I looked down at my hand in dismay and blood dripped from my wound and onto my dress.

"Why for a certain fairy tale to be stopped, of course. You refused to cooperate with my other methods of sabotage, so I was forced to put a stop to it tonight at the ball."

My hands started to shake, whether from out of fear or anger or pain I wasn't certain. I heard Cressida whimper behind me. "How much do you know about the fairy tale?" I whispered, low enough for only the two of us to hear.

"Everything." She pulled out a long, golden scepter from beneath her cloak. I could feel dark magic hum within it. "Librarian, I know what you are. I know what you are trying to do. Your mother tried to do the very same thing to stop my own mother from coming to power long ago." She paused and shot me a menacing look, fingering the glittering scepter and sliding her hands over the crystal sphere adorning the top of it.

The roaring in my ears was too loud, too overwhelming. *Fix this, Felicity. Fix this.* I fought the urge to run away from Alana and charge her at the same time. It was one of those moments in a person's life when suddenly everything and nothing made sense all at once.

Alana's eyes flitted to Cressida and then back to me. "I intend to stop this fairy tale, to keep this kingdom from the fairies' rule or the humans rule, from anyone's rule other than mine. I intend to succeed where *my* mother did not."

"Your-your mother?" My voice broke at the sudden realization. "Your mother was *Bruna*? Impossible."

At that moment Cressida wrenched away from the monster holding her. She turned to run, but Alana raised her specter and a menacing claw-like hand snaked out from it and clasped Cressida around the neck, holding her in an ironclad grip.

I sprung to my feet. "Cressida!"

"Stay where you are," Alana commanded coolly. "Or she dies."

I froze mid-step.

Alana reached out and brushed a gloved hand across Cressida's cheek, which, to my horror, was turning a shade of purple as she struggled for air. "Don't look so dismayed, librarian. What does it matter if I kill her?"

Cressida made a gagging noise in response as she made futile attempts to pry the claw away.

Alana paced around Cressida, circling her like a vulture stalking its prey.

"*Stop!*" I screamed. I took another step forward, but the magic only seemed to grasp Cressida even more tightly. I paused again, my hands falling helplessly to my side. "Please, Alana, stop this madness. Your fight is with me. You'll kill her."

"As I should. She was supposed to make sure Cinderella married Lord Reginald, but even that was too difficult of a task for her. I needed the stupid scullery maid to marry anyone but the prince. Yet a certain librarian couldn't leave things alone."

I shook my head, tangled curls bouncing around my eyes as I did. My hair had long since come undone and spilled out around my face.

Alana continued. "The humans in this realm really are troublesome, what with Jack trying to thwart my plans with the giant realm and you being so stalwart in your dedication to seeing this fairy tale through to the end. Even after all my attempts to rid myself of you, to either break your bones or your spirit, you managed to evade me at every turn." Her eyes slithered over to mine. "You've made my revenge difficult to complete."

"Revenge," I whispered. The word was bitter in my mouth. "Are you really so filled with hate that you would stoop to kill innocent people?"

The claw tightened around Cressida's neck in answer to my question.

Fix this, Felicity! She's going to die!

I threw myself at Alana, knocking the scepter from her hands and breaking whatever chain of magic was between them. The claw around Cressida's neck disappeared and she slumped to the steps. Alana and I rolled over each other, her black cloak twisting around my ankles and her fingernails scratching at my face.

Enraged, I fought back. I threw punches with my good fist and kicked with my legs. The thickness of Queen Briar's dress and the layers of petticoats somewhat impeded the impact my flailing legs made against Alana. Pretty the dress was, conducive for fighting it was not. I pushed Alana off me with a grunt, rolling over onto my feet.

"Felicity!"

I turned my head at the sound of my name. Jack and two other knights crashed through the doors leading down the staircase, only to freeze on the top step as they took in the shrouded monsters and Alana's form sprawled out before me. I didn't care how much Jack hated me for accusing him of betraying Valencia, I was never happier to see him in my life.

Alana rose to her feet, steaming with rage. She whispered a strand of ancient magic in some unidentifiable language. The actual words were lost on me, though the meaning wasn't. They were dark, dangerous words that held power. She swung her cloak over her body in a dramatic flourish, and in a flash of smoke and mist she and her monsters disappeared. Seconds later a great, seismic wave rolled over the palace and a *boom* that sounded like thunder echoed over the ground. I nearly tumbled down the stairs as the earth shook beneath me.

Jack reached out to steady me and we exchanged a startled glance. The knights surrounding us unsheathed their swords with wary glances of their own. Screams of hysteria erupted from the guests inside the ballroom—the trample of feet and the sound of shattering glass filled the air. Somewhere inside I heard a woman yell for help much in the same manner I had earlier.

We heard another *boom.* It was followed by more screams, more cries, and more pleas of mercy.

Chaos. Mayhem. Destruction.

CHAPTER 26

"What have I done?" I whispered to myself. I watched in a daze as guests began pouring out of the ballroom, pushing and screaming their way past us. Jack seized me by the elbow, so I wouldn't get caught up in the rampage.

A knight helped Cressida to a standing position. Her eyes widened when she saw the guests fleeing the ball.

"Where is my sister?" she asked softly.

Jack tried to propel me down the stairs. "You need to get out of here."

"Where is Agatha?" Cressida said, louder this time. She pulled away from the knight and clasped my hand. "You have to help me find her."

"I haven't seen her," I replied. A frantic duke pushed past me, slamming into my shoulder.

"Please!" Cressida yelled. She tugged on my arm and pointed to the palace. "My sister is in there somewhere!"

Jack tugged me in the opposite direction. "Felicity is leaving now. Both of you are. If you two had any sense, you'd get out while you can."

I looked between the two of them.

Cressida, whose eyes were usually so icy, silently pleaded with me to help her. She looked so helpless, so real, I felt some of my disdain toward her chip away. "*Please*," she begged.

I tried to pull away from his grasp, but Jack's grip was firm. "Jack, I have to stay and fix this. I have to try to help."

"Fix this?" Jack's eyebrows shot up as if I had just told him I was going to fly to the moon.

I used his moment of hesitation to pull away. Cressida and I raced up the stairs to the ballroom with as much coordination as a fish swimming upstream.

Jack caught up with me, shouting over the madness, "Alexander will kill me if he finds out I didn't get you out of this mess!"

"Well, I have to—"

My next sentence was cut off as we squeezed through the ballroom's door, and the deafening blast of hysteria and rampaging screams filled our ears. I shrank back in horror, and Jack stared at the wreckage before us.

The giant chandeliers hanging above the ballroom had fallen and shattered into thousands of jagged pieces of glass. The banquet tables had been turned over, sending platters of foods and fine china plates scattering across the once polished floor. Instruments from the orchestra were strewn about the room, broken and useless. People were still pouring out of the ballroom in pandemonium, fighting their way through the crowd. Alana's minions, with their eerie black armor and horrifying faces, ransacked and attacked.

Cressida shoved past us, shouting her sister's name.

"Wait!" I cried, reaching out to stop her.

I was a moment too late. One of the monsters appeared and grabbed Cressida by the arm, hauling her across the room as she screamed and fought back. Jack charged forward. With a yell of rage, he sank his sword deep into the heart of the monster. The blade slid out of the decaying body covered in thick, black liquid.

"Are you hurt?" I asked, helping Cressida to her feet.

Her only reply was a soft cry as she stared at the ground in horror. I followed her gaze until I saw another girl lying crumpled and still on the floor, and I mourned the fact that perhaps it was too late to do anything.

Cressida touched the dead girl with a shaky hand. "Agatha," she whispered.

"Felicity! Jack!"

I looked up as Queen Briar ran into my view. She sidestepped around the broken china and crystal that littered the floor, worry and confusion etched across her face.

"Your Majesty, you shouldn't be here!" I called over the commotion. I pulled her aside as a windowpane shattered behind her. We ducked as the glass crashed around us, and I felt a shard stick into the soft underside of my arm.

"Where is your guard?" I asked her.

Queen Briar's beautiful blue eyes held none of their usual serenity as she shook pieces of glass from her skirt. "Felicity, what's going on?" she asked frantically. There was an unmistakable edge of hysteria in her voice. "Alana just showed up with all of these awful creatures and started attacking our guests. I don't even know where Frederic is right now or if he's alive... and my son... oh, my son."

An escaping guest pushed past the queen, almost knocking her to the ground. I followed her gaze as she looked down and saw Cressida crying over her sister, whose arms were twisted around her body and her hair matted with blood.

Queen Briar knelt on top of glass and debris. "This poor girl is no older than Alexander," she whispered, pushing back one of the Agatha's bloody curls. She reached out and closed the girl's eyelids, which caused Cressida to sob wildly.

Jack hauled the queen back up to a standing position. "Aunt Briar, you must leave. It's not safe in the palace right now."

"Jack, dear, it's not safe anywhere right now." The queen turned to me. "Does this catastrophe have something to do with the fairy tale?"

I nodded, pulling Queen Briar closer to me and away from Jack. I whispered, "Alana is Bruna's daughter. She's out for revenge against Valencia. She seems to think if she intervenes, then the fairy tale won't be able to succeed, giving her control over the kingdom instead of the fairies."

Jack stepped between us. "*Your Majesty*, I must insist, as a knight of the realm and your nephew, that you leave immediately."

"What needs to be done?" the queen asked me, ignoring Jack.

"I need to find Cinderella, the girl Alexander left with earlier. I need to get her out of here. She has to leave before midnight." We both glanced at the mangled clock on the wall. It was twenty minutes until twelve.

"We don't have much time," Queen Briar said with quiet determination. She reached down and picked up a fallen sword. She looked as though she had every intention of coming with me to find Cinderella.

"*We?* Your Majesty, do you know how to use that?" I asked, pointing to the sword in her hands.

"You don't think you were the only person Alexander taught how to use a sword?"

"Fair enough." I reached down for Cressida's hand, pulling her to her feet. "We need to go."

"I'm not leaving without Agatha!" she demanded, sinking back down on the floor next to her sister.

I groaned. Of course, she would choose now, of all moments, to act like a human being and stir my sympathy for her.

I crouched down next to her and picked Agatha's lifeless body up by the shoulders. "Grab her feet," I ordered Cressida. "Jack, protect the queen. Let's get her out of this place."

We ran toward the palace steps once more. The scene outside was maddening as guests rushed to their carriages, collapsing over each other and spooking the horses as they struggled to leave. My eyes scanned the crowd. Where were Cinderella and Alexander?

Cressida released her sister, setting her feet gently down on the ground. "They went to the courtyard," she said, as if she could read my thoughts.

"What?"

"If you are looking for the prince and my stepsister, they went to the courtyard. Before you met me on the stairs earlier, I saw them go that direction. I was angry and didn't want to tell you the truth."

I laid Agatha's body into her outstretched arms. "Thank you," I whispered.

A tear dropped from her eye as she stroked her sister's face. "No. Thank *you*."

"Come on," the queen urged me. "If they are in the courtyard, we need to find them."

I nodded once to Cressida and then took off after Jack, who had already started toward the courtyard, ducking and weaving in and out of the crowd. Queen Briar kept up with me step for step. Determination lined her lovely features, and she gripped the weapon in her hand tightly.

Just as we turned the corner into the courtyard, we heard Cinderella's cries ring out across the night.

We all froze at the courtyard's entrance. Cinderella was surrounded by a swarm of Alana's minions, but she stood over a body, protecting and shielding it with her own. The long cascading branches of a weeping willow dipped down over her face, but they did nothing to muffle her cries. The creatures inched closer to her, their swords drawn, and still she would not abandon her position.

I noticed then who she was guarding. Alexander's body was lying on the ground, unmoving; a dark crimson gash on his side marred his once pristine jacket.

The queen saw her son's body, too. "Alexander!" she yelled, agony seeping into her voice.

Please, I prayed. *Let him not be dead. Let him live.* Though even as I uttered my prayer, I remembered Katrina's words from that stormy night weeks ago: *If you steal from Death now, it will certainly steal from you later.* Was this my punishment from stealing Max back from Death? Had I sacrificed Alexander's life instead?

Cinderella shrieked in pain. One of the creatures grabbed her by her hair, jerking her into its slimy arms.

Jack darted forward, but Queen Briar held him back.

"Enough!" the queen shouted at the monsters. "Let the girl and my son go."

They creatures turned their hollowed in heads around to face us, murmuring to each other in their low, foreign language.

Cinderella looked at me helplessly. Her arm was twisted behind her back, and she winced as she whispered, "Help us."

I started towards them, but the queen pulled me back, too.

"Let the girl and my son go," the queen repeated, handing me over to Jack. "And perhaps you shall live if you obey my command."

"Bold words from a queen whose palace is falling right before her eyes."

We spun around and found Alana standing behind us, closing off the only exit from the courtyard.

Panicking, I took a step back and crashed into Jack's chest.

We're trapped.

"We welcomed you into our home," Queen Briar said, the sword in her hand shaking. "I trusted you, Alana. My son trusted you."

"Obviously, your son is a fool," she replied, gesturing to Alexander's fallen body. She watched Cinderella struggling under the grasp of her captors and grinned wickedly.

"If you've killed him, I swear—"

"You'll what?" Alana gestured to the queen's sword. "Run me through with your little blade? I'd like to see you try. I'll enjoy watching the spineless, meek Queen of Valencia meet the same end as her son."

A storm passed over the queen's usual tranquil face. "Why are you doing this?"

"The fairies aren't the only realm who want the humans under their control." Alana turned to address her minions, flicking her wrist. "I see you've already killed the prince. Kill the girl, too."

Cinderella moaned and dropped to her knees.

"*No!*" I shouted, wrenching from Jack's grasp. I began to run towards Cinderella, but Alana raised her scepter and a bolt of lightning rose out, striking the ground in front of me. The earth shook under my feet and I fell to my knees.

I heard a clash as Queen Briar's sword rose to meet the scepter; the *clang* of the two metals meeting rang across the night. The queen pushed against Alana with a grunt. For a moment, she looked like some mystical goddess as she wielded the sword around, the silver blade flashing as it caught a beam of moonlight.

Jack started toward the fight, his own blade unsheathed, but Queen Briar called out, "Stay back! She's mine!" Her sword caught the side of Alana's hip, slicing into it.

Alana screamed as she felt the sword's edge. She reached down and touched the blood that pooled from her side, her face contorting with rage. Queen Briar, more confident now, attacked again but with too much force, and Alana used the queen's momentum to her advantage. She swerved under Queen Briar's next blow and her scepter came crashing down across the queen's head. Alexander's mother crumpled instantly to the ground in a heap of silky skirts. I pushed myself to my feet, horrified to see a trickle of blood sliding down the queen's temple. Her body went suddenly still, and I feared the worst.

Alana turned to Jack, sneering triumphantly. "Your family is dying off by the minute."

"*You are a monster!*" I screamed.

"And *you* have been a nuisance since the moment I laid eyes on you!" Alana shouted.

She raised the scepter again, but I darted out of the way, tucking and rolling onto the ground, before her magic could hit me. The magic ricocheted off a marble statue of King Frederic, sending stone and debris hurtling in every direction. A piece of stone collided into the monster holding Cinderella, knocking it off its feet and taking her to the ground as well. I ran toward Cinderella and pulled her up.

Grasping Cinderella's arm, I yelled, "Come on! You need to get out of here!"

Using his adrenaline from the fight, Jack picked up Alexander and hoisted his body over his shoulder with relative ease.

They followed me as we threw ourselves behind a fountain in the middle of the courtyard.

"You cannot hide forever," Alana called out. "Though it does make the chase more fun for me."

Jack placed his cousin's body against the fountain. I crawled over to him, placing my hand over the wound in Alexander's side to apply pressure. For the first time since entering the courtyard, I let myself consider the option that he might really be dead. His face was gray, ashen, his body frighteningly still. This lifeless person was not my Alexander. My Alexander was a force to be reckoned with.

"No, no, no," I whispered frantically. Thick tears blurred my vision. "This is not how your story ends, Alexander. You are supposed to live."

Cinderella muffled a sob. "He stepped in front of a blade that was meant for me when those things attacked us. He saved my life."

Jack reached out and placed two fingers against Alexander's neck. His eyes brightened for a moment. "There's a pulse. He's only passed out. He's lost a lot of blood."

New hope surged within me just as the ground started to shake beneath us. Alana's rage and dark magic radiated off her as we heard her call out ancient spells, and our bodies shook as we fought to remain low to the ground. The sky swirled with dark mist and bolts of lightning crashed from black, angry looking clouds, striking the ground mere feet from where we were. Instinctively, I hunched over Alexander's body, shielding him from whatever else Alana was about to throw at us.

Cinderella's eyes widened in fear as she whispered frantically, "Felicity, what is going on?" She peeked over the fountain. "We cannot leave the queen—"

I yanked her back down as another deadly burst of magic shot in our direction.

"Listen to me," I ordered. "I'm going to create a diversion to distract Alana. When that happens, you must run. You must escape this place as soon as you can. Stop for nothing or no one. If you can't find Thomas with the carriage, run home. Don't turn back for—"

"What about you?"

I shook my head. "No! Did you hear me? Don't even turn back for me." I turned to Jack. "You must go with her. Make sure she leaves the palace before midnight."

Cinderella looked over her shoulder toward the courtyard's exit. Her eyes focused on it as if she were in a trance.

Jack glanced at Alexander. "I can't leave—"

"I believe you, Jack," I whispered, cutting off his sentence. I tore at the petticoats under my dress, wrapped the strips of cloth around Alexander's middle, and spoke quickly as I worked. "I believe you about the giants and the beanstalk. Whatever you've seen or whatever you've done, I believe you." I grasped his hand and placed it over Cinderella's, pulling her attention back to us. "Now you must believe in me. You must trust me when I say that it is crucial Cinderella gets out of here."

I had to get Cinderella to leave before midnight. There was still a chance I could save the fairy tale—to preserve Valencia. It was better for the fairies to control Valencia from a distance with their fairy tales than to have Alana control Valencia from the throne with her dark magic and her obsession with revenge.

"Do you understand?" I asked them both, more urgently this time.

Jack nodded.

"Y-y-yes," Cinderella stammered. "I mean, no—but I trust you. I always have."

I brushed Alexander's hair out of his eyes before I left my friends, hoping this would work, and began inching around the fountain on all fours, crawling over clods of dirt and the remains of the statue. Stray pieces of stone stabbed into my knees and the dirt felt damp and slimy beneath my palms.

"You think you can stop me, librarian?" Alana called out into the night. The ground shook even harder, and my body tensed under the strain of trying to stay upright. "Well, you cannot. You are not your mother, and I am not mine."

Another bolt flew from Alana's scepter, this time taking off the top of the fountain. The explosion made my ears ring. For a moment, all my senses shut down and there was only the constant ringing. Icy water sloshed over onto my dress, spurring my senses back to life and drenching me while adding more weight to my thick petticoats. I paused and covered my head with my hands as more debris broke off. I felt a shock of pain as stone pelted me and a jagged edge grazed the side of my head. Warm blood trickled down my face, a stark contrast to the frigid fountain water, which continuously lapped over the edge of the fountain as I inched around it.

Alana started toward the side of the fountain where Cinderella and Jack were crouched and Alexander's body lay, and before she could raise her scepter once more, I shot to my feet and sprang forward. I threw myself into Alana, pummeling her from behind. Our bodies rolled over each other, but she landed on top of me.

"You fool!" she whispered with venom.

From the corner of my eye, I made out Cinderella's silvery form dashing across the courtyard with Jack in close pursuit. She had a slight limp in her step, and she stumbled to the ground. Before Alana could raise her scepter and catch Cinderella in her moment of weakness, I lunged for it. We both struggled over control of the scepter. My arm muscles screamed as Alana tried to yank it from my grasp.

Buy her time, my mind urged me. *Buy Cinderella enough time to get away. Fix this. Fix this. Fix this.*

Alana hit me hard across the face, and my grip on the scepter loosened from the pain of my teeth biting down on my tongue and the sheer shock of her action.

Alana pulled herself off me but kept the scepter pointed at my head. I saw the vengeance in her eyes, the determination—and fear. Perhaps she was just realizing Valencia could not—*would not*—be taken so easily.

Despite the circumstances, I breathed an easy sigh of relief as I noticed one thing that gave me a small ray of hope: Cinderella had escaped.

Alana laughed as she shoved her scepter at me once more. The tip of the sharpened crystal adorning it was inches from my throat, prepared to slice if the need arose.

She hummed an ancient language under her breath, the same one she had used earlier to summon dark magic. Her words floated through the night as if they were one with the impenetrable black mist that continued to plague the air. A white orb of light poured out from her scepter, shining brilliantly against the mist.

I knew whatever was next would prove to be fatal. I thought of all the people I still needed to say goodbye to before I left—Max, Katrina, Cinderella, Queen Briar, Jack... *Alexander*—and my heart lurched painfully in my chest.

Alana moved the scepter an inch and tipped my chin up with the end of it, smiling. I wanted to run, but I dared not for fear she would follow me and recapture Cinderella.

Give her time to get away.

Alana pressed the pointed crystal into the tender flesh under my neck. I felt blood, hot and sticky, seep down my throat. Then, to my utter shock, she whispered something that frightened me more than any ancient magic she might have summoned. "You could join me," she murmured.

Startled, I gazed at her with wide eyes. "Join you?"

She chuckled. "I guess it never occurred to me what we might accomplish together."

"What?"

"Join me," she urged once more. "Maybe this doesn't have to end with your death. In fact, I'd rather it didn't end with your death." She ran a finger down my cheek, stopping at the pulse in my neck, an idea sparking to life in her eyes. "Knowing what I know about you, about your family, I think I'd rather have you as an ally than as an enemy."

Family. Was she referring to my mother? Was she referring to my *father*?

"What do you know about me?" I whispered. Then, coming to my senses, I answered, "It doesn't matter. I would *never* join you."

I closed my eyes, so that at least in the end I would not have to see Alana's face crowing over me, but she didn't move to harm me.

"Dear librarian, we'll see about that." I could hear the smile in her voice.

Whoosh.

Just then I heard the distinct sound of a sword sliding out of its sheath. My eyes popped open to find Alexander standing behind Alana. Though he swayed slightly on his feet and his face was ashen, he pointed the tip of his sword towards her throat with precision.

Alana lowered her scepter an inch.

"I would think hard before you kill her," he whispered in a dark, vicious voice that sounded nothing like him. "I can assure you, the repercussions will be quite painful."

"Your threats do not scare me, Your Highness."

He pressed the tip of his sword into her flesh though he did not draw blood.

Alana wavered a moment, peering into his eyes to weigh the depth of his threat. "Very well." She lowered her scepter completely. "I promise not to kill your librarian," she whispered.

At that moment, I heard Queen Briar begin to stir. I looked over my shoulder to watch her sit up slowly. Blood continued to drip from the cut on her forehead, but she was alive and able to move.

She saw that her son was also alive, and a shaky smile spread across her face. "Alexander," she whispered through tears.

There was a shout beyond the courtyard, the sound of footsteps running closer to us, someone calling out Queen Briar and Alexander's names. I heard King Frederic's voice, loud and clear.

He was coming for us. We would be saved.

A flash of relief surged through my veins.

"It sounds as if your monsters have not managed to take all of Valencia," I said.

Alana glanced from me to the queen—her eyes darting between the two of us. "I promised not to kill the librarian..."

Alexander's hand tightened around the hilt of his sword. "Stand down, Alana. You don't have much time before this courtyard is swarming with guards. You can fight off a few, but you won't be able to take them all down. You'll eventually have to answer to the king's justice for the crimes you've committed tonight."

"I promised not to kill the librarian," she said again, louder this time.

I realized a moment too late what was about to happen. "NO!" I screamed.

Quick like the flash of one of her lightning bolts, Alana shoved the end of her scepter into the wound in Alexander's side. He let out a terrible yell as he fell to knees and dropped his sword. Alana raised the crystal end of her scepter and another final blast of magic shot from it. There had been no time to prepare, and the flash of light, bold and brilliant, charged into the center of Queen Briar's chest—and the queen collapsed once more.

Alana laughed evilly, like a crazed madwoman half out of her mind. Her face twisted manically and her eyes flashed as her cackle ricocheted through the night. In her moment of triumph, I charged into her, knocking the scepter from her hands. We wrestled to the ground again. She was strong and fueled by revenge, but I was fueled by something even stronger. I reached for the scepter; it was cold and heavy in my hands. I swung it around in a wide circle, knocking it into her skull with a satisfying *crack*.

Alana crumpled to the ground in a heap of black mist.

"Mother!" Alexander limped toward the queen, wrapping his arms around her. I stared in horror at her unmoving, unblinking face. Her vibrant blue eyes, Alexander's eyes, were still and lifeless. She couldn't be...

Alexander shook his head over and over again. "This can't be..."

"*Briar!*"

I looked up and saw King Frederic running toward his family, a group of guards following. He had arrived, a moment too late, but he had finally found us.

I stared down at Alana's unconscious form—too shocked to say anything. How could she take the life of another with so much ease?

"Briar!" the king called out again. When he reached his wife's side, his cry echoed through the night. He fell to the ground next to his son and his sobs pierced me harder than a thousand arrows aimed at my heart.

Queen Briar was dead.

CHAPTER 27

King Frederic murmured soft pleas, begging his wife to return to him, as he rocked back and forth while pulling her into his arms. I knew then that Queen Briar had been wrong—King Frederic had loved her. They had both realized it too late.

The guards ran to Alana, circling around her form. I dropped the scepter like it was a poisonous snake and backed out of their way. "Your Majesty," one of the guards called to the king. "What should we do with the prisoner?"

The king didn't answer, or maybe he was unable to. He continued to hold his wife.

It was Alexander who spoke up. He stood, squaring his shoulders with authority. "Take her to the dungeon. Post at least two guards with her at all times. Let me know when she awakens. I need to question her before whatever sentence my father decrees is carried out."

As the guards hoisted Alana's ragdoll form away, I began to follow them out of the courtyard. Alexander's eyes were transfixed on the sight of his mother and father before him. As I brushed past him he whispered hoarsely, "Are you hurt?"

I looked down at the scrapes and bruises littering my arms, guessing that I probably had a few more covering my face, but I shook my head.

I gestured to the giant pool of blood on his side. I couldn't imagine how he was still able to stand. "You should see about that wound, though."

He acted as if he didn't hear me and turned away. I watched with overwhelming sadness as Alexander sank down next to his parents and began to cry.

There were many things I was capable of bearing with grace. The sight of my best friend, the next ruler of Valencia, crying over his mother, was not one of them. It was enough to send me over the edge, so I pushed my dirty fist into my mouth to keep from sobbing out loud and fled the scene. They needed to be alone to grieve, and I needed to be alone with the guilt that was welling up inside of me.

As I left the courtyard, the faint sparkle of glass nestled into the damp earth caught my attention. I leaned down to gingerly pick up one of my mother's glass slippers. It must have come off Cinderella as she fled from Alana's attack. I grasped the slipper tightly, it's smooth surface cool against my palm. I clasped it as if it were a memory from a different world, a world that wasn't filled with destruction and betrayal and death.

I trudged up the long staircase to the palace and was acutely aware of the bodies littering the ground around me. I shuddered and held back tears once more. Some were old, some were young, but they were all still bodies. Alana's monsters had vanished, but not before they left proof of their evil behind them. Frantically, my eyes wandered. Where was my uncle? Surely, he wasn't lying amongst the fallen?

"Felicity!"

As if he could sense my panic, I looked up to see Max running down the steps. I picked up my mangled skirts and met him halfway. Max had survived the night! He was alive. When we reached each other, I wrapped my arms around him tightly.

"Thank goodness, I thought you were dead," he whispered. "I've been looking for you."

"Oh, Max." I didn't try to hold back the tears this time. I let them flow freely. "Max, everything is so messed up. I'm not sure what I did wrong or what I could have changed—"

"Hush now," he consoled me. He awkwardly patted my back. "You did everything you could do. This was not your fault."

"Then why does it feel like it is?" I whispered into his shoulder. The soft fabric of his jacket soaked up the tears from my cheeks.

Max pushed me out at arm's length, so I was facing him. He reached down to wipe away a tear that threated to drip off my chin. "Because the pain is still fresh."

"Max, the queen is dead."

"I know. A guard just told me. The entire palace will know soon enough."

The guilt seemed to overpower me. It pierced my aching soul. "I should have been able to do something to stop this from happening. If I had only suspected Alana sooner, the queen might not have died for nothing."

"You cannot control who lives and dies, Felicity," Max reminded me.

"I cannot control anything." I choked back more sobs.

He pulled me back into his arms, and I welcomed the embrace of something familiar.

* * *

Hours later, after we helped the healers tend to the wounded, Max and I headed back to the library. It was early in the morning when I reached my bedroom, sometime just after dawn, and I almost screamed when I caught my reflection in the mirror. I was disgusted with what I saw. There were swollen cuts and dark bruises all over me. My hand, the one Alana had smashed with her boot, was almost unrecognizable it was so black and blue. Thankfully, no bones seemed to be broken. It would be impossible to squeeze it into a fist for days, though.

Queen Briar's dress was torn in almost twenty different spots and covered in blood and dirt. I hastily pulled it off. I threw it to the floor angrily, stomping on it for good measure. Just looking at it reminded me of the queen's death.

I washed the filth from the night off me, bandaged my battered hand, cleaned the cuts on my neck, face, and arms, and changed into a white nightgown.

As I started to pull back the covers to my bed, my eyes caught the flash of silver hanging from the chain around my neck. I fingered my mother's wedding band, tracing over the intricate designs engraved into the metal.

Knowing what I know about you, about your family, I'd rather have you as an ally than as an enemy.

Alana's words rang through my head. What did she know about my family? I clinched the ring tightly. Why had my mother hidden my father's identity from me?

"Who did you fall in love with?" I asked aloud, as if my mother was sitting across the room from me and not long gone from existence. "Would it have been so terrible to at least tell me his name?"

I heard a knock at the door.

"Come in," I called wearily.

Max opened the door. "How are you feeling?"

"About as good as I look."

Max caught me twisting the ring around the chain on my neck. "Rosalind's wedding band," he said softly. His eyes filled with sadness and he sighed deeply.

"Did you know who he was, Max?" I asked. "Tell me the truth. I need to know if you knew who my father was."

Max shook his head. "Rosalind never told me. You have all the information I do."

"And you were okay with that?" I grounded out. "*You were okay with so little information? As a man whose life's work revolves around research and facts, I find that hard to believe.*"

"My sister had returned home. It was enough that she was alive. Everything else seemed unimportant."

"I wonder how he died. I wonder who he was..." I looked away from the ring and found Max staring at me. "Half of me is missing, Max. I don't know who I am," I said.

"You are Felicity. You are a librarian. You are my niece." He shrugged his shoulders. "For now, that's all you need to be." He reached into his jacket pocket and pulled out an envelope. "This just came for you."

"From who?"

"Jack. I told him you were resting though and not to be disturbed."

I reached for the letter, tearing it open with haste.

Fliss,

Cinderella is home safe, for now. She asked that I send you word. Her stepmother and a certain Lord Reginald were waiting for her at the manor. I couldn't make out much of what was said, but I do know there was a fair amount of yelling. Most importantly, Cinderella wanted you to know that her wedding day was moved up to today.

Jack

I reread the letter three times just to make sure I had understood it correctly. After the third time, frustration built up inside me like a violent thunderstorm and I slammed the letter down on my bed, though the satisfying impact I had wanted was somewhat muffled by my quilt containing downy goose feathers.

"What's the matter?" Max asked.

"Only more bad news to top off a spectacularly horrible evening." I thrust the letter into his chest. "Here. Read it for yourself."

A minute later Max looked up. "What are you going to do?"

"I'm going to stop that wedding, that's what I'm going to do." I hastily began rifling around for a clean dress in my trunk. "I'm getting dressed."

"You need rest. You've had a trying day—"

"No!" I snapped. I slammed the trunk lid closed and whirled around to face my uncle. "What I need is to put this fairy tale behind me! I'm going to stop Cinderella from marrying that awful, brutish man."

Max raised an eyebrow, but he didn't argue. "What's your plan?"

"I'm going to tell Alexander the truth."

A throat cleared behind me. "Well, it's about time."

Max and I turned to find Alexander standing in the doorway, leaning against the doorjamb. His shoulders were hunched over, his hair disheveled, and there was no mistaking the red rims around his eyelids. Yet, despite it all, his commanding presence quickly filled my small bedroom.

"Alexander!" I backed up and almost stumbled over my trunk.

I reached for a robe and quickly put it on. When Alexander offered no explanation for his arrival, I spoke, "What are you doing here?"

I noticed he had taken the time to clean up and change out of his formal jacket and pants from the night before. His simple cotton shirt was tucked into dark breeches. He had replaced his polished dress boots for dull, dusty ones that were normally used when he rode out with patrols.

Alexander glanced at Max. "Could you give us a minute? I need to speak with your niece alone."

Max looked to me. "Is that okay?"

"It's fine. Wait down stairs. I'll be along shortly to, um, finish that task I was telling you about."

Max nodded and left without another word. When the door clicked quietly behind his exit, Alexander turned back to me. I gazed up at him, feeling the harsh weight of his stare. I tugged absentmindedly on the sash of my robe to give my hands something to do. I stood there, thinking he might say something first and hoping that he would.

Instead, he narrowed his eyes as he watched me fidget.

I noticed the wound on his side had reopened. It was seeping through the bandage under his shirt, leaving a small splotch of red on the otherwise clean fabric. "Your wound..."

"Forget about the wound. I came for the truth. Imagine my surprise when I came up here and found that you were finally willing to give it to me."

"I'm sorry."

"Sorry for what?"

Without hesitation, I leaned forward and wrapped my arms around him, taking care to avoid his injured side. "For your mother's death. I know what that loss is like. I wouldn't wish it on my enemy and certainly not on you."

He answered my embrace with one of his own. We held each other for what seemed like hours, just grasping—maybe grasping for something intangible too. We rocked side to side, almost as if we were dancing. Even as the world fell apart, everything made sense when I was with Alexander.

"You broke my heart last night," he whispered in my ear.

"I wasn't sure how I'd ever be able to face you again. After the way I treated you at the ball, I just knew you hated me..." I swallowed a lump in my throat. "Then, after what happened to your mother. I thought you might blame me."

Alexander's chin settled on top of my head, and I felt the faint pounding of his heart beneath my cheek through the fabric of his shirt. "There was nothing you could have done."

"It should have been me," I whispered into his chest. My shoulders shook as I choked down a sob. "I was the one who should have died."

His hold on me tightened. "Enough, Felicity. Do you think I want to ponder your death any more than I want to come to terms with my mother's?"

"But—"

"This was not your fault. The blame lies with Alana alone, and I swear on my father's crown she *will* answer for what she has done."

"I should have told Queen Briar not to follow me when I left the ballroom. Perhaps she would be safe now if she hadn't."

"Mother would not have listened. She was famous for making up her own mind."

"I still feel like I could have stopped her. If only I had known—"

"You, my dear, are capable of many things, but you cannot predict the future. I trusted Alana, too. She betrayed us all." He pulled away to look me in the eyes, but his hands remained on my shoulders. There was a warmth to them that I could feel even beneath my robe. "I did not come up here to speak of Alana, though. I'll deal with her soon enough."

I tilted my face up to see him better. "Why are you here then?"

"If last night has shown me anything, it is that life is precious. I lost a lot of things yesterday. But do you know what I fear losing most of all?"

I shook my head.

"Losing you. You said you'd tell me the truth. Tell me here and now if you have any feelings stronger than friendship for me."

I tried to put even more distance between us, but Alexander followed me as I backed away from him. "Well, the truth is I don't."

"So I've heard." Alexander turned his palms out as if he were surrendering something over to me. "*Why?* That's the part that doesn't make any sense. You've never actually given me a reason. What would be so terrible about loving me?"

Nothing. There was nothing terrible about it. Terrifying, yes. Terrible, definitely not.

"Alexander..."

"I need a reason, Fliss. I need to know what's driving you away from me."

He needed a reason. I knew he wouldn't leave without one, and I knew I had to give him the only true reason.

I walked over to the dresser where I kept the copy of *Cinderella* that Max had given me so long ago, and I pulled the book out of the top drawer. I brushed some dust off the cover, which tickled my nose and caused me to sneeze. I turned and beckoned for Alexander to join me on the bed.

"What's this?" he asked curiously. Alexander sat down next to me, his weight caused the bed to groan and sag underneath us, and took the book from me. He flipped through a few of the pages and then made a puzzling face. "There are no words in this book."

"When the story's finished, there will be." I paused, gathering my wits. "I have so much to tell you. I'm not even sure where the proper place to start is."

"The beginning?" he offered.

I smiled as I hugged my knees to my chest, taking every ounce of the boy sitting next to me in before I uttered the words that would change everything and nothing between us. "You should know that I love you. I am tired of denying it because it is so untrue and goes against the deepest desires of my heart. I love our friendship, Alexander. I love the way I can meet your eyes across a crowded room and know exactly what you are thinking. I love how you challenge me. I love that you respect my uncle. I love that you see me as your equal even though I am a librarian."

"Oh, Fliss." He cupped my bruised cheek with his hand. "You were never just a librarian to me."

"Most importantly, I love you for being you and loving me in return." His eyes grew wide and he opened his mouth to reply, but I continued. "Wait. There's more. You should know that I am no ordinary librarian."

"I don't care what you are," he said. "As long as you'll be mine."

He tilted my chin up and his lips pressed soft kisses into every part of my face. "You love me," he whispered as his lips glided over my eyelids, my cheeks, my forehead, and finally my lips. I didn't want him to stop. I wanted to cherish his kisses and stay like this forever: in his arms, holding him close, and running my fingers through his hair until it felt as if we were the only two people left in this world.

"*You love me. You love me. You love me.*" His voice murmured those words repeatedly, until it became almost a mantra, a dizzying mantra that left me breathless. "You love me!" he finally shouted.

I felt a blush stain my cheeks as I hastened to shush him. "Calm down. Max will hear you."

"Let the entire world hear me." His hand trailed down the curve of my neck. He leaned in closer to me. His deep breaths tickled my skin as he whispered, "You love me, and I feel as if my insides will burst from joy."

I swatted his hand away, and Alexander's eyes laughed at my gesture. "What are you more pleased about? The fact that I told you I loved you or the fact that you were right all along?"

"Both."

"I love you, Alexander." I took the book off his lap. "Which is why I must tell you the truth, why we can never truly be together—not in the way we both might want. You are meant to be with someone else."

"Impossible." Alexander shook his head at the notion. "I am meant to be with you. You just said you loved me—"

I placed my fingertips over his lips, silencing him before he could say more. "No. Listen to me. No matter how crazy or ridiculous this story sounds, you *must* hear me out."

Alexander pulled my hand away from his mouth. "What story? Why are you telling me this?"

"Because you have to fix this in a way I cannot. You must go after her. We only have a little bit of time and if I don't tell you the truth now, there's a certain Lord Reginald who is going to ruin the fairy tale."

"You aren't making any sense. Who do I need to go after? Who is Lord Reginald? And did you say something about a *fairy tale?*"

"Yes, the most extraordinary, heartbreaking fairy tale," I answered softly, conceding to my fate. I held up the book. "This fairy tale. Your fairy tale, Cinderella's fairy tale, Valencia's fairy tale, and—in a way—my fairy tale, too."

Then, I did what I promised King Frederic and Max that I would never do. I did what I promised myself that I would never do. I told him about his destiny.

CHAPTER 28

Alexander sat quiet and pensive through most of my tale. I began the story with his father's anxious arrival in the library, followed by Max's revelation about seven different realms and how the fairies tried to control the humans out of vengeance for our past mistakes, and I finished by telling him the details of his own fairy tale.

When I reached the end, I leaned back against my headboard and stared at him. "Well, there you have it."

Alexander took the book from my hand and flipped through its pages. "There are no words in this book. The pages are blank."

"They won't be after the fairy tale is finished. I'm the only one that can read it right now."

"You are saying this is *my* fairy tale?"

"Yes." I sighed and closed my eyes. "Well, yours and Cinderella's, I suppose." I pried one of my eyes open and found him staring at me. "You think I'm crazy, don't you? You think I've lost my mind."

Alexander didn't respond.

"See! I knew it." I snapped up into a straight position. "But you must admit that it does make a little sense, especially after the night we just had. After Alana's attack tonight, you must at least admit that there's such a thing as magic."

Alexander nodded, reluctantly.

"So," I continued, "if there's such a thing as magic then there's got to be such things as fairy tales." I tapped on the book in his hands several times. "This is real."

Alexander's hand stilled my own. "I believe you."

"You do?"

"Of course."

"Why?"

"If it had been anyone else that told me this story, I would have laughed in their face or called them a liar. You've never given me any reason to doubt you, though. Except for when you declared your love for Jack, but I knew that was a lie. It broke my heart and frustrated me to no end, but I was still fairly certain it was a lie."

I tilted my head and my hair spilled down around over my shoulders. "Just as you know this fairy tale is not?"

"Yes." Alexander stood up, and I found his sudden height imposing as he loomed over me. "Though I wish you had confided in me sooner."

"I wasn't allowed to tell you. I couldn't give you a choice. You might have chosen not to follow the fairy tale."

"I wouldn't have done that," he whispered. A stark look of hurt dashed across his face, darkening it for a moment. He was truly offended. "I wouldn't have put all of Valencia in jeopardy. I have more honor and love for this kingdom and its people than that."

"But your father didn't follow—"

"I am not my father, Felicity."

"I-I couldn't take the chance that you might refuse the fairy tale," I said, feeling guilty for assuming he wouldn't put Valencia first.

"But you took it now."

"Only because I had no choice. Cinderella is about to marry another man..."

"And I need to stop her," he finished.

"Yes. To complete the fairy tale."

"To save Valencia."

"To save Cinderella, too," I said. "You have no idea what her life's been like. If any girl needs you to save her, it's Cinderella. That man she's about to marry is a complete brute."

Alexander scratched his chin. "She might not have me, though."

"What?"

"I said Cinderella might not have me."

"Don't be ridiculous," I snapped. "She'll have you. Who wouldn't want to marry a prince when they've lived all their life treated like a slave?"

Alexander shook his head. "She may have no desire to marry me. We only talked for a short while last night. It wasn't long into our conversation before we were attacked in the courtyard. We hardly know each other. How can I stop her from marrying a stranger when in all likelihood she may not even want to marry *me*, someone who is also a stranger?"

I rose to my feet. We faced each other, the rise and fall of our chests synchronized.

"You are called Prince Charming in your fairy tale for a reason," I explained with a sardonic edge in my voice. "Use that charm and convince her to marry you."

"More importantly, how do I propose to one woman when I'm in love with another?"

Our eyes met.

"You do it for Valencia," I whispered.

"Ah, yes. Valencia." Alexander ran his fingers down my arm, stopping when he reached my palm to grasp it within his own. "Are you going to be okay with what happens next? Are you going to be okay if I marry Cinderella?"

"I always knew you could never be mine. This comes as no shock to me."

"You didn't answer the question."

"Yes, I'll be fine." I squeezed his hand, trying to reassure him and desperately trying to reassure myself. "Will *you* be okay? Everything is going to change."

He said nothing for a moment. Instead, he pulled my hand up to his lips and placed the faintest of kisses on it. "It's hard to say. Do I at least get to keep you as a friend?"

"Of course. You will always be my friend. No fairy tale can change that." I brushed an errant lock of hair from his eyes. "In any other lifetime, we would have been good together. If we had been anyone else, it might have worked. If you hadn't been a prince and I hadn't been a librarian..."

"Listen here, we are good together—in *this* lifetime, in the one before us, in the one after us, or in any other. We will always be good together," Alexander said. He tugged on my arm and pulled me toward the door, breaking a moment between us that felt like it was now lost forever.

"Come on," he called over his shoulder.

"Where are we going?" I asked.

"We are going to find Cinderella. We are going to stop this wedding. I believe we have a fairy tale to fulfill."

I followed him, remembering only at the last moment to snatch up my mother's glass slipper before we left to find Cinderella and finish their story.

CHAPTER 29

Where do you think you are going in your nightgown, young lady?" Max asked as we came thundering down into the library. He shut the book in his hands with a distinct *snap*.

Alexander looked down at me. "He's right. We can't have a proper rescue with you dashing about in a nightdress."

"Oh. I didn't realize—" I made a face as I touched the starchy fabric of my gown beneath my robe. "I'd better change first."

"I'll send word down to the stables to see that horses are saddled for us." Alexander strode to the door and opened it with a painful hiss. He clutched his side. "I'd better have a healer bandage this wound again though. It's soaking through my shirt." He peeked over his shoulder. "I'll see you in the stables in fifteen minutes."

After he left, I turned to go change clothes, but Max stopped me. "What's going on?" he asked.

"I'm about to change the course of my life, not to mention Cinderella's and Alexander's, in one fell swoop." I took a deep breath. "We are going to stop Cinderella from marrying that horrid oaf and convince her to marry a prince instead."

Max raised an eyebrow. "*We?*"

I hastened to explain. "Yes, I told Alexander about the fairy tale. I didn't have much of a choice."

Max rubbed a hand over his weary face.

"It was the only way to make him pursue Cinderella."

He slumped down into a nearby chair.

"I didn't see any other way. If you were me—"

He raised a hand, silencing me. "I'm not saying it wasn't a difficult choice to make."

"You aren't saying anything at all."

"I suppose what's done is done. But know there are certain things now that cannot be undone."

"Alexander promised to follow the fairy tale. I believe in him." I turned to go upstairs to my bedroom, stopping at the railing to glance at Max. "He will not make the same mistake as his father."

"Perhaps not. But you have already made the same mistake as your mother by telling the next ruler of Valencia about the fairy tale. Tread carefully, my dear."

Max stared at me with his sharp, unyielding eyes for a long moment before placing the book in his lap on a table. He stood up and started towards the library's exit.

"And where are you going?" I asked.

"You've inspired me to go change the course of my own life. I'll be back later tonight. Don't wait up."

Max left the library without looking back.

* * *

Max's warning to tread carefully still rang through my mind like the blare from a loud trumpet when I left for the stables. I was greeted by the overwhelming scents of hay and manure, the latter of which caused me to wrinkle my nose. Alexander saw me approaching and waved to me over the top of a stall that belonged to a red roan mare.

I turned into the stall and stopped short when I saw Jack saddling the horse. I looked over at Alexander. "What is he doing here?"

"He's coming with us. I told him."

Max's warning in my head went from a trumpet solo to an entire fanfare in the split of a second. "You told him about what precisely?"

"The fairy tale."

I groaned. "What part of keep it to yourself did you not understand?"

Alexander walked around the horse and patted her softly on the nose. "Jack deserved to know the truth after last night. What else was I supposed to say to explain what happened with Alana?"

"Practically anything else!"

Jack leaned over, making a great show of buckling and looping things together, pretending all the while we weren't arguing in front of him.

"You said that the fairy tale pertains to the royal family." Alexander cast a stern glare in my direction, no doubt frustrated with me for rebuking him. "Well, Jack is a part of the royal family," he said before going in search of his own horse.

I bit back another retort. "I suppose what's done is done," I replied, echoing Max's words from earlier.

Jack reached out to help me mount the mare, his hands light and gentle around my waist. I paused before I pulled up onto the saddle. "I'm sorry I accused you of terrible things last night," I whispered.

"Forget it. There's no need—"

"Yes. There is. I shouldn't have accused you of being a traitor, of trying to harm the people you care for or this kingdom. It's unforgiveable."

"I forgive you though."

I hoisted myself into the saddle. "I don't deserve it."

Jack handed me the reins. "I forgive you anyway."

Alexander led his horse out of the stables. "Well, are we ready?" he asked.

I refused to answer his question as I urged my own horse from the stables. "Follow me. I'll lead the way."

* * *

Alexander, Jack, and myself stood before Lady Maura's manor. I hugged my arms around my chest to fight off the cold.

"You didn't need to bring your sword," Alexander said, gesturing to the weapon hanging from my side. "There will be no need for it here. We aren't slaying dragons, you know."

"You haven't met the stepmother yet."

He glanced around the exterior, brows furrowed in thought. "I thought you said there was a wedding going on here? There's only one carriage in the drive."

"They aren't exactly what you would call a celebratory family," I explained.

We had already dismounted and tied up our horses to a nearby tree. I walked down the long drive with the boys on either side of me, the gravel beneath our feet crunching loudly enough that I couldn't even hear myself think. My thoughts crashed into each other, causing one thought to shift to another before my mind could properly wrap itself around the first. But it was Alexander who voiced my biggest concern.

"What if she doesn't come with me?" he whispered.

"Why would she not?" Jack replied.

"I don't know." Alexander dug his hands into his pockets as he kicked at the gravel, probably annoyed with the loud crunching just as I was. "Maybe she doesn't want to marry a complete stranger. Maybe she wants to have a say in her own destiny." He paused for a moment before continuing. "Maybe she loves another."

Jack sighed.

I turned to Alexander. "You should tell her."

"Tell her what?"

"Tell her about the fairy tale."

"Did you or did you not just scold me for telling Jack?"

"Cinderella's going to be your wife, though. Like it or not, she's going to be a part of the royal family. She deserves to know the truth. She deserves to know where your intentions lie."

Alexander thought for a moment, pondering my request. Finally, he said, "No."

"No?"

He charged forward to the front door. "No."

"Be reasonable."

"I am being reasonable. You saw the effects a fairy tale had on my parents' marriage. I won't have Cinderella thinking that she's only required to marry me because of the fairy tale."

"So, you are going to lie to her?"

"I'm going to spare her years of hurt and pain."

"Stop. Wait." I grasped Alexander by his sleeve and pulled him back to me. "You don't know what this girl has been through. You'll hurt her more in the end if you aren't honest. She deserves the truth. Don't treat her as if she were a pawn in all of this."

Alexander plucked my hand from his sleeve and continued toward the manor. "There was always a point of contention between my parents that I could never understand. I finally figured out what it was; it was the fairy tale. My mother left this world thinking that my father didn't love her because he was forced by some book to marry her. I won't have my own wife thinking the same of me."

I chased after him. "She'll find out someday. When she does, she'll never forgive you for keeping something like this from her."

"Felicity." Alexander's voice held a hint of a warning. "Enough."

"Just tell her the truth."

"*Felicity.*"

"If you don't, I will!"

Alexander stopped suddenly, turning around so sharply he almost crashed into me. "I forbid it."

I blinked, shocked by his words. I stumbled back a few paces. "W-what?"

Even Jack looked momentarily startled.

"I forbid you to say anything to Cinderella about the fairy tale."

I shook my head and let a beat of silence slip by between us. "Is that a request from a friend?"

"No, it's a command from a prince. I don't often pull rank on you, but I am today. You *will* obey my command. You are not to say nor hint nor breathe one single, solitary word about the fairy tale to Cinderella. Do you understand?"

"Alexander, you don't—"

"Do you understand?"

"No. You are being stubborn and foolish. I do not understand at all. I will never for the life of me understand why you would keep something like this from Cinderella." I paused and bit my lower lip, holding back more of what I wanted to say. I gave a mock curtsy. "I will honor your command though, *Your Highness.* I would hate to disobey the powerful and mighty Prince Alexander of Valencia."

Alexander turned around. "I'm choosing to ignore your dramatics." He reached the door first, pounding on it heavily.

When no one came to the door after a few moments, he tried again. "Open up!" he shouted. "We are here to see Cinderella." Yet still no one answered the door. Jack and Alexander exchanged worried glances. I gave the doorknob a jiggle, only to find it securely locked.

"What if we've come too late?" Jack asked.

"What if they can't hear you shouting?" I offered.

"What if they are avoiding us?" Alexander muttered.

I gave a great intake of breath as I placed my hand over my heart. "Who would dare dismiss a *command* from Prince Alexander of Valencia?"

"Still ignoring your dramatics, Fliss."

I stepped off the porch and tried the door to the servants' entrance through the kitchen. To my dismay, it was locked as well. I trudged back around to the front, while Alexander pounded on the door once more. I tilted my head up as I surveyed the manor and the flash of the morning sun sparkling against the windows caught my attention. I noticed a trellis leaning up the house. Intrigued, I placed a shaky foot between one of the crevices and after a moment I tried both of my feet, testing to see if it would hold my weight.

"Felicity?" Jack stepped off the porch. "What are you doing?"

"Climbing up to that window." I pointed to the window in the music room, the one Cinderella and I had hidden from Lord Reginald beneath days ago. "It's slightly cracked open. I can pry it open the rest of the way. Once inside, I'll come let you two in."

Alexander pulled me off the trellis. "That's a bad idea."

"It's better than pounding on the front door to no avail. Tell him, Jack."

Jack made a face. "I'm inclined to agree with Alex on this one. It's too dangerous."

"I don't care. Cinderella needs us."

Alexander gently moved me to the side. "I'll climb up." He placed both of his feet on the trellis, only to break two of the wooden planks as soon as all his weight was on it. He stumbled to the ground.

"You are going to reopen that wound in your side if you aren't careful. Besides, you are too heavy," I said. Jack opened his mouth to intervene, but I beat him to it, knowing what would come next. "As are you, by the way. It has to be me." I started up the trellis, gingerly sampling my weight on the wooden planks once more. Much to my relief, they held. I climbed higher, wincing as a thorn from one of the wild vines stabbed my thumb.

"Let us in the moment you get inside," Alexander called up to me. "Don't meander and don't try anything foolish."

"I wouldn't dream of it, *Your Highness*."

"I'm serious, Felicity!"

"Quit distracting me."

I was a few feet away from the window when my foot became tangled up in my skirts, slipping out from under me. I latched on, my feet flailing. The sword at my side banged into my leg, and the wood beneath my palms made a creaking noise, as if the nails holding the planks together were being slowly pulled apart.

"Come back down!" Jack shouted. "This isn't worth breaking your neck over."

"He's right. We'll just kick the front door down instead," Alexander said.

"Almost there," I muttered, taking a few more steps before reaching the window. While grasping tightly onto the trellis with one hand, I tried pushing the windowpane up. It was stubborn and didn't budge. I pushed again, harder this time. The window eased itself open, but the extra pressure against the trellis caused it to give away beneath my feet. Before I knew what was happening, the whole thing made a loud *pop* and collapsed in a heap of wood and thorny vines onto the ground. I dangled from the window's ledge. If Cinderella's stepmother didn't hear us pounding on the door, I was almost certain she heard me bring down part her house's exterior.

"Felicity!" the boys shouted my name in unison.

"I'm fine!" I called down. I pulled myself up, swinging my legs over as I crawled through the opening. Once inside the music room, I peeked my head out the window. "I made it!"

Alexander's face was ashen as he yelled, "Well, go let us in!"

"Be right there."

I turned around and ran to the door. Pushing it open, I made my way down the hall and the familiar staircase that I had cleaned and polished more times than I cared to remember. I was just about to start toward the front door when I reached the bottom step. Until I heard a voice from the sitting room say, "We are gathered today to witness the marriage of this couple."

I gasped.

The wedding had already begun.

CHAPTER 30

I charged through the sitting room doors, throwing them open wide and banging them into the wall. "Cinderella!" I shouted.

A room full of eyes swiveled around to greet me. The only ones I cared about were Cinderella's though, and hers filled with disbelief as she took in my presence with bemusement spreading across her features. Her golden hair was pulled behind her neck with a few tendrils escaping around her cheeks and a gauzy veil hung limply from her bun. She looked like some celestial being in a simple white dress that fell to the floor in soft folds.

Lady Maura and Cressida were the only witnesses present and they both shot to their feet at my intrusion. Somewhere, in the back of my mind, I registered a distinct knocking on the front door and someone calling my name.

"Felicity," Cinderella whispered. She started toward me, but Lord Reginald hastily pulled her back to his side. She collided into his gut. Scrunching up her face, she shouted, "Let me go!"

"What is going on?" Lady Maura demanded, marching over to me. After a moment, she recognized me. "Who invited the scullery maid to this wedding?" She gave Cinderella a venomous look. "I told you that you were not allowed any guests!"

I pushed past her, closer to Cinderella. The knocking on the front door turned into thunderous pounding. "You call this farce a wedding?" I made pointed eye contact with the palace official conducting the ceremony. "The bride is being forced to marry this ogre against her will."

The official blinked. "I beg your pardon?"

Lord Reginald puffed out his chest. "Now see here!"

"Don't bother denying it." I pried his hands off Cinderella's arm. "Tell the official, Cinderella. Tell him that you don't want to marry Lord Reginald. Tell him that he's abusive and cruel. Tell him that the man does not deserve to even wipe the mud from your boots much less secure your hand in marriage."

Cinderella's eyes widened at my bold words. "I-I don't..."

Just then a *crash* came from another room, causing everyone to snap their attention back to the doorway once more. A moment later, every single person gasped as Prince Alexander strode into the room, dusting debris from his pants.

Alexander paused in the doorway and his eyes landed on me first. "You were told not to meander."

I raised an eyebrow at his dramatic entrance, vaguely aware of Lord Reginald and the official bowing to Alexander while Lady Maura and Cressida offered small curtsies. "What exactly did you do? Kick down the door?"

"Yes. I told you we would." Alexander walked into room with Jack trailing close behind his heels. He paused mid-step and winced, covering his side with his palm. "If you've made me reopen my wound, I'm not going to be happy."

"Jack!" Cinderella cried out. Once more she tried to come forward, but Lord Reginald yanked her back again.

I reached for the sword at my side, unsheathing it with relish. "Go ahead. Lay another hand on her. I look forward to watching you lose it."

Lord Reginald's second chin wobbled as he fumbled for his own weapon. It was only then that I heard the sound of more swords being drawn.

Jack and Alexander stepped forward, placing themselves before Lord Reginald.

"You dare raise your sword to a lady!" Alexander cried.

"Coward," Jack spat.

Lady Maura stepped forward. "Your Highness, there is no quarrel here. We were only having a simple, respectable country wedding before this wench," she jerked her head in my direction, "interrupted the ceremony."

"That's right!" Lord Reginald huffed. "The wedding is perfectly respectable."

"*Respectable?*" Alexander frowned in disbelief before turning to Cinderella. "And what does the bride have to say about this wedding?" Cinderella didn't meet his gaze, so he slowly tipped her chin up. "Speak now or forever hold your peace, my dear," he said softly.

"I-I do..."

"Yes?" Alexander prompted.

"Not wish to marry this man," she finished.

"You will do as you are told!" her stepmother shouted.

"She shall do as she pleases," I barked back.

"She's coming home with me with or without a proper wedding! I have paid good money for the girl," Lord Reginald bellowed.

Alexander's eyes glinted dangerously. "You should not have said that."

Cinderella, gaining a spark of courage, stepped around Alexander and shoved a finger into Lord Reginald's chest. "I am not chattel that can be bought and sold. I am a human being with feelings and emotions of my own. I refuse to cower in your presence or submit to your demands any longer." She turned her head sharply towards her stepmother. "That goes for you, too."

Lord Reginald raised his hand back, ready to strike. "See here!"

Before his hand connected with her face, Cinderella reared back and threw a mighty punch squarely into his nose. Blood gushed forward and dripped down his face, and I gave a *whoop* of satisfaction. Everyone else stared at Cinderella in silent shock for a moment while she took a few hesitant steps backward. Her eyes met Jack's, wild with something new, something bold in them.

"Good girl," Jack whispered encouragingly with a satisfied nod.

She yanked off her veil, throwing it at Lord Reginald's feet. "I am tired of being used," Cinderella said evenly before she stormed past the group and out the door.

"Stop!" Lady Maura yelled, starting after her stepdaughter, but she was silenced when Cressida, who had remained uncommonly quiet until now, pulled her back. "What is the meaning of this?" she snapped at her daughter.

"Let her go, Mother," Cressida pleaded.

"Think of the money Lord Reginald is paying us!"

Cressida's eyes were strained and red-rimmed from the tears she had shed since last night. She shook her head ruefully. "How could any of this matter after what happened to Agatha last night? You should be mourning your daughter's death right now, not plotting the demise of another."

"That brat is no my daughter of mine."

Cressida blinked once slowly and then several times more rapidly. "Neither am I," she finally said. She turned to me. "I am sorry for how we have treated your friend. She has shown us nothing but kindness over the years."

"You should try telling her that."

Cressida nodded solemnly. "I will."

Alexander cleared his throat and tipped his head toward the door. "You should see to Cinderella, Fliss. Make sure she hasn't run off for good."

"Will you see to him?" I glanced at Lord Reginald, who was still doubled over, moaning about his bloody nose. I hoped it was broken.

"Gladly. I'm having him and Lady Maura arrested."

"Marvelous idea," Jack chimed in, his sword still aimed at Lord Reginald's neck.

"Whatever for?" Lady Maura cried, outraged. "I've committed no crime."

"Did I or did I not hear you two say that you traded money for Cinderella?"

"We had an agreement! It was for an offer of marriage!"

"The buying and selling of humans is called slavery," Alexander said through clenched teeth. "Something that is not condoned in this kingdom."

"It was a dowry of sorts," Lady Maura hastened to explain. "There is nothing illegal about that."

"My father, King Frederic, has final say over every criminal sentence that is brought before him, rest assured your charges *will* be brought before him, and I can personally guarantee that he will not agree with your sentiments."

Satisfied with Alexander's words, I turned to find Cinderella, hoping that we had not rescued her only to lose her again.

I found her standing on the front porch amidst the rubble and debris of the broken door, staring out at the road that ran in front of the manor. I leaned up against the doorway and crossed my arms over my chest.

She shifted slightly as she heard me come up behind her. "I wanted to run away so many times in the past." Her head scanned from left to right as she looked down the road, as if trying to decide which way to go. "As you can see, this time I only made it as far as the front porch." She turned slowly to face me, a sad smile on her lips. "This is the farthest I've ever gotten though."

"At least you are headed in the right direction."

"I have to start over somewhere, Felicity. I can't stay here."

"I agree."

She bit her lip, struggling to hold back tears. "You came for me."

"Of course. I am your friend." I reached out for her hand and she clasped mine tightly. "I always will be."

"When I saw you standing in the doorway, I thought I was dreaming. I thought surely my mind was playing tricks on me. You saved me."

"I think you saved yourself. Who knew a scullery maid could deliver such an impressive right hook?"

For a moment we stood quietly on the porch, neither saying much of anything. Eventually, she looked at me with solemn eyes. "So you and Jack?"

"Huh?"

"Why didn't you ever tell me you had feelings for Jack? I would have understood."

"Oh. Yes." I faltered for a moment, forgetting that she thought I was in love with the boy she loved. What did I tell her? That I had been lying to make Alexander mad enough to chase after her at the ball? That would lead to all sorts of questions about the fairy tale that I was *forbidden* to explain.

"I forgive you for not telling me that you cared for him. I should not have overreacted," she said.

I winced. I didn't deserve her forgiveness.

"I understand why you and Jack are here, but I *still* don't understand why the prince is here. He hardly knows me."

"What if I told you he came to ask you to marry him?" I offered.

Cinderella gave a brittle, hard laugh that bordered on the edge of hysteria. "Why would anyone want to marry me? I'm broken."

My heart ached for her. "We're all broken in our own way."

"Yes, but I'm *really* broken."

"I guess that just means you have more pieces to work with when you start over." I hesitated for a second, debating whether I should tell her about the fairy tale. Alexander would be furious. I swallowed a lump in my throat and spoke up before I could lose my courage. "As for your question, the real reason Alexander is here—"

"Perhaps I can answer that."

We both turned to find the prince standing in the doorway, watching us with those unsettling blue eyes of his.

"Your Highness," Cinderella breathed. She dipped into an unsteady curtsy.

I decided to forgo a curtsy. Instead, I stared at him with pleading eyes, silently begging him to tell Cinderella the truth.

"Fliss, could you give us a moment?" Alexander asked, ignoring my not-so-subtle look.

I stood rooted on the spot. My pleading stare turned into a full-fledged glare.

"Felicity."

I glanced at Cinderella, who raised an eyebrow at my hesitation, and then back at Alexander, who matched me with a glare of his own.

"*Felicity.*"

"Fine," I yielded. "Yes, Your Highness." I backed into the manor once more, my anger rising as I went. "I'll just wait somewhere in here."

I had good intentions of not eavesdropping on their conversation, grand intentions even. Except when it came down to it, I couldn't seem to pry myself away. I hid behind the nearest corner, listening in keenly to their conversation.

"What are you doing here, Your Highness?" Cinderella asked.

Alexander sighed and kicked a stray piece of door with the tip of his boot. I heard it bounce down the steps and land on the lawn with a *thump.* "Would you believe me if I told you I came here to ask you to marry me?"

"No."

I peeked around the corner, watching as Alexander raked a hand through his dark hair. He turned around to face Cinderella, a sheepish expression on his face. "I didn't think so, but it's the truth."

She blinked. "I don't understand. What Felicity said was true?"

"Yes. What else did Felicity say?"

"Nothing more, really."

Alexander took a step towards her. "Cinderella, I—"

"Why me?" she asked.

"Excuse me?"

"Why *me?* You could have any other girl in this kingdom. Last night there was a ballroom of women willing to throw themselves at your feet. You should go choose one of them. Choose a refined lady that possesses a title and some measure of wealth, one that knows how to navigate life at court. You don't want the girl with dirt and cinders under her fingernails."

Alexander was quiet, pensive as he looked at her. I thought he might not answer her. When he did, his voice was unwavering. "Last night this kingdom was brought to its knees. My people are frightened and too scared to leave their homes now. My mother, the queen, died last night along with many others. I know my subjects are wondering how I can protect them when I could not even protect my own mother. I don't have any answers for them right now, because I don't have any for myself. All I know is Valencia needs me to rise to this new, frightening occasion that has come before us. It also will need another queen, someone who is willing to stand by their future king and lead these people, someone who is willing to offer to them *hope*. If that person has dirt and cinders under her fingernails, so be it."

"I don't believe in false hope, Your Highness," Cinderella whispered.

"I'm not asking for false hope. I'm asking for the kind of hope that people can't live without," Alexander replied. "I am also asking for you to give me a chance. When I look at you, I see goodness and honor and strength—all things my kingdom needs. For you see, in as much as I choose a bride for myself, I also choose a future queen for this kingdom."

"Are you saying *I* am what Valencia needs?"

"*Yes*," he breathed gently. "I should warn you that it would not be an easy thing to be married to me. The royal family will always have enemies, as you discovered last night. Though I can promise you if there is breath in my body, I will protect you. Valencia's enemies will not be the only challenge. Valencia itself will prove the biggest obstacle between us. You will demand things of me, but Valencia will demand more. I will give to you, but I will always have to give a little more to Valencia. We will not just belong to each other, but to—"

"Valencia," Cinderella finished for him. "I understand." She looked up at him and the morning sunlight swept over her features, brightening them radiantly.

Alexander was a fool if he missed the obvious beauty in front of him, a fool if he let her get away.

"Is this your proposal?"

Alexander nodded. "I think I'm supposed to get down on one knee. I'm also without a ring at the moment. Men have been doing this for centuries, and I'm the first one to forget to get down on one knee *and* bring the ring." He reached into the bag swung over his shoulder and pulled out my mother's glass slipper. "Will this do for now?"

Cinderella ran her finger gingerly over the smooth glass. "I thought I lost this slipper last night. How did you find it?"

"I think I was always meant to find it."

Cinderella looked over her shoulder at the manor and then toward the road in front of her. For a moment, I thought she was going to take off running down the road and never stop. I wouldn't have blamed her for running away. Instead, she surprised me by saying, "I have to start my life over somewhere else. I suppose I could start over with you."

Alexander squinted down at her uncertainly. "Is that a *yes*?"

"That's a *yes*. Under two conditions though."

"Name them."

"First, I want my own music room in the palace. I want it filled with all my father's instruments, his music, and my mother's harp. It was sold a few days ago. I want it found and brought to me."

"Done. The second?"

"I don't need your admiration or your attention or even your love. I've lived without those things for quite some time and I think I can continue that way. I do, however, need your trust and I need to be able to trust you in return. I value honesty and trust above all things." She paused for a moment and tilted her head as she gave him a sharp look. "Well?"

"Yes?"

"Can I trust you?"

Alexander nodded carefully.

"Very well then." She offered him her hand. "I accept your proposal, Your Highness."

He laughed as they sealed the deal by shaking hands, the boyish grin that had captured my heart so many times in the past resurfaced. His handsome smile must have had some effect on Cinderella, too, for her eyes softened.

"If we are going to be married, you should at least call me Alexander."

"Perhaps in time, Your Highness."

I watched them step off the porch together. With a pang in my chest, I turned around, only to collide into Jack.

"You were eavesdropping," he said.

"Apparently, so were you," I pointed out. "Anyway, I'm the librarian in charge of this fairy tale. That was my moment as much as it was theirs."

"I think you were just being nosy."

"Aren't you are supposed to be arresting Lord Reginald and Lady Maura?"

"The palace official has agreed to escort them back to the palace. I had to see for myself how things played out between those two." Jack looked over my shoulder at their disappearing forms, his face impassive. "I guess this is it then? We just let them go?"

"Truthfully, they were never ours."

"For a moment they were." He smiled down at me, though it didn't reach his eyes. "Come on, Fliss. I'll see you back to the palace."

"Aren't you forgetting something?"

"What?"

"You never told me about those giants and that beanstalk. I'm tempted to see them for myself."

"We just survived one ordeal. Let's not dive head first into another. Haven't you had enough adventure to last a lifetime?"

"Hardly. Besides, if I can handle a vengeful sorceress, I think I can manage a few giants." I nudged him playfully in the ribs. "Maybe you can tell me about them tomorrow, though. Today I think I'd like to go home, drink a cup of tea, and read a book from my library that doesn't have anything to do with a fairy tale."

And that's exactly what I did.

ACKNOWLEDGMENTS

First, the biggest acknowledgment goes to my husband. Dallas, thank you for not laughing when I told you I wanted to write a novel. This story would have never seen the light of day without you. It would still be buried in the back of my mind or hidden in a file on my computer. Also, thanks for taking care of our kid all those times I went off to write. You are a wonderful husband and father. I'll love you for the rest of forever.

Calvin, you are too little to know that Mama wrote a book. You helped me finish it, though. I knew one day I'd tell you to dream big dreams and finish what you start— even if it feels scary and impossible. I decided I'd better follow my own advice before I try to dole out any to you. I love you, little man.

Thanks Mom and Dad for loving your kids unconditionally. That's all any parents can truly do, and you guys do it well. Thanks for all the books you read to me and bought for me when I was growing up—those books laid a foundation for this dream. I figured if I loved reading stories so much, I'd probably love writing them too. This wouldn't have been possible without you both.

Amanda, you inspired Cinderella's compassion and quiet courage. I'm immeasurably blessed to have you in my life.

Thank you, a hundred times, to all my extended family—Memaw, Papaw David, Grandpa Fix-It, Troy (my jovial father-in-law), and Kayrene (my kind-hearted mother-in-law). Also, thanks to all the amazing bonus siblings that I received over the years: Josh, Melissa, Jason, Danny, and Chelsi. We've been blessed with some wonderful family.

I have a lot of fantastic friends who made this dream possible. Elizabeth, thanks for being the first person outside of my family to read this novel and offer me guidance and support. I can never adequately tell you how much I appreciate all the time you put into helping me. A heartfelt thanks to Audrie and Becky, my Swamp girls, who read this novel while it was still a rough, *rough* draft and told me they liked it anyway. I'd like to think Felicity has a little bit of Swamp girl in her, too. Also, thanks to my friends Rachel, Hailey, Holley, and Jen. Y'all have always been my faithful cheering squad.

Michaela and Kirsten, thank you for being kind, generous with your time, and just generally cool critique partners. I'm happy to return the favor someday.

Carla P., I appreciate all your notes and encouragement. I'm so glad we share common interests in books, television, and movies. I always know you'll give me a good recommendation on what to watch or read next. Also, thanks to my friend, Jessica A., and my cousin, Maranda, for being beta readers and slogging through my very first attempts at writing. You guys rock.

Many thanks to my high school English teachers, Melinda Bacon and Kathy Adkins Aslin, who told me I had the makings of a writer. Writers are nothing without the people who teach them to write. I've never forgotten your kind words. Also, thanks to Kim Cheek for always inspiring her students to use their imaginations. Every day you show your students that a little imagination goes a long way.

Editor Cassandra, you are amazing at what you do. You deserve all the editing accolades for helping me turn a jumbled mess of words into a story. I'm so glad our paths crossed.

I know it seems cliché to thank the reader, but I'm going to do it anyway. After all, books don't read themselves. Dear Reader, unless you've written a novel yourself, you won't know how much it means to me that you've spent time reading my story and getting lost between its pages. *Thank you.*

Hey guys, I really hope you enjoyed *Magic by Midnight*! I would love to hear what you thought about the book. You can find me on Facebook and Instagram.

Another way you can show support is by leaving an Amazon review!

ABOUT THE AUTHOR

Allison grew up a voracious reader who daydreamed about stories filled with romance, adventure, and magic. One day, she decided to put those stories on paper. Her debut novel *Magic by Midnight* is the result. Like any 21st century fairy tale heroine, she met her own prince via the Internet. They do not live in a castle, but they have a beagle who acts like a court jester. When she's not spending time with her husband and son, she enjoys finding new stories for her personal library.